O9-BRY-884

BOOK YOUR PLACE ON OUR WEBSITE
AND MAKE THE
READING CONNECTION!

We've created a customized website just for our very special readers, where you can get the inside scoop on everything that's going on with Zebra, Pinnacle and Kensington books.

When you come online, you'll have the exciting opportunity to:

• View covers of upcoming books

• Read sample chapters

• Learn about our future publishing schedule (listed by publication month *and author*)

• Find out when your favorite authors will be visiting a city near you

• Search for and order backlist books from our online catalog

• Check out author bios and background information

• Send e-mail to your favorite authors

• Meet the Kensington staff online

• Join us in weekly chats with authors, readers and other guests

• Get writing guidelines

• AND MUCH MORE!

**Visit our website at
http://www.kensingtonbooks.com**

THE FIRST MOUNTAIN MAN
PREACHER'S QUEST

William W. Johnstone
with J. A. Johnstone

PINNACLE BOOKS
Kensington Publishing Corp.
www.kensingtonbooks.com

PINNACLE BOOKS are published by

Kensington Publishing Corp.
850 Third Avenue
New York, NY 10022

PUBLISHER'S NOTE
Following the death of William W. Johnstone, the Johnstone family is working with a carefully selected writer to organize and complete Mr. Johnstone's outlines and many unfinished manuscripts to create additional novels in all of his series like The Last Gunfighter, Mountain Man, and Eagles, among others. This novel was inspired by Mr. Johnstone's superb storytelling.

All Kensington titles, imprints, and distributed lines are available at special quantity discounts for bulk purchases for sales promotions, premiums, fund-raising, educational, or institutional use. Special book excerpts or customized printings can also be created to fit specific needs. For details, write or phone the office of the Kensington special sales manager: Kensington Publishing Corp., 850 Third Avenue, New York, NY 10022, attn: Special Sales Department; phone 1-800-221-2647.

PINNACLE BOOKS and the Pinnacle logo are Reg. U.S. Pat. & TM Off.

ISBN 0-7860-1739-2

First printing: January 2007

10 9 8 7 6 5

Printed in the United States of America

Chapter One

If there was ever any doubt in the mind of the man called Preacher that the frontier was truly where he was meant to be, it was erased as he rode slowly down a wooded hillside toward a long, green valley. He felt a sense of contentment growing within him. He felt as most men do when they return from a long journey to the place where everything dear to them resides.

Preacher felt like he was coming home, and that was the simple, God's honest truth of it.

Rugged, snowcapped mountains loomed all around the valley, starkly beautiful against the deep blue vault of sky. The snow on the peaks was a reminder that although the weather down in the valley was warm and sunny on this late spring day, winter was never very far off in this mountainous region.

Tendrils of gray smoke from dozens of campfires rose into the air above the valley. Tents and tepees dotted the valley floor on both sides of the little stream that meandered through it. A couple of hundred people were crowded into the encampment, mostly bearded, buckskin-clad men, although quite a few Indian women in beaded buckskin dresses were in evidence, too, most of them stirring the contents of iron pots that simmered over the flames of the campfires. The men stood and talked and smoked their pipes or played cards or passed around jugs. They argued with the representatives of the fur trading companies who had come out here to bargain for their loads of pelts. A few wrestled or competed at throwing knives and tomahawks.

A grin creased Preacher's lean, weathered face as he looked down the hill at all the goings-on. There was only one word to describe these festivities.

Rendezvous!

Twice each year, at the end of the spring trapping season and also at the end of the fall season, the mountain men who had come here to the Rockies to harvest beaver pelts gathered together to sell the results of their labor to the agents of the fur companies. However, Rendezvous was a lot more than just business. It was also the most important social occasion—often the *only* social occasion—each spring and fall. Friends who hadn't seen each other for months slapped each other on the back and called each other obscene names and roared with laughter. Fiddles scraped and mouth harps wailed and the valley fairly shook from the stomping feet of the mountain men as they danced and capered. The party lasted for three days and nights, and when it was over the buckskinners, most of whom led solitary lives the rest of the year, went their separate ways, hungover, sore from laughing and fighting, back to their lonely existence until the time came for them to head once again for the Rendezvous.

Preacher knew that sometimes the men who lived in these mountains went crazy from the solitude. A lot more probably would have lost their minds if it hadn't been for the Rendezvous twice a year.

With the grace of a natural-born horseman, Preacher rode a rangy, ugly mount known as Horse. At his side padded along a big wolflike cur called Dog. Like Preacher, the animals were starting to get some age on them. Not that any of them were actually *old,* far from it. Preacher, who had been born as the eighteenth century slipped into the nineteenth, hadn't seen thirty-five winters yet. But the rugged life he'd led had put a few silver strands in the thick black hair under the floppy-brimmed hat he wore. The mustache that hung over his mouth and the beard stubble on his lean cheeks were dotted with silver as well.

He led a packhorse that carried the pelts he had taken. This time he had fewer than usual because he hadn't been able to spend a full spring season in the mountains. After wintering in Texas, he had been on his way back to the high country when he'd gotten delayed by some trouble in the Sangre de Cristos, down New Mexico way. He wasn't particularly worried, though. A man who could live off the land like Preacher could didn't need a lot of money.

A frown creased Preacher's forehead as he noticed a large, striped tent near the river. Mountain men usually didn't go in for anything that fancy. The tent probably belonged to some of the fur company representatives, Preacher decided.

As he reached the bottom of the slope and started across the valley floor toward the encampment, several dogs noticed him coming and bounded toward him, barking. The big cur beside him growled low in his throat, and Preacher said, "Behave yourself, Dog. I don't want to have to be pullin' you out of a ruckus ever' time I turn around."

Dog just looked up at him.

"I know, I know," Preacher said tolerantly. "You're bigger and tougher'n those other dogs. But you know that and I know that, and I reckon that's all that matters."

With dignity and only the occasional growl, Dog padded on, ignoring the canine commotion that went on around him.

Some of the men attending the Rendezvous noticed Preacher's impending arrival, too, and they stopped what they were doing to stride out a short distance from the edge of the encampment and wait for him, long-barreled Kentucky rifles cradled in the crooks of their elbows. Preacher lifted a hand in greeting as he approached them.

"As I live and breathe," one of the buckskin-clad men called, "if it ain't Preacher." He nudged the man next to him with an elbow. "See, I told you I smelled somethin'. Smelled like rotted bear grease, so I knew it had to be Preacher."

"Rather smell like rotted bear grease than a three-hole privy like you, Stump," Preacher said.

The grin disappeared from the man's face and was replaced by a scowl. "Damn it, Preacher, you know I don't like bein' called that." The nickname had come about not because the trapper had lost an arm or a leg or because he was short—although he was—but rather because nature had been less than generous to him when it came to his masculine endowment. Quite a bit less than generous, in fact.

"Yeah, you're right," Preacher said as he reined Horse to a halt and the packhorse stopped, too. He held up a hand with the thumb and forefinger only a couple of inches apart and went on, "It ain't really your fault that you only got—"

Another man had walked up behind the ones who had come out to meet Preacher, and now shouldered through their ranks. That wasn't much of a chore because he was taller and heavier and had broader shoulders than any of them except for Preacher himself.

"Preacher!" the newcomer bellowed. "Nobody's killed you yet? I'm plumb amazed!"

Grinning, Preacher swung down from the saddle and stepped forward to shake hands with the man. "Howdy, Rip," he said. "Good to see you again."

"Good to see you, too, you old scalawag." The man pulled Preacher closer and pounded him on the back before retreating a step.

Rip Giddens was a little younger than Preacher, with shaggy blond hair that hung around his shoulders and a beard of the same shade. He and Preacher had been friends for several years, although the only place they ever saw each other was at these Rendezvous.

Looking past Preacher at the packhorse, Rip commented, "Doesn't appear that you had a very good spring."

Preacher grimaced. "I only got up here in time to trap for a few weeks. I spent the winter in Texas, and when I started back I had to stop for a spell in New Mexico."

"What for?" Rip asked bluntly.

Preacher shrugged. "Helped out a few folks, and shot some others."

"Damned if that ain't just like you."

"Hey, I was talkin' to Preacher!" the trapper called Stump interrupted. He crowded forward, his rifle clutched in both hands now.

Rip turned and said, "Sorry, Stump," ignoring the baleful look the smaller man gave him. He waved a hand at Preacher. "You go right ahead."

Stump glared. "Well, I was just sayin' that, uh, you shouldn't make fun of a fella because of his, uh, shortcomin's that he don't have no control over—"

He had to stop because all the other trappers were laughing now, not just Preacher and Rip. Looking mad and frustrated, Stump fumed and muttered under his breath as he stomped off.

Rip put a hand on Preacher's shoulder. "Come on," he said. "I want you to meet the folks I'm workin' for."

"Workin' for?" Preacher repeated as he fell in step with Rip and led the two horses across the encampment. "Ain't you trappin' this year?"

"Oh, yeah, sure. Got a good load o' plews durin' the spring, in fact. But I've got another job comin' up for the summer, guidin' some pilgrims—"

Preacher didn't know where Rip intended to guide those mysterious pilgrims, and didn't get a chance to find out right then, because a frightened scream rang out from not too far away.

A *woman's* scream.

"Damn it!" Rip said. "That sounds like Miss Faith!"

He broke into a run, and Preacher saw that Rip was heading for that fancy striped tent he had noticed earlier.

Preacher followed at a more deliberate pace, not running because he was still leading the two horses, but not wasting any time, either. As he approached the tent, he saw a knot of people in front of the canvas flaps that formed its entrance. Two knots of people, rather, with Rip Giddens between them, evidently trying to keep them apart.

One group, the bunch that Rip faced angrily, was made up of men in buckskins and coonskin caps and floppy-brimmed hats. They were trappers, and Preacher recognized most of them. He wasn't particularly fond of them, either, especially the man who appeared to be their leader. His name was Luther Snell, and Preacher had had a few run-ins with him before. Once he had even suspected Snell of raiding his traps, but he'd never been able to catch the man at it.

The half-dozen or so men with Snell were the same sort, no more honest than they had to be and given to brutality.

It was the group of people clustered behind Rip that drew most of Preacher's attention, though. He knew immediately that they must be those pilgrims Rip had mentioned.

There were four of them, and one of them was a woman— a *white* woman, maybe the only one in more than a hundred miles. She was tall and on the slender side, with a thick mass of auburn curls that tumbled around her shoulders. Her eyes were a vivid, almost startling shade of green. Standing next to her with an arm protectively around her was a slight, sandy-haired man who was several inches shorter than her. On the woman's other side stood a handsome, dark-haired man in his thirties, and behind that trio was a taller man with brown hair. He looked to be the most physically fit of the group, but the spectacles that perched on his nose gave him a bookish look, and he seemed to be the one of the four who was the most nervous.

Preacher's keen eyes took in the whole scene and the players involved at a glance. Rip was saying, "Look, Luther, there ain't no call for trouble. I'm sure that Miss Faith didn't mean to offend you—"

"She called me an uncouth lout!" Luther Snell interrupted angrily. "I ain't exactly sure what that is, but it can't be nothin' good!"

"Perhaps I should have added uneducated as well," the woman said with a defiant look on her pretty face, and Preacher winced a little. Clearly, she wasn't going to go out of her way to ease the tension here.

"If you mean I ain't had no schoolin', that ain't true," Snell shot back. "I went to school for a whole year. I can read a little and cipher some."

"Oh, well, then, you're ready to apply for admission to Oxford."

The man with his arm around her said, "Faith, dear, you're not really helping matters—"

"Oh, hush," the woman snapped at him. "If you were any sort of a decent brother, Willard, you would have stood up to this bully when he first accosted me." She glared at the other two men in their party. "And the same is true for the pair of you. My God, you must have *some* backbone, if you're brave enough to come out here to this filthy wilderness in the first place."

"I didn't have that much choice," the smaller dark-haired man said. "The newspaper for which I work insisted that I come along with your brother's expedition, Miss Carling. A journalist goes where he's told to go, you know."

Faith Carling looked at the third man, who refused to meet her accusatory gaze. Despite his muscular build, he was obviously a peace-loving sort.

That wasn't exactly the same thing as being a coward, Preacher thought—but it wasn't far from it, either.

"Look," Snell said, "I didn't do anything to get the gal upset. I just asked her if she'd be willin' to write one of her pomes about me."

"Poems," Faith said distinctly and scornfully. "I write poems, not *pomes*. And as an artist, I can't be commanded what to write. I have to follow the urgings of my muse."

One of the other trappers said, "I thought the little prissy fella was the artist."

"My brother Willard is a painter," Faith replied. "He captures the beauties of nature in oils, while I use words. But both of us are artists." She looked at Luther Snell. "And you, sir, are *not* one of the beauties of nature."

"That does it!" The burly, black-bearded Snell drew back a fist. "Sorry, Giddens. Since I can't wallop no female, looks like I got to beat the hell outta you!"

Chapter Two

"Hold it, Snell." Preacher's deep, powerful voice wasn't loud, but it cut through the atmosphere of impending violence and stopped Snell before the trapper could launch a punch at Rip Giddens.

Snell and his friends hadn't noticed Preacher coming up behind them. At the sound of Preacher's voice, Snell's head snapped around. "Preacher!" he said in surprise. "I didn't know you'd got here to the Rendezvous yet."

"Just rode in a few minutes ago," Preacher said mildly. "And I'd take it kindly if you'd stop threatenin' my friend Rip, Snell."

Reluctantly, the angry trapper lowered his arm, but he didn't unclench his fist. "This ain't any o' your business, Preacher. I know you like to meddle in other folks' affairs, but this is one time when maybe you ought to back up."

"Funny thing about that," Preacher said as he dropped the reins he had been holding. The horses weren't going to wander off. As Preacher stepped forward, he continued. "When the Good Lord made me, He clean forgot to put much back-up in me."

"Now look here," Snell began to bluster.

"No, *you* look," Preacher said, and his tone was cold and

angry now. "You and your pards just leave these folks alone and move on. There's been hard feelin's but never any real trouble between us, Snell. Let's keep it that way."

Snell looked like he wanted to continue the argument, but one of his companions said, "Come on, Luther. We never figured on Preacher bein' mixed up in this. You know what a lobo wolf he is."

"Yeah, well, I can be a wolf, too," Snell said obstinately. But the look of wanting to fight had gone out of his small, piggish eyes, and Preacher knew Snell was going to back down. He wouldn't like it, but he'd do it.

Snell couldn't leave without getting in a parting shot, though. He sneered at Rip and said, "If I was you, Giddens, I'd be ashamed about havin' to get Preacher to fight my battles for me."

With that he turned and stalked away, followed by his friends, before Rip could make any sort of reply.

Rip didn't look happy, though, and Preacher wondered suddenly if he should have stayed out of the confrontation. Ignoring trouble wasn't the sort of thing he was good at, though, especially when the fella threatening to raise a ruckus was a no-account bastard like Luther Snell.

"I appreciate the help, Preacher," Rip said tightly, "but you didn't have to do that. I ain't scared of Snell."

"Nobody said you were," Preacher pointed out. "But him and me don't like each other, and it goes back a while. Still, I didn't mean to mix in where I hadn't ought to."

The woman took a step toward him. "On the contrary, sir, your participation in this contretemps was quite welcome. Men such as that have no concept of fair play. I'd wager that they would have ganged up on poor Mr. Giddens and given him the thrashing of his life had you not intervened."

Preacher saw Rip's bearded jaw tighten even more, and he wanted to echo what Faith Carling's brother had told her a few minutes earlier—that she wasn't helping the situation. But his natural frontiersman's politeness made him just nod and tug at the brim of his hat. The way words spewed out of this redheaded gal's mouth, he doubted if he could ever keep up with her.

"Preacher, this here is Miss Faith Carling," Rip said, evidently deciding it was better to just move ahead rather than dwelling on what had happened.

She stuck out her hand like a man and asked, "Are you a minister, then? A man of God? A purveyor of the Gospel?"

"No, ma'am," he said as he took her hand. It was surprisingly strong, and her grip was firm. "I'm just a fur trapper like all these other fellas at the Rendezvous."

"Then why do they call you Preacher?"

He didn't much want to rehash the details, but the story would be new to her. "Some time back, a bunch of Blackfoot grabbed me, took me prisoner, and figured on liftin' my hair. Funny thing about Indians, though, they generally won't bother a man if they think he's touched in the head. I'd seen a street preacher one time, back in Saint Looey, so I started doin' like he would've if he'd been there, preachin' at those heathen Blackfeet at the top o' my lungs. Kept it up all night and the next day, too, until they didn't have any choice but to believe that I was pure-dee crazy." He shrugged. "They let me go, and once the story got around, folks started callin' me Preacher. The name's stuck all this time."

"But what's your real name?" Faith persisted.

"After all these years, I sort of disremember."

That wasn't really true—his name was Arthur, and he knew that perfectly well. But he didn't particularly feel like sharing it with this woman, who he had already sized up as being rather obnoxious, despite the fact that she was good-looking.

Beauty and being a decent human being didn't always go hand in hand.

The short, sandy-haired man introduced himself. "I'm Willard Carling, Mr. Preacher. As my sister mentioned, I'm a painter."

"Pleased to meet you, but it's just Preacher. No mister." Preacher paused, then waved a hand at the magnificent scenery surrounding them. "I reckon you came out here to paint all this?"

"Yes, and the savages, too. It's becoming all the rage back East for artists to paint Western landscapes and portraits of the Indians. I like to see my subjects at first hand before I attempt to capture them on the canvas."

That made sense to Preacher. He was no artist, but he figured it would be a lot easier to paint a picture of something if you'd seen it for yourself, with your own eyes.

"And this is Jasper Hodge," Carling went on. "He's a journalist, you know. Plans to write a book about this expedition, as well as the stories for his newspaper."

"That a fact?" said Preacher as he shook hands with Jasper Hodge.

"Yes, indeed," Hodge replied. He smiled jauntily. "If you'd like, I can put you in the book, Preacher. Wouldn't it be something for your friends to read about you in such a volume?"

"It sure would, considerin' that most of 'em can't read a lick," Preacher said dryly.

Hodge's smile went away and was replaced by a frown. Preacher could tell that the Eastern journalist wasn't sure if he was being made fun of or not—but if he was, he didn't like it.

That just left the bigger, bespectacled man, who wasn't quite as well dressed as the others. "Chester Sinclair," he introduced himself as he briefly shook hands with Preacher. "I'm Mr. Carling's assistant."

"I have to have someone lug all my paints and canvases about, you know," Carling said. "And for that I need a big strapping mule like this lad here."

"Chester may be big, but he's obviously not any more courageous than you two," Faith said. "Otherwise, he would have volunteered to help Preacher and Mr. Giddens when they confronted those ruffians."

"Sorry, Miss Faith," Sinclair said with his eyes downcast. "I didn't think it was my place to interfere."

"That's a handy excuse, anyway," Faith said caustically.

Preacher frowned at her. There weren't many things in this

world more annoying than a bossy, tart-tongued woman, he thought. But he didn't say anything. These Easterners were Rip's problem, not his.

At least, he supposed that was the case. He said, "These are the folks you've hired on with for the summer, Rip?"

"That's right," Rip replied with a nod.

"Yes, Mr. Giddens has agreed to be our chief scout and guide," Willard Carling said. "We're all quite pleased about that."

Faith gave out with a ladylike little snort. From what Preacher could tell, she wasn't very pleased with much of anything about this trip to the Rocky Mountains.

"I've got Sparrow to cook for us," Rip told Preacher. "You remember her?"

Preacher remembered the Indian woman called Sparrow quite well. She must have gotten the name back when she was a youngster, he had reflected more than once, because there was nothing birdlike about her now. She was short and broad, just about as wide as she was tall. But she was a fine cook, he recalled, and he nodded and said, "That's good, Rip. You folks will be well fed." A concern occurred to him. "What about other fellas to go along and help you watch out for trouble?"

"I've got four gents lined up for that. Switchfoot, Hammerhead Jones, and the Ballinger brothers. But if you're offerin', Preacher, I reckon I could talk Mr. Carling into hirin' you on, too." Rip turned to Carling and added, "I don't want to embarrass him, Boss, but when it comes to the frontier, Preacher's worth more'n all them other boys put together."

"Why, that sounds excellent," Carling said. "Join our little expedition, Preacher, do."

Preacher almost wished now that he hadn't asked Rip who else was going along on the journey. He didn't particularly like any of these four pilgrims, and he surely didn't desire to spend a few months around Faith Carling and her shrewish ways.

But it was true that he didn't have nearly as big a load of pelts to sell this time as he usually did. Whatever Willard Carling would pay to hire him, the money would come in handy sooner or later. But would it be worth the aggravation?

Preacher reached a decision and shook his head. "I appreciate the offer," he said, "but I just come here to sell my plews and move on. I ain't lookin' for work."

"Oh, dear." Carling looked disappointed. "Are you sure?"

"Rip and the others you've hired are good men. They can handle just about any problem that comes up."

"Very well. But I wonder . . . would you be interested in posing for a portrait before we part company, Preacher?"

Preacher's eyebrows went up in surprise. "You want to paint a picture of *me*?"

"Yes, indeed. You're the quintessential woodsman, a perfect archetype."

Preacher wasn't sure exactly what Carling was trying to say, but he figured it was better than being called an uncouth lout. He said, "What would I have to do?"

"Simply stand still."

"I reckon I could do that."

"Excellent! We'll get started this afternoon, if that's all right with you."

Preacher nodded. "Fine. That'll give me time to talk to some of the agents about my furs and get somethin' to eat."

"Come back here whenever you're ready. I'll have Chester set up an easel and a fresh canvas."

Carling went back into the fancy tent, accompanied by Jasper Hodge. Faith and Sinclair remained outside. Faith sat down on a stool at a small folding table that held a pad of paper, a pen, and an inkwell. Now that she wasn't paying any attention to him, Sinclair's eyes followed her with almost dog-like devotion, Preacher noted.

He gathered up the reins of his horses and started back across the encampment toward the tents set up by the fur buyers. Rip trailed along with him.

"Sure you won't change your mind about comin' along, Preacher?" Rip asked. He inclined his head toward the fancy tent where the Easterners were. "Havin' you around might make it a heap easier for me to ride herd on that bunch."

Preacher laughed softly. "I'm afraid that's your lookout, Rip. The lady ain't what you'd call shy and retirin', is she?"

Rip sighed and didn't answer the question. "It's a good job. Mr. Carling's payin' me a mighty good wage."

"You tryin' to convince *me* . . . or *you*?"

"I said I'd take 'em on into the mountains, and I figure on doin' what I said I'd do." A stubborn edge had come into Rip's voice.

"I wouldn't expect any less of you. Still, if that gal lets out a scream just because Luther Snell comes up and talks to her, I don't know what she'll do if you run into any real trouble."

"He didn't just talk to her," Rip said. "When she told him to go away, he grabbed her arm and wanted to know what made her think she was so much better'n him."

Preacher stopped and looked over at his old friend. His eyes narrowed. "Is that so? I didn't know he'd laid hands on her." He might not like Faith Carling, but he'd been raised to believe that a man didn't lay hands on a woman in anger.

Rip nodded and said, "That's what she told me when I first come runnin' up, and Snell didn't deny it. I was almost hopin' he'd take a swing at me, so's I'd have an excuse to wallop him some." His broad shoulders rose and fell. "But Miss Faith was prob'ly right. Snell's bunch would've jumped me, too."

They might have discussed the matter further, but at that moment several of the fur company agents noticed Preacher and advanced toward him holding out their hands, ready to shake and make offers on the pelts Preacher had on the pack-horse. Rip added, "See you later," and moved on.

Preacher spent the next hour negotiating with the various representatives of the fur companies and finally settled on a price with one of them. He was always glad to get that trans-action concluded. He didn't like haggling over money.

The agent counted out the agreed-upon amount in gold coins. Preacher put them away in a small leather pouch that he stowed under his buckskin shirt. Then the fur company man's hired helpers unloaded the packhorse and carried the pelts into the tent that was serving as a temporary warehouse. Later, when the Rendezvous was over, they and all the other pelts the agent had bought would be loaded on pack animals and started on the long trip back to St. Louis.

Preacher shook hands with the man, who said, "Pleasure doing business with you." As Preacher turned away, he wondered briefly what he was going to do next.

That question was answered unexpectedly as he found his arms suddenly full of woman and a pair of warm, demanding lips pressed themselves eagerly against his mouth.

Chapter Three

Preacher pulled back and said, "What in blazes?"

It wasn't that he minded being kissed so much as that he liked to have a say in such things.

The woman looked hurt and said, "Preacher, do you not remember me?"

"Of course I remember you. You're Mountain Mist."

She was Shoshone, around twenty summers old and mighty good to look at with her long, straight, black hair and dark eyes and features that were strong but attractive. The buckskin dress she wore was tight enough to reveal a sturdy, well-curved body.

"Are you not glad to see me?" she demanded.

"Sure I am. I'm just, uh, surprised, that's all. I figured for sure you'd be hitched up to some lucky Shoshone brave by now."

"None of the men of my people can compare to you, Preacher."

He muttered a curse under his breath. Years earlier, a beautiful young woman named Jennie had helped him across the threshold of manhood, and Preacher—who had still been Arthur then—had fallen in love with her. Over the years he had known her, he had always loved her.

But they hadn't always been together during that time, and

occasionally he had shared the blankets of some other woman—including Mountain Mist. He hadn't seen her for quite a while, and he had been telling the truth when he said he would have thought that she'd be married by now. He sure as blazes hoped she hadn't been waiting for *him*.

"What are you doin' here?" he asked her.

She pointed toward one of the tents. "Working."

Preacher's jaw tightened. He knew what she meant by that. She was whoring. There were always plenty of Indian women at the Rendezvous who sold themselves to the trappers.

Preacher wasn't hypocritical about such things. Jennie herself had been a whore when Preacher first met her, forced into a life of prostitution at a young age by the cruel man who had taken her in after her folks died. And she had remained in that line of work for most of her life, eventually becoming a madam in a house in St. Louis. That was just business and didn't have anything to do with what was between her and Preacher.

He hated to see Mountain Mist going down that road, though. Jennie had been strong enough so that the life she'd led had never broken her spirit. Preacher wasn't sure the young Shoshone woman was that strong.

She caught hold of his hand and tugged eagerly on it. "Come with me," she said. "We will go in the tent and—"

Preacher shook his head as he gently worked his hand out of her grip. "I don't reckon that'd be a good idea."

"But we have lain together in the past," she pointed out with a puzzled frown.

"That was a while back. You shouldn't be doing such things, Mountain Mist."

Her frown deepened. "But why not?"

Preacher muttered and mumbled some more. He couldn't tell her a good reason why not. He just knew it was so.

Suddenly, Mountain Mist's frown went away and her face lit up with a smile. "I know now," she said. "You think I should not work in the tent, Preacher. You think I should lay only with you." Her head bobbed up and down in a nod. "That is what I will do. I will stay with you and be your woman from now on."

"Hold on there just a minute!" Preacher lifted his hands to stop her excited babbling. "I didn't say—"

Her face fell.

He spat out a heartfelt, "Oh, hell!" He had gone and hurt her feelings. It was her fault for jumping to a conclusion that wasn't anywhere near what he'd had in mind, but he felt guilty about it, anyway. He thought about the money in the pouch under his shirt and then caught hold of her hand again. "Listen, stay with me during the Rendezvous. You can be my woman until it's over, and I'll pay you what you would have made in the tent. But after that we go our separate ways, understand? I ride on, and you go back to your people and find yourself some sturdy young fella to marry."

"None of them will be like you, Preacher." Mountain Mist sighed. "But as your people say, I will take what I can get."

The trapper called Stump was sitting by himself later that day, with his back pressed against the trunk of a tree, his hat tilted down over his eyes, and a jug in his lap. He wasn't drunk, just . . . relaxed. Mighty relaxed.

But not so much so that he didn't notice the shadow that fell over him.

Stump looked up and saw a burly man in buckskins looming over him. He recognized the rugged, bearded countenance and asked, "What do you want, Snell? This is *my* jug, if you had in mind askin' for a nip, and I ain't in much of a mood to share."

Snell said, "I don't want your whiskey . . . Horace."

Stump's face lit up in surprise. "You know my real name?"

"Horace Pendergast, originally from Cairo, Illinois."

"Yeah, that's me," Stump said, warming up to Snell. They had never been friends, only casual acquaintances. Snell didn't have a very good reputation among the buckskinners. But if Snell had gone to the trouble of learning his real name and where he was from, thought Stump, maybe the fella wasn't so bad after all. "Sit down. Have a drink."

"Maybe later. Right now I want to ask you something."

Stump waved a hand. "Ask away."

"I hear you had a run-in with Preacher this mornin'."

"Well, I wouldn't go so far as to call it a run-in," Stump said with a frown. "It's just that he called me St . . . He called me that name I don't like."

"How'd you like to get even with him?"

"With Preacher?" Stump sounded like the idea had never occurred to him. "I don't know about that. Preacher's one ol' boy who's rough as a cob. . . ."

"He's human, just like you and me," Snell said, "and I'm gettin' mighty damn tired of him lordin' it over ever'body and actin' like he's better'n any o' the rest of us. Somebody needs to take that son of a bitch down a peg . . . and I'm just the ring-tailed roarer to do it."

Stump didn't disagree with anything that Snell was saying—but he noticed that Snell wasn't saying it within earshot of Preacher, either. Still, he was intrigued enough to ask, "What did you have in mind?"

"You've got some friends you can call on to help you, haven't you?"

"Sure, I've got friends," Stump declared. He didn't know how many of them would be willing to risk getting on Preacher's bad side, but for now he was going to play along with Snell and tell the man what he wanted to hear.

"All right, then. The word around camp is that he's taken up with one o' them Injun whores, the Shoshone squaw called Mountain Mist. Now, here's what we're gonna do. . . ."

The prime spots along the river were already taken, so Preacher went the opposite way in setting up his campsite. He got off to the edge of the encampment, sort of off away from everybody, and pitched his tent there. Mountain Mist moved in like a new wife in a just-built cabin, lugging Preacher's gear into the tent and unpacking it and setting up housekeeping. She spread his blankets and buffalo robe, then patted them and smiled up at him.

"We will warm these very well tonight, Preacher. Are you as ready as I am?"

To tell the truth, he *was* getting a mite worked up just watching Mountain Mist as she moved around the tent. If he had been the sort of man to settle down with one woman and start a family, he could have done worse than her, he told himself.

But he just said, "We'll let tonight take care of itself. In the meantime, I thought I'd sort of circulate around the camp and say hello to everybody I ain't seen since last fall."

"I will wait here and prepare a meal for you."

"You can come along, too," Preacher offered.

Mountain Mist shook her head. "No, my place is here, making sure everything is good for you, Preacher."

"If you say so." He was already unsure if he had done the right thing by taking her in like this. He thought that maybe if he left her alone for a while, she would realize that she had made a mistake and would slip out of his tent and go back to what she had been doing.

The afternoon passed pleasantly as Preacher renewed acquaintances with many of the trappers who had come to the Rendezvous. He swigged from jugs, told jokes, swapped stories about what was going on elsewhere, and laughed a lot. Over the course of the day, he didn't really think much about Rip Giddens and the Easterners Rip had signed on with, or Luther Snell or even old Stump.

When he finally returned to his tent as the sun was going down, a campfire blazed merrily in front of it, and delicious aromas drifted up from the pot that Mountain Mist was stirring. Not only was she still here, but it looked like she had settled in just fine. Preacher's nebulous plan—more of a hope, really—hadn't worked.

"I have food," she informed him. "And the horses and your dog have been cared for."

In fact, Dog was sitting on his haunches beside her, and he

appeared to grin as she lowered a hand and scratched between his ears. It took a lot to win over the big wolflike cur. Preacher thought that maybe he ought to reconsider his decision to part company with Mountain Mist after the Rendezvous was over.

They sat and ate together, and the stew that Mountain Mist had prepared lived up to its enticing aroma. It was mighty tasty. When the meal was over, Mountain Mist insisted on cleaning up while Preacher sat and smoked a pipe. Darkness had settled down over the valley, and the encampment was quieter than it had been earlier. Preacher still heard fiddle music and somewhere men were laughing, but it wouldn't be too much longer before folks began to turn in for the night.

He wondered briefly how those pilgrims in the fancy tent were doing. The noises of the night probably made folks like that nervous. Rip was going to have his hands full, not only keeping them safe but also keeping them calmed down.

Mountain Mist went into the tent, and a few minutes later he heard her call softly, "Preacher."

With a faint smile on his face, he tapped out the dottle from his pipe into the embers of the campfire and then put it away. He stood up and turned to go into the tent. There was a small fire inside, too, to ward off the nighttime chill, and as Preacher swept back the entrance flap, he saw by the flickering light of the flames that Mountain Mist was stretched out on the buffalo robe with one of the blankets pulled up over her. The blanket rose only as far as her smooth, bare shoulders, though.

"I am happy to be here with you, Preacher," she said with a smile.

"And I'm happy you're here," he told her. He was a little surprised to realize that his words were true. Maybe this was going to work out after all.

Mountain Mist pushed the blanket aside, her smile widening as she revealed that she wore nothing under it.

Preacher stepped into the tent and let the entrance flap fall closed behind him.

* * *

When they had finished making love, Mountain Mist fell into a deep sleep, but Preacher took his time about dozing off. He lay there with her in his arms and listened to the night sounds—the call of an owl, the distant howl of a wolf, the trumpeting of an elk. Lonely sounds in their way, but also reminders that a man was never truly alone out here on the frontier. Even though there might not be another human within a hundred miles, life still surrounded everyone who came here. Vibrant, ever-changing life, often full of beauty and peace, but sometimes touched with blood and sudden violence as well, as the squeal of some sort of rodent as it was snatched to its death by a hunting owl reminded Preacher.

When he finally drifted off, it was into his usual light slumber, where he rested despite the fact that a part of his brain remained alert for any warning signs of trouble.

He couldn't have said how long he had been asleep when he abruptly came fully awake. Preacher glanced around the inside of the tent, not sure what had roused him.

Everything looked all right. The fire, small to start with, had burned down to a tiny circle of faintly glowing embers. They gave off just enough light for his keen eyes to see that nothing was out of place and no one was moving around inside the tent.

But something had wakened him. Mountain Mist lay snuggled into his side, her nude body soft and warm against his leaner, more muscular shape. Preacher hated to leave her warmth, but he knew he couldn't rest until he figured out what had disturbed his sleep. Carefully, so as not to awaken her, he slipped out from under the blankets.

He had pulled on his buckskin trousers and was reaching for one of the pistols he had placed next to the buffalo robe when he heard the hissed voice from outside the tent. "Preacher!" it summoned. "Preacher, you in there?"

The voice was muffled so that Preacher couldn't be sure who it belonged to. He thought maybe the man calling him was Rip Giddens, but he wasn't certain about that. He knew plenty of other men at this Rendezvous who might be trying to get his attention for one reason or another. He stood up, padded in his bare feet to the entrance, pushed the flap aside, and stepped out into the night to see what was going on.

With a crashing impact, what felt like the entire world fell on his head, driving him down into a darkness so vast and deep, it dwarfed the massive mountains rising around him.

Chapter Four

Preacher swam up out of that ebony sea an unknown time later, struggling toward consciousness. The fact that he was still alive surprised him a little; anybody foolish enough to have walloped him over the head like that should have gone ahead and killed him, because when he caught up to the son of a bitch . . .

Well, whoever had hit him would pay for it, that was for damned sure.

There was no doubt he was still alive. His head hurt too much for him to be dead. With a groan, he forced his eyes open and lifted his head from the ground. The world spun crazily around him and the throbbing in his skull grew worse, as if all the imps of Hades were in there pounding on it with sledgehammers.

Preacher let his head fall back to the ground and closed his eyes again.

But he didn't allow unconsciousness to reclaim him. He was still aware of what was going on around him, and he listened intently, trying to pick up some clue as to what had happened to him.

The encampment sounded perfectly normal. A quiet voice here and there, raucous snores coming from a nearby tent, the occasional bark of a dog. The tranquil atmosphere that hung over the Rendezvous told Preacher that the hour was very late, because some of the trappers who came to these gatherings never stopped celebrating until exhaustion overwhelmed them.

A wet tongue suddenly lapped against his beard-stubbled jaw. Preacher groaned and levered his eyelids open again. Dog stood over him, licking him. Preacher cast his mind back to earlier in the evening. Dog hadn't been around when he had crawled into the blankets with Mountain Mist. The big cur had been out somewhere prowling around. Preacher might have worried about him being gone if they had been in a city, where man and dog both had unnatural enemies, but not out here in the wilderness. Dog could take care of himself here.

Preacher groaned again and rolled onto his side as Dog moved back a step. After letting his head settle down for a few seconds, Preacher got his hands and knees under him and pushed himself off the ground. He staggered to his feet and held his hands to his pounding skull. As he took an unsteady step toward the tent, one of his bare feet struck something painfully. He looked down and in the light from the moon and stars he saw his pistol lying on the ground. He must have dropped it when he got clouted over the head.

Even though it made him dizzy again to bend over, Preacher reached down and picked up the gun. When he straightened, he felt a little better because he had a weapon in his hand. He didn't like being unarmed.

A low moan came from the tent and made him jerk his head around. The dizziness and the throbbing in his head were instantly forgotten. That sound of pain had to have come from Mountain Mist—!

Fear and anger growing at almost equal rates inside him, Preacher lurched to the tent and thrust his way through the flap. "Mist!" he rasped. "Mist, are you all right?"

There was no answer except another soft moan.

Preacher couldn't see. He dropped to his knees beside the embers of the fire and carefully stirred them with a stick until a tiny flame leaped up. He fed more twigs into it. The fire caught and burned strongly enough to send a glow spreading out over the inside of the tent.

That flickering light showed him a hellish scene he would never forget. Mountain Mist lay on her back on the buffalo robe, still nude, her arms and legs outflung, her body covered with already-darkening bruises and streaks of blood on the inside of her widespread thighs. Her swollen face was stained with blood, too. A stream of it trickled from the corner of her mouth.

Preacher lunged to her side and grabbed her shoulders. "Mist!" he said as he tried to lift her and shake her back into consciousness. "Oh, Lord, Mist!"

She didn't awaken. Her head lolled loosely on her neck. But she cried out as Preacher tried to raise her into a sitting position, and he knew then that she must be broken somehow inside. He eased her back down, as gently and carefully as possible.

He knew as soon as he saw her what had happened. Somebody had lured him outside and knocked him unconscious, and then that somebody—several somebodies, more than likely—had come in here and attacked Mountain Mist, raping her and beating her, probably kicking her until she was all busted up inside. The bastards. The unholy bastards.

Maybe there was somebody here at the Rendezvous who could help her. Mountain men had an amazing variety of backgrounds. Many were illiterate and had never been anything other than farmers or laborers before coming to the high country. But others were educated men, and numbered among them were lawyers, teachers—and doctors. Preacher pushed himself to his feet and turned toward the tent's entrance, intending to go out and see if he could find anyone to help Mountain Mist.

Her voice stopped him. "P-Preacher!" she gasped as she regained consciousness. "Preacher, are . . . are you here?"

Instantly, he was beside her again, kneeling and catching hold of one of her hands.

"I'm here, Mist," he told her. "I'm right here."

"P-Preacher . . . there were men . . . bad men . . . they hurt me. . . ."

"I know." This wasn't the time to be asking questions, but he had to find out if she knew the identity of her attackers. "Did you see who they were? Did you know them?"

"C-couldn't see . . . they threw . . . a blanket over my face . . . held me down . . . choked me . . ."

Preacher could tell that from the sound of her voice as it came through her tortured throat.

". . . they . . . did things to me . . . hurt me . . . over and over . . . then started hitting me . . . and k-kicking me . . ."

She started to cry and writhe around as the memories came back to her, and moving like that must have sent pain shooting through her because she gasped and shuddered and whimpered. Preacher put his hands on her shoulders to hold her still and said soothingly, "It's all right now, Mist. It's all over. Nobody's gonna hurt you again."

He was all too afraid that was true. More blood had welled from her mouth while she was moving around. She had to have broken bones inside, ripping her to pieces. Preacher had seen a lot of people die, and he sensed that life was slipping away from Mountain Mist.

He didn't want to leave her now. It was too late for anyone to help her, too late for him to do anything except say good-bye.

And make a promise to her.

"I'll find them, Mist," he whispered. "I'll find the men who did this to you, and I'll see to it that they pay for hurtin' you."

"Preacher . . ." Her fingers tightened on his hand.

He leaned closer. "What is it?"

"I would have been . . . your woman . . ."

"Yes," he said, and meant it. "I think I knew that all along. You would have been my woman, and I would have been your man."

"We would have been . . . happy together . . ."

"Very happy," Preacher whispered.

She squeezed his hand hard and then sighed. The strength left her fingers and her grip slipped away.

"Damn it, Mist," he grated. "Damn it . . ."

But she didn't hear him. She was gone. He knew it even before he gently placed a hand on her chest and felt that her heart had been stilled.

He sat there beside her for a long time as the fire slowly burned down again, until only embers were left once more.

But those embers continued to glow hotly, as did the desire for vengeance in his heart.

The Rendezvous was just stirring to life again in the morning when Preacher came out of the tent. He was fully dressed now, and so was Mountain Mist. He cradled her in his arms as he walked slowly toward the center of the encampment. Indian women who had poked cooking fires back to life and were about to begin preparing breakfast stopped what they were doing when they saw Preacher walking by with the lifeless, buckskin-clad bundle in his arms. Some of the women hurried back into their tents and tepees to shake awake the men with whom they shared the hide and canvas dwellings. Others fell in behind Preacher, following him to see what he was going to do.

The representatives of the fur companies were the closest thing to civilization out here, the only ones who could even remotely be said to stand for law and order. Preacher intended to settle the score for Mountain Mist himself, but he wanted everybody to know what he was doing and why he was doing it.

He stopped in front of the largest tent and called, "Judson! Wake up in there! Judson!"

Benjamin Judson was the agent Preacher had sold his furs to the day before. The man generally bought more furs and paid the best prices, and if the group from St. Louis could be said to have a leader, Judson would be it. A few minutes after Preacher had shouted for him, he came out of the tent, rubbing sleep from his eyes with one hand and pulling up his suspenders with the other. He stopped short when he saw Preacher standing there holding Mountain Mist's lifeless body.

"My God! What happened?"

"She was murdered," Preacher said. "Attacked and murdered."

"Isn't she one of those Indian—" Judson stopped abruptly, but Preacher knew he had been about to say *whores*.

"What she was before don't matter," Preacher said. "For the rest o' this Rendezvous, anyway, and maybe after that, she was my woman. That's why I'm tellin' you, Judson, and everybody else in this camp, that I'm gonna find the men who did this to her . . . and kill the bastards."

"But Preacher," Judson exclaimed, "you can't think that *I* had anything to do with . . . with . . ."

"No, I know you ain't the sort to do anything like this. But you can see to it that word of what happened gets back to St. Louis, so that if there's ever any question of what I'm gonna do bein' justified, folks will know that the skunks had it comin' to them."

The word had spread rapidly, and quite a few people were gathered behind Preacher now, including the group of pilgrims from back East. Rip Giddens stepped out from among them and said in a hollow voice, "Lord, Preacher, I'm sorry. Do you know who did this?"

"I got a pretty good idea. I've only had trouble with one varmint since I got here." He turned, his eyes seeking a familiar, bushy-bearded face in the crowd. But he didn't see Luther Snell anywhere.

"Oh, my God, that poor woman." Preacher was surprised to see Faith Carling coming toward him. He hadn't liked Faith very much the day before, but this morning he saw mostly compassion on her face. She went on. "There should be a proper funeral service—"

"She'll be laid to rest proper," Preacher said. "The Shoshone way."

"But surely there should be a minister—"

Faith's brother came up behind her and laid a hand on her arm. "We shouldn't interfere in things we know little about," he said. "One reason we came out here to the frontier is to learn, isn't it, Faith?"

"I suppose so," she said. "Still . . . that poor woman."

Willard Carling approached Preacher. "What will you do? What ritual is involved?"

"Not much ritual," Preacher said. "I'll wrap her up in a blanket and find a cave up in the hills where I can lay her to rest. Most of the tribes put their dead up in a tree or build a special scaffold for the burial, but the Shoshones do it different."

"Fascinating," Carling said. "I don't suppose that outsiders would be allowed to observe—" At the look on Preacher's face, he broke off and then added hurriedly, "No, of course not. How rude of me to ask. You have my deepest sympathy, sir."

Preacher nodded curtly and started to turn away, but then he stopped and unexpectedly thrust Mountain Mist's body into Rip's arms. Rip looked startled, of course, but he took the body, a little clumsily but as carefully as he could.

"Preacher," he said, "what the hell—"

Without a word, Preacher stalked off. His hands went to the butts of the pistols thrust behind his belt, and as he pulled the weapons out, the members of the crowd began to scatter, getting out of his way and giving him plenty of room for whatever he intended to do.

He had spotted the ugly face he had been looking for a few minutes earlier. Luther Snell had just stepped out of a tepee, yawning prodigiously and stretching. He didn't seem to notice his doom bearing down on him until Preacher stepped up, thrust the barrels of both pistols into his face, and said coldly, "Snell, in about a minute I'm gonna blow your damned head clean off."

Chapter Five

Snell's eyes bulged in apparent shock. "Preacher, be careful with those guns!" he said. "You're gonna hurt somebody!"

"Damn right I'm gonna hurt somebody. You, you bastard." Preacher's voice shook a little from the depth of the emotions that gripped him. "You killed Mountain Mist. First you raped her, then you beat and kicked her to death."

"Mountain Mist?" Snell repeated. "Who . . . Preacher, I don't have any idea what you're talkin' about. I been in this tepee all night long. Never came out until just now."

"You're a liar," Preacher said coldly. "You and probably some of those no-account friends of yours are responsible for a good woman bein' dead."

"Wait just a minute, Preacher." The voice belonged to Benjamin Judson, who had come up behind Preacher and spoke carefully, lest the furious mountain man whirl around and open fire on *him*. "You've made a serious accusation against Snell," Judson went on. "You should let him answer it."

"Anything he says'll be a lie," Preacher growled. The guns in his hands were still rock-steady, and the muzzles were only inches from Snell's face, which had gone pale from shock and fear under its tan.

"It's the truth, Judson," Snell said desperately. "I don't know what Preacher's talkin' about."

Rip Giddens said, "This is what he's talkin' about," as he stepped forward with Mountain Mist's body in his arms. He had a better grip on her now.

Snell shook his head vehemently. "I didn't do that," he insisted. "I don't know nothin' about it. I swear!"

"Swear all you want to," Preacher said. "Nobody else had any reason to hurt her."

"What reason did *I* have? I didn't even know her!"

"You knew she was with me. You were gettin' back at me for what happened earlier in the day."

"For what happened . . . you mean that little run-in over those pilgrims? Hell, Preacher, that didn't amount to anything. I wouldn't have hurt nobody over that."

"I don't believe you. And I've held off on killin' you long enough—"

Someone else came out of the tepee behind Snell. He heard the entrance flap being pushed out of the way and said, "Wait a minute! Don't shoot, Preacher! Just ask the squaw. Ask her if I wasn't with her all night!"

The stocky woman who had emerged from the tepee wore a buckskin dress and had her black hair in two braids that hung over her shoulders. Preacher recognized her as one of the women who had come to the Rendezvous to sell her body to the trappers. A look of fear appeared on her face as she saw Preacher pointing the pair of pistols at Snell.

"Ask her!" Snell said again, his voice rising as an edge of hysteria crept into it.

"Preacher, you really should," Judson said. "It's the civilized thing to do."

Problem was, Preacher wasn't so sure he wanted to be civilized right now. The way he saw it, the spread of so-called civilization across the frontier wasn't necessarily a good thing. Civilized men were more likely to lie, cheat, and steal. Civilized men thought they could get away with anything because their society and its laws would protect them. In

Preacher's view, men who were regarded as barbarians by most Easterners were more likely to be honest and polite—because they knew that being *dis*honest and *im*polite could get them killed in a hurry.

So Judson's argument about doing the civilized thing didn't carry much weight with Preacher. But he had tried to live his life in a fair, honest manner, so he supposed it wouldn't hurt anything to ask the woman about Snell.

"Was this man with you all night?" Preacher put the question to her in her own tongue.

To his surprise, she nodded. "He paid for me to stay with him all night and did not leave this tepee," she answered in the same language.

Preacher frowned. "That's impossible. He must've left with some of his friends—"

The squaw stopped him by shaking her head. "He was with me."

"You see?" Snell said in English. "I told you, Preacher! I done told you I didn't hurt nobody!"

Preacher's jaw tightened. He still didn't believe it. The squaw was lying. Snell had either paid her to back up his story, or she was too afraid of him not to. Snell had to be to blame for what had happened to Mountain Mist.

Judson said, "Preacher, it appears that your accusations were unfounded." The fur company agent spoke enough of the tribal dialects that he had been able to understand the gist of what the squaw was saying.

"No, it's a lie," Preacher insisted. "Snell told her to lie."

"You just don't want to admit that you're wrong about me," Snell said. "Come on, Preacher, put those guns down. One of 'em's liable to go off."

Preacher's fingers tightened on both triggers as a snarl of hatred contorted his face. But he didn't fire. He eased off on the pressure as Rip said, "Maybe Judson's right, Preacher. I hate to say it, but you, uh, don't have any proof that Snell had anything to do with what happened to this poor gal."

"Proof! Since when does a man need any more proof than *knowin'* in his heart that he's right?"

Judson said, "That's not the way things work in a civilized society."

"Maybe you ain't noticed, Judson, but we're a hell of a long way from Saint Looey."

"I know that. But this is still American territory, and America is a nation founded on laws."

He wasn't quite correct about that, Preacher thought. America was a nation founded on doing what was right, and the law be damned. After all, having a revolution had been against British law, hadn't it?

But as Preacher glanced over his shoulder, he saw the same look on a lot of the faces that were staring at him, waiting to see what he was going to do. They believed Snell, he realized. Even though Snell wasn't well liked, he had a witness who said that he couldn't have committed the awful crime that had taken place.

Nobody would try to stop Preacher from pressing the triggers and blowing Snell's head off as he had threatened. Probably there wouldn't be any legal repercussions at all, considering that the closest authority was hundreds of miles away.

But if he killed Snell, Preacher knew that some of the trappers would always believe that he had been wrong to do so. Preacher wasn't the sort of man who lived his life according to what other folks might think of him. A fella could drive himself crazy doing that. He respected most of the other trappers, though, and knew that they respected him. For some of them, that would change if he killed Snell.

He growled a curse and lowered the pistols, looping his thumbs around the hammers so that he could lower them carefully off-cock. "I still think you done it," he said to Snell.

"I didn't. You got my word on that, Preacher."

"Your word don't mean shit to me," Preacher said curtly. "Stay outta my way the rest o' this Rendezvous. If I see you again, I might just go ahead and kill you, just on general principles."

Snell's jaw clenched. He was a proud man, and Preacher

knew he didn't take kindly to being threatened. But Snell just said, "We'll stay out of each other's way, how about that?"

Preacher didn't answer. He turned away, stuck the pistols behind his belt again, and went over to Rip Giddens.

"I'll take her now," he said as he held out his arms for Mountain Mist's body. "Thanks, Rip."

With great care, Rip placed the young woman's body in Preacher's arms again. "You want me to come with you up into the hills?" he asked.

Preacher shook his head. "No, this is somethin' I got to do by myself. You can get Horse saddled for me if you would, though."

"Sure, Preacher."

Ten minutes later, Preacher rode out of the encampment, leaving his tent set up and most of his gear behind him. He would be coming back when he finished the grim chore that awaited him. With Mountain Mist wrapped in a blanket and cradled in front of him on Horse's back, Preacher headed for the hills overlooking the valley.

Behind him, most of the people who had come to the Rendezvous watched him go, including the four Easterners. "What a tragedy," Faith Carling murmured. "So typical of this savage wilderness."

"You don't know that," her brother pointed out. "We haven't been out here long enough to know what's typical and what isn't."

"I fear that we'll find out, Willard, before we ever see home again," Faith said with a sigh.

Preacher carried the shrouded figure into the cave and placed it with great care on the bed of pine boughs he had prepared. Then he backed away, removed his hat, and murmured a few words in the Shoshone language, a plea to Mountain Mist's Creator that He welcome her into the land where the sky was always fair and the breezes always warm.

Then he added gutturally in English, "Lord, have mercy on

the soul of this gal. Most folks would've considered her a
heathen, but You know and I know that ain't true. I ain't fool
enough to think that all trails lead to the same place when it
comes to the hereafter, but I figure since you made these
mountains and led her people here, You ain't gonna turn Your
back on her now." Preacher put his hat on. "Amen."

He left the cave, which sat on a small bench that shouldered out from the side of a hill, several miles from the valley
where the Rendezvous was being held. There were quite a
few large rocks nearby. Preacher picked up the ones he could
carry, his ropy muscles straining against the weight, and carried them over to the mouth of the cave. He had to use a rope
on some of the larger ones and get Horse to drag them into
place before he stacked the smaller ones on top of them. As
the morning grew warmer, Preacher found himself glad that
the opening into the cave wasn't any larger than it was. He
was able to pile up enough rocks to close it off in about an
hour's worth of hard labor.

With that job concluded, there was nothing left here for
Preacher to do. He mounted up, nodded toward the cave, and
said, "So long, Mountain Mist. You didn't deserve what you
got, and I swear to you, somehow I'll settle the score for you."

He nudged Horse into motion and rode back toward the
Rendezvous, the need for vengeance still smoldering in his
heart.

Around midday, Stump came up to Luther Snell and asked
anxiously, "Is Preacher back yet?"

"I ain't seen him," Snell replied. "Besides, you don't have
to worry about Preacher."

"But he was mighty mad when he rode out, mad about
what happened to that Injun gal—"

"Shut up!" Snell said, casting his eyes around. He and
Stump stood near the big rope corral where some of the trappers had their horses penned. No one was close enough to be
within earshot, but that didn't make Snell any less cautious.

"You know we didn't have nothin' to do with what happened, and the less said about it, the better."

Stump took off his hat and ran a hand over his balding head. "I wish I'd never listened to you," he practically moaned. "I didn't know you was gonna kill her. I thought we'd just bust Preacher over the head and then have some fun with his squaw. That's all you said we'd do, Snell." The little trapper was almost crying.

Snell grabbed Stump's shoulders and leaned closer to him. "Shut . . . the hell . . . up!" he said in a low, dangerous voice. "Nobody except you, me, and the other boys know what we done. They ain't gonna say anything, and neither are you!"

"But Preacher knows—" Stump blubbered.

"Preacher don't know shit! He just thinks he does. He can't prove a damned thing, because *my* squaw told him I was with her all night, and half the folks here heard her. Preacher can't touch us."

"But he knows she was lyin'. He's gonna come after us and kill us anyway. He'll come for us in the night and slit our throats, you just wait an' see if he don't—"

Snell hauled off and walloped Stump in the face.

The blow knocked the little trapper back a couple of feet. Stump lost his balance and sat down hard on the ground. Tears sprang into his eyes as he looked up at Snell.

"Aw, hell," he said. "What'd you go and do *that* for?"

"To knock some sense into your head," Snell said. "Listen, Stump, the only thing we have to worry about is you goin' off and runnin' that mouth of yours. If you don't, Preacher can't touch us."

"I dunno. . . ."

"I do," Snell said confidently. "We're all in this together, so we got to trust each other. If we can't do that, then we'll just have to make sure some other way that nobody talks." He glared ominously at Stump.

With a scared gulp, Stump said quickly, "I won't say nothin', Luther. You can count on me. I got a mite spooked there for a minute, but I'm over it now."

"Good. See that you stay that way." Snell rubbed his bearded jaw. "I got somethin' else in mind you might want to be part of, Stump. You've seen those folks from back East, haven't you?"

"That prissy little artist feller and his sister and the rest o' that bunch? Sure, I seen 'em."

"The gal's sort of pretty, and I'll bet her brother's got a heap of money," Snell said speculatively. "He must have, if he was able to mount a big expedition out here and afford that fancy tent. I'll bet he could raise a heap o' cash if he had to buy his way outta trouble."

Stump frowned. "But what sort o' trouble could he get into all the way out . . . Oh, no, Luther. You ain't thinkin' what I think you're thinkin'. Are you?"

A wolfish grin stretched across Snell's face. "Hide an' watch, Stump, that's all I got to say. Just hide an' watch."

Chapter Six

Rip Giddens must have been keeping an eye out for Preacher, because he came striding over as soon as Preacher had ridden back into the encampment and dismounted.

"Get it taken care of?" Rip asked.

"Yep," Preacher replied tersely. "Now I've got other things to do."

"If you're talkin' about Luther Snell," Rip said, "you're gonna have to leave him alone, Preacher. Everybody's sorry about what happened to Mountain Mist, but most folks are convinced that Snell didn't have anything to do with it."

Preacher snorted. "I don't care all that much what most folks think." He had been brooding about Mountain Mist's death all the way back from the cave where he had laid her to rest. The injustice of it all gnawed at his guts like a beaver at a log.

"I know that, but Judson's been talkin'."

Preacher stiffened. "About what?"

"About how if you kill Snell, he's gonna tell the law about it back in Saint Looey and swear out a warrant for your arrest."

Preacher gave a humorless laugh and said, "No lawman's gonna come all the way out here to serve that warrant."

"No, you'd be safe enough as long as you stayed in the

mountains. But if you ever went back to Saint Looey or any other town, you'd have that murder charge hangin' over your head. Now, I ain't sayin' that any jury would ever find you guilty once they heard the whole story, but you can't never tell about things like that. You might find yourself facin' a hangin', Preacher."

"So, it don't matter what's right and wrong anymore, is that it?" Preacher demanded. "The only thing that counts is what some foolish law says?"

"Hell of a note, ain't it?" Rip asked with a gloomy shake of his head.

Preacher gripped his friend's arm. "We both know Snell and his pards are guilty as hell. I can't let 'em get away with it."

"Then you'll be an outlaw the rest of your life, Preacher. I'm sorry, but that's just the way it is."

Preacher let go of Rip's arm and stepped back, his face bleak.

"Look, remember that job I offered you?" Rip went on. "Come with us, Preacher. Put all this behind you. Mr. Carling plans to spend all summer out here, visiting the Injuns and paintin'. I'm hopin' everything will go smooth, but if it don't, I'd sure like to have you along."

"I don't think so—" Preacher began.

"At least come and eat dinner with us," Rip broke in. "Don't make up your mind yet. Get to know those folks better before you decide what to do."

Getting to know a bunch of greenhorns from back East didn't exactly sound like something Preacher really wanted to do. He had better ways to spend his time. But Rip was an old friend, and he had to eat anyway, Preacher told himself, so he supposed it wouldn't hurt anything to accept the invitation.

"All right," he said. "But that don't mean I'm comin' along on this here expedition o' yours."

Rip grinned. "Shoot, right now I'll settle for that."

As they walked across the encampment toward the big striped tent beside the river, Preacher's narrowed eyes searched for Luther Snell but didn't see any sign of him. Nor

did he spot any of the half-dozen or so trappers who were
Snell's friends. It didn't surprise him that they were all lying
low. Guilt would make a man hide quicker than anything else.

A table had been set up in front of the tent, and the rotund
Indian woman known as Sparrow was dishing out fried elk
steaks to the four people sitting at the table. Willard Carling
looked up with a smile and said, "Preacher, welcome! I'm
glad you decided to join us."

"Just for dinner," Preacher said as he and Rip pulled up stools
and sat down. "I still ain't goin' along on your expedition."

"That's a shame. Mr. Giddens tells me that you know more
about the flora and fauna of the frontier than anyone else."

Preacher knew Carling was talking about plants and animals. He said, "I don't know if that's true or not. I've been out
here a while, but not my whole life like the Injuns. I reckon
they know more'n I do."

"Where are you from?" Jasper Hodge asked.

"I was born in Ohio, and grew up there on a farm."

"How did you come to be out here?" Hodge seemed very
interested, but Preacher didn't know if that interest was genuine or if the man just wanted to talk about him in that book
he planned to write.

"I had the urge to wander," Preacher said, "to see what was
on the other side of the hill or down the river. So when I got
old enough, I left the farm and went to travelin' around."

"How old were you?" Faith asked.

"Thirteen."

They all stared at him, except for Rip. "Thirteen?" Carling
repeated. "My goodness, you were still just a child!"

"I felt like a man full-growed," Preacher said with a shrug.
"I reckon that's all that counts in the end, how a man feels
about himself."

"Yes, but how did you take care of yourself?"

"Worked on keelboats and such for a while, and then I
joined up with the Army."

"The Army?" Hodge asked in surprise. "But you were just
a lad."

"Yeah, but we was fightin' the British then, and the company I fell in with didn't much care how old a fella was as long as he could shoot a rifle and hit what he was aimin' at, which I did most of the time."

"So you took part in the War of 1812?" Carling asked avidly.

"Just the Battle o' New Orleans, mainly. And we found out later that the war was actually over before we fought that battle. Nobody told the British, though, and we sure as blazes didn't know."

"Fascinating," Carling said. "What about after that?"

Preacher wasn't the sort of man who enjoyed talking about himself, and the way the Easterners were staring at him and hanging on his every word didn't help matters, either. On top of that, he was still filled with rage and sorrow over Mountain Mist's murder. But he suppressed those feelings for the moment and said, "I met up with some fellas who were comin' out here to trap beaver. Sounded like a good way to see some country I hadn't seen before, so I decided to come with them."

Faith said, "And you've never been back to civilization since then?"

"Well . . . I've been to Saint Looey. Does that count?"

She laughed. "Barely."

"You should visit Boston," Carling said. "That's where we're from. An absolutely wonderful city."

Preacher shook his head. "I don't know. I reckon there'd be too many people there for me. I get a mite antsy when folks go to crowdin' me."

"I can testify to that," Rip said. "I recollect a time when Preacher got out of sorts with me 'cause I was trappin' in a valley twenty miles from the one where he'd run his lines."

"Oh, come now," Hodge said. "Surely you don't mean that he knew you were there, when there were that many miles between you?"

"Preacher knows things. I don't ask how."

With a grunt, Preacher said, "Ain't no trick to that. I saw

the smoke from Rip's campfire one day. I knew that fire didn't light itself, and there hadn't been any lightnin' storms lately to start a blaze, so there had to be somebody over there. I didn't know it was Rip until I went to visit."

"Well, if that bothered you," Carling said, "you probably *would* be uncomfortable in Boston."

"*I* always was," Chester Sinclair said.

The other three looked around at him, as if they hadn't expected him to speak. Preacher recalled that Sinclair had been pretty quiet every time he had been around the man. Sinclair looked a little embarrassed at the attention, but he went on. "I never liked having a bunch of people around me, either."

"Well, I can't imagine living in such solitude all the time," Faith said. "It's fine for a while. An artist sometimes needs to be alone for a time to do his or her best work. But being alone in this wilderness would drive me mad."

"You haven't been alone out here," Preacher pointed out. "A Rendezvous like this, well, it's plumb crowded compared to what life in the mountains is usually like."

A delicate shudder ran through Faith. "Spare me from that, please."

Carling shouldn't have brought his sister with him, Preacher thought. If he'd been bound and determined to see the West and paint what he found there, he should have come alone—or at least left Faith back in Boston where she belonged.

But it was too late for such considerations now, Preacher told himself. And anyway, it was Rip Giddens's problem, wasn't it?

The Rendezvous went on for another day and a half, and during that time Preacher didn't see Luther Snell or any of Snell's cronies. Snell was still around—Preacher talked to several men who had seen the trapper—but obviously he was keeping an eye peeled for Preacher and ducking out of sight any time Preacher came around where he was.

To Preacher that was just one more indication that Snell was guilty of the atrocity that had been carried out against Mountain Mist, but he figured most of the others at the Rendezvous wouldn't see it that way. They knew about the bad blood between the two men, and would think that Snell was just being careful not to provoke Preacher into a fight.

On the evening of the gathering's third day, everyone began making preparations to pull out the next morning. It had been a more subdued Rendezvous than usual, probably because folks had been sobered a little by Mountain Mist's death, and the trappers were anxious to get back to their work. The prime season for beaver wouldn't come again until the fall, so the buckskinners would spend their summer hunting, repairing their equipment, and trapping a little. They would keep busy until the weather began to cool off and the pelts again grew thick and lush.

Rip Giddens and his helpers packed up most of the party's gear, including the canvases that Willard Carling had worked on during the Rendezvous. Carling had painted several rough scenes of the festivities. Preacher had given Carling his word that he would pose for him, so even though he didn't feel much like it, he had stood still for several hours, his rifle cradled in his arms and his eyes lifted to the mountains, feeling a mite foolish, while Carling first sketched him in pencil and then did an actual painting of him. Carling seemed prissy and ineffectual most of the time, but put a pencil or a brush in his hand and he was somehow transformed, turning into a man who knew what he wanted to do and had the skills to accomplish it. His movements were assured and confident as he created images on paper and canvas.

Carling worked in silence for the most part, only occasionally giving Preacher instructions such as "Turn your head a bit to the left, please," and "Raise your chin just slightly." Preacher had no idea why those little adjustments were important, but he tried to go along with what Carling wanted.

Late in the afternoon, as the artist was finishing up, Faith emerged from the tent and watched for a while. Preacher felt her eyes on him, but didn't return the look.

When Carling was done and began putting his gear away, Faith came over to Preacher and said, "It was kind of you to pose for my brother."

"I told him I would," Preacher said with a shrug. "I like to keep my word."

"Yes, you're as much a noble savage as any of those redskins, aren't you, Preacher?"

He bristled a little. "I never claimed to be noble, and all the Indians ain't savages, neither. In fact, some of them have been the best friends the white men out here could have. There's been many a trapper who wouldn't have survived if it hadn't been for the kindness of some Indians . . . even though it might've been in their own best interests to let every white man west o' the Mississippi die from his own foolishness and stupidity."

"You have such a low opinion of civilization that you'd rather have seen this whole part of the country remain a pristine wilderness, isn't that true?"

"If you mean am I worried that we'll take all this territory that was fine the way it was and mess it up somehow . . . then, yeah, I reckon that's true, all right. But there's no stoppin' folks from wantin' to do better for themselves, and for some of 'em that means comin' west."

"But the others should stay back East, right? Like my brother and I?"

"You said it, Miss Carling, not me."

She smiled. "You know, Preacher, I get the feeling that you don't like us very much."

"It ain't up to me one way or the other."

"Come to supper tonight. Give us one last chance to win you over."

"It don't really matter," Preacher said. "After tomorrow, we'll probably never see each other again."

"All the more reason to spend this last evening with us."

Preacher shrugged. "All right, if that's the way you want it, ma'am."

"That's the way I want it. And don't call me ma'am. It makes me feel old."

"Sorry," Preacher said. And he was already a little sorry, too, that he had agreed to share one last meal with the party of pilgrims from back East.

But as he had told Faith, after tomorrow they would never see each other again, so Preacher thought he could stand them for a little while longer.

Chapter Seven

Sparrow outdid herself when it came to fixing that last meal of the Rendezvous. She made a tasty stew full of chunks of tender elk meat and wild onions. There was also fried trout caught fresh out of the river and some of the best biscuits Preacher had eaten in a long time, plus a chokecherry pudding that was good enough to make a man's mouth water. If nothing else, the expedition would eat good as long as they had Sparrow as part of the company.

Rip Giddens had given up asking Preacher to go along with them, and Preacher was glad of that. He didn't like having to refuse an old friend.

Willard Carling wasn't so easily dissuaded. Over dinner he said, "You're an excellent subject, Preacher. Are you sure I can't convince you to accompany us? I think I'd like to do an entire series of portraits of you, capturing you in a wide variety of moods."

Rip chuckled from the other side of the table. "Preacher ain't got but one mood," he said. "Touchy."

"That ain't true," Preacher said. "Sometimes I'm downright surly, like an ol' possum."

"Regardless, I wish you'd reconsider your decision," Carling said.

Preacher shook his head. "Nope. Sorry."

Carling shrugged and said, "Well, you can't blame a man for trying."

Preacher never had quite understood that sentiment. It seemed to him that depending on what a man was trying to do, you sure as hell *could* blame him if it was something bad.

When the meal was over, Carling told Chester Sinclair to go in the tent and fetch a bottle of brandy. Carling turned to Preacher and went on. "You'll stay and have a drink with us?"

Preacher didn't see what harm it would do. He nodded and said, "Sure."

Sinclair brought the bottle and tin cups. He poured the brandy and passed the cups around the table. When Faith took hers, she made a face and sighed. "It's come to this," she said, "drinking brandy from a tin cup rather than from a snifter of fine crystal."

"I reckon the stuff's got the same kick, no matter what you drink it from," Preacher said.

"I suppose." She lifted her cup and smiled at him over it. "Cheers."

Preacher nodded to her and raised his own cup.

He was used to drinking cheap trade whiskey, the sort of panther piss that was brewed in a washtub. The brandy was a lot smoother but still pretty potent. It went down easy and kindled a nice warm fire in his belly. After a couple of cups, he felt relaxed enough to ask Willard Carling, "What made you want to come out here in the first place? Weren't there enough things to paint back in Boston?"

"Of course, but not the things I *wanted* to paint." Carling leaned forward on his stool, warming to the subject. "You see, I'm interested in man's struggles with himself, with other men, and with nature. What else personifies those struggles better than this magnificent wilderness that's all around us?" He smiled. "Besides, I've never seen anything more *colorful* than these savages. My God, their clothing, their headdresses, their decorations . . . they're a veritable *riot* of hues! An artist with a good eye, such as myself, is in heaven trying to match all the delicates shades and blends of colors."

Preacher grunted. "If you say so. I never thought of it that way."

"Of course you didn't. You're too close to the subject. Why, you might as well be one of them yourself."

Preacher glanced at Faith, remembering the way she had called him a noble savage that afternoon. He hoped her brother wouldn't start down that same road.

Carling didn't. He went on. "Often, it takes a fresh eye to see the truth and capture it. That's what I bring to the West, Preacher . . . a fresh eye. And I want to capture everything I see and take it back East with me, so that everyone else can see it, too."

"Well . . . that ain't a bad goal, I reckon," Preacher had to admit.

The conversation went on a while longer before everyone was ready to turn in and get a good night's sleep. Rip intended for the party to make an early start in the morning.

Preacher shook hands with his old friend and said, "If I don't see you in the mornin' before you leave, good luck with this expedition, Rip. I got a feelin' you may need it, mother-hennin' a bunch o' chicks like these."

Rip grinned ruefully. "Aw, they ain't bad folks. They're just ignorant in a lot o' ways."

"Reckon we all are, in some ways," Preacher said.

He sketched a casual salute, then turned to walk off into the night. Dog padded along beside him as Preacher headed for his tent at the edge of the encampment. The big cur had lain at his feet during the meal and enjoyed the occasional bit of food that Preacher tossed to him.

Almost in spite of himself, Preacher had enjoyed the time he had spent with Rip and the group of pilgrims from back East. They were . . . interesting. Not really Preacher's sort of folks at all, but he supposed they had their good qualities.

And they had kept his mind off what had happened to Mountain Mist. But his outrage was always there in the back of his mind, and so was the vow he had made to her to see to it that the men responsible paid for their crime. It might take a while, but he intended to keep that promise.

As Preacher mulled that over, Dog suddenly stopped, looked behind them, and growled. Preacher stopped, too, trusting Dog's senses and instincts. His hand went to the butt of one of the pistols as a dark shape came toward him.

Before he could pull the gun, a woman's voice said softly, "Preacher? Is that you?"

He recognized Faith Carling's husky tones and relaxed. "Blast it, ma'am," he said, "you shouldn't be wanderin' around camp in the dark like this."

"Why not?" she asked as she came up to him. "Am I in danger? I had the impression that most of these men would never harm a woman."

"Think about what happened to Mountain Mist," he said, his voice deliberately harsh. "Most men on the frontier won't bother a decent woman . . . but that don't hold true for all of them."

"No, I don't suppose it does," she admitted. "But I wanted to talk to you while I still have the chance."

"We just talked durin' supper."

"What I have to say is more personal."

Preacher frowned, feeling a stirring of unease inside him.

"You see," Faith went on, "I've written a poem about you."

He had to make an effort not to laugh. "A poem?"

"That's right."

"I don't reckon anybody's ever written a poem about me before. It don't hardly seem like I'm worthy of anybody doin' such a thing."

"Oh, I beg to differ. Will you let me recite it for you?"

Preacher had to admit that he was curious. "Sure, go ahead," he said, reaching down to scratch Dog's head between the ears.

Faith straightened her back and lifted her chin, as if she were standing on a stage about to perform for an audience. "I call it 'Ode to a Forest Denizen.'" She took a deep breath. "'He stands like a statue, bedecked in the hides of the creatures he has slain, as sunlight and shadow play through the boughs of the trees and a fragrant breeze wafts up from the plain. Stripped of civilization, as wild and as free as any russet-skinned savage, this frontier godling . . .'" Her voice trailed off. She tried to pick up where she had left off, saying, "'This frontier godling, strong as Hercules, swift as Mercury, bestrides his wilderness Olympus much as Zeus bestrode the Olympus of yore. . . .' Oh, the hell with it!"

And as that frustrated exclamation burst from her, she stepped forward, threw her arms around the neck of a startled Preacher, and pressed her lips to his in a kiss.

Preacher didn't think much of Faith's poem. He had heard the little trapper called Audie recite line after line of Shake-speare's plays and sonnets, and Faith didn't have near the way with words that old Bill Shakespeare did. But all thoughts of such things went out of Preacher's head in that moment, driven out by the surprise he felt at the idea of Faith Carling kissing him.

No matter what he thought of Eastern gals, Faith was attractive, no doubt about that. Her slender body felt good as she molded it to his. But it was too soon after what he had shared with Mountain Mist, too soon after what had happened to the Shoshone woman, and Faith must have been able to tell that from the way he stood there stiffly, not returning the kiss or even putting his arms around her. After a moment, she pulled back and said quietly but angrily, "I know the poem was terrible, Preacher, but don't you like me, even a little bit?"

Preacher wasn't much good at lying. That was why he was in the habit of telling the truth, as he did now when he said, "No offense, ma'am, but not particularly."

"Oh! Well, we'll just see about that!"

Then, instead of letting go of him the way Preacher had figured she would do, she grabbed on to him tighter and kissed him again.

This one was interrupted by Chester Sinclair, who bounded up and yelled, "Let go of her!"

If Preacher could have gotten his mouth free, he would have

pointed out that Faith was the one hanging on to him, not the other way around. But he didn't get a chance to say anything before Sinclair took hold of her, pulled her away from Preacher, and then swung his right fist at the mountain man's jaw.

Preacher saw the wild, looping punch coming in plenty of time to duck under it. Sinclair's fist went harmlessly over his head as Preacher stepped in, grabbed Sinclair, and spun him around. His arms went around Sinclair from behind in a bear hug. He didn't want to hurt the young fella, just talk some sense into him.

"Settle down, Chester," he said. "There ain't no call for you to be mad."

"You . . . you were attacking Miss Faith!" Sinclair panted between clenched teeth. "I . . . I have a responsibility to protect her . . . to protect everyone in Mr. Carling's party!"

Preacher suspected there was a little more to it than that. He had already noticed the way that Sinclair looked at Faith Carling, especially when she wasn't paying any attention to him. Sinclair was sweet on Faith, Preacher thought—and she didn't even know that he existed except as her brother's assistant.

"Chester, what are you doing?" Faith asked, sounding more annoyed than anything else. "Have you lost your mind, attacking Preacher that way?"

Her words seemed to have the opposite effect on him from what she might have hoped. A rumble of anger sounded from deep inside him, and he suddenly threw himself backward, carrying Preacher with him.

Sinclair was just as tall as Preacher and packed more weight on his bones. He drove them both backward. Preacher lost his balance and fell. Sinclair crashed down on top of him. The impact drove the air out of Preacher's lungs and made him go limp for a second.

Sinclair rolled over and his hands groped for Preacher's throat. Even though Sinclair was a novice at this sort of rough-and-tumble fighting, anybody could get lucky, and Preacher knew that if Sinclair's hands locked around his neck, he might not be able to get them loose in time to keep from blacking out. So even though he didn't want to hurt Sinclair, he brought a knee up sharply, driving the point of it into Sinclair's belly. As Sinclair grunted in pain, Preacher grabbed hold of his shirt and heaved him to one side. Freed from the bigger man's weight, Preacher rolled and came up on his hands and knees.

He saw that Sinclair was struggling to get up. Preacher made it to his feet first. By now some of the trappers had taken note of the commotion and come on the run to see what was happening. Shouts of "Fight! Fight!" rang over the encampment, and more men hurried to watch the entertainment. Somebody caught up a burning branch from a campfire and carried it with them as a makeshift torch. The flickering light illuminated the scene as Preacher and Sinclair faced each other. Sinclair wobbled upright, hunched a little over the pain in his midsection. But his fists were still bunched, and he started toward Preacher again.

"Damn it, Sinclair, don't do this!" Preacher urged. "We got no reason to fight."

"Miss Faith—" Sinclair began.

"Was just sayin' some poem she's written."

"That's not true," Sinclair accused. "I saw you kissing her!"

Preacher glanced at Faith, who stood by watching the confrontation, her face pale and tense. It wouldn't do her reputation any good if word got around that she had thrown herself at him. Not sure why he should care about such a thing, Preacher asked through gritted teeth, "How about if I apologize to her?"

Sinclair halted his unsteady but inexorable advance. "Well," he said, "that would be a start, I guess."

Preacher extended a hand toward him, palm out. "Stay right there." He turned toward Faith. "Miss Carling, I sure do beg your pardon and hope I didn't cause you any offense by my behavior."

Faith sniffed and said haughtily, "That's quite all right, I suppose. It would be a mistake to expect too much in the way of proper behavior from men such as yourself."

Dog growled, and Preacher felt a mite like growling himself. But he swallowed his pride and said, "Thanks, ma'am." Looking back at Sinclair, he went on. "It's all over now. No need for any more ruckus."

Sinclair straightened and pointed a finger at Preacher. "You say away from Miss Carling in the future," he warned.

"Believe you me," Preacher said, "that's exactly what I intend to do."

Chapter Eight

There was some grumbling from the other trappers because the fight hadn't amounted to much, but Preacher didn't care. He was just glad he'd been able to head off the trouble before he was forced to do any serious damage to Chester Sinclair. The poor fella couldn't help it that he was smitten with Faith Carling, just like he couldn't do anything about the fact that Faith was such a . . . well, bitch was the word that came to mind, Preacher thought.

He tried to forget about the whole thing as he went on to his tent and rolled up in his blankets. The thought that he had shared these blankets with Mountain Mist only a few nights ago made it easy for him to put Faith, Sinclair, and the rest of that bunch out of his mind.

Didn't make it any easier for him to go to sleep, though.

He woke up early the next morning, as usual. As he stepped outside his tent to stretch, he looked toward the river and saw that the fancy striped tent wasn't there anymore. It had been taken down and packed up. Movement caught Preacher's eye, and when he glanced up at the hills, he saw a line of riders moving along the nearest slope, trailed by a group of packhorses and mules. Despite the early hour, the Carling expedition was on the move.

Good riddance, Preacher thought. He took a moment to hope that things worked out for them, for Rip's sake.

All over the encampment it was the same story, trappers moving out, some on foot, some on horseback, most of them trailing pack animals. Some of them took squaws with them, too, "summer wives." Most of the buckskinners had "winter wives," as well, and not necessarily the same women who spent the summers with them. The arrangements were casual and produced nothing lasting except a passel of half-breed kids.

Preacher brewed some coffee and ate a stale biscuit for breakfast, then took down his tent and got the rest of his gear stowed away on the packhorse. He saddled up Horse and then paused for a last look around the valley. He wouldn't be taking fond memories away from this Rendezvous. Although it had been good to see Rip Giddens and some other old friends, too many bad things had happened. When he thought about this Rendezvous, Preacher would always have a sour taste in his mouth.

He swung up into the saddle. After three days of rest, Horse was anxious to hit the trail again. The rangy mount danced a little to the side, skittish and eager to get moving.

That skittishness saved Preacher's life. He heard the distant boom of a shot and then the flat wind-rip of a rifle ball passing close beside his ear, right where his head had been a second earlier.

Knowing from the sound of the shot that it had come from somewhere behind him, Preacher whirled Horse around. His eyes scanned the landscape, looking for the telltale powder smoke that would tell him where the rifleman was located. He spotted a gray haze floating above a clump of trees on a hillside about two hundred yards away. With an angry shout, Preacher drove the heels of his moccasins against Horse's flanks and sent the animal lunging into a gallop.

Preacher leaned forward over Horse's neck, making himself a smaller target as he raced toward the trees where the would-be killer was hidden. He figured the man would try again, so after a few seconds, long enough for the rifleman to reload, Preacher veered Horse back and forth. Sure enough, a rifle ball kicked up dirt to his left. He hadn't been able to hear the shot over the pounding of Horse's hooves, but he knew the rifleman had fired.

And now the son of a bitch, whoever he was, wouldn't have time to reload again before Preacher reached him.

The rifleman must have realized that, too, because when Preacher reached the trees he didn't see any sign of the man. He reined Horse to a stop and sat tensely in the saddle for a few seconds, listening intently. He heard a swift rataplan of hoofbeats coming from farther up the hill and bit back a curse. The man who had taken those shots at him was running.

The bastard would find that he couldn't run far enough or fast enough to get away from Preacher.

Stump's heart slugged so heavily in his chest, he thought it was going to bust right out of his body and fall to the ground to flop around like a fish out of water. That was crazy, of course, and Stump knew it. He also knew that he was out of his mind with fear.

He should have listened to Luther Snell, he told himself. Snell had insisted that Preacher wouldn't come after them. But Stump didn't have Snell's confidence, and even though he planned to join up with Snell in the man's latest scheme, Stump wanted to get rid of Preacher first.

He would have, too, if that damned horse hadn't chosen the exact wrong second to move. . . .

Now Stump was on the run, and he knew that if he didn't get away from Preacher, he was a dead man. He couldn't take Preacher in a fair fight. Ambushing him had been the only chance Stump had. And now that was ruined, all because of bad luck. Bad luck for Stump, anyway. He supposed it was good for Preacher, because without it Preacher would be dead now, his brains splattered all over the campsite.

Stump kept his horse moving, heading up the hill where he had hidden to take his shot at Preacher. He knew that beyond the hill was a series of rough hogback ridges. If he could reach that rugged terrain, he might have a chance of giving Preacher the slip. A slim chance, to be sure, but right now Stump would take any chance at all and be glad to get it.

He never should have believed Snell in the first place. He knew that now. Snell was a vicious, lying bastard, and Stump should have known that he had more in mind than knocking out Preacher and bedding Preacher's squaw. That wouldn't have been enough to satisfy Snell's twisted need for revenge.

And why had Snell felt that way? Because Preacher had interfered when he started bothering that redheaded gal from back East, and Snell had been forced to back down in front of half the folks at the Rendezvous. That had been such an insult to Snell's pride that he had been willing to sink to murder to settle the score.

Stump knew about wanting to get even with somebody. Hell, he'd been mad at Preacher for making fun of him, too. All his life, people had been making fun of Stump because he was short. He had gotten used to that. But then one of the squaws he'd been with had told some of her friends about his lack of size in a certain area, and those squaws had told other squaws, and it had gotten back to the trappers they consorted with, and suddenly, before you knew it, he was a laughingstock, an object of ridicule from one end of the Rockies to the other. All for something that wasn't his fault, something he really hadn't had anything to do with.

Damn them, Stump thought. Damn all of them.

And suddenly, he didn't care what had happened to Mountain Mist. He was glad that Preacher had suffered over it. Preacher deserved that pain for making sport of him. Preacher didn't really know what pain was—but Stump did.

Stump reined in and looked around. He was several miles from the valley where the Rendezvous had been held. He had reached the first of the ridges where he had hoped to hide from Preacher.

After a moment, he plunged into that rugged, desolate terrain, but he no longer thought of it as a place to hide.

Now he told himself it was going to be a good place for a trap. A trap for Preacher . . .

Preacher hadn't come in sight of the fleeing bushwhacker by the time he reached the rocky spines of the ridges that twisted their way across the landscape. Those sharp, steep folds of stone and earth were dotted here and there by scrubby pines and clumps of hardy brush. The ground was too hard to take many prints. With his rifle across the saddle in front of him, Preacher proceeded more slowly now, aware that he might be riding into an ambush. But he knew, too, that if the mysterious rifleman *wasn't* laying for him, there was a good chance that the man was increasing his lead at that very moment.

This wasn't the first time Preacher had been between such a rock and a hard place. He pushed on, determined not to let the man get away.

He had a pretty good idea who he would find when he caught up to the bushwhacker—Luther Snell. Snell knew Preacher's reputation, knew that he would never be truly safe from reprisals for Mountain Mist's death as long as Preacher was alive.

So he had decided to take care of that little problem by shooting Preacher from ambush. That was the coward's way—but then, Snell was a coward. He had proven that by attacking a woman.

Most of Preacher's senses came into play now as he stalked his quarry. He looked, he listened, he even sniffed the air, searching for the smallest hint that the bushwhacker had passed this way. He was careful not to skyline himself on top of any of the ridges. His path twisted back and forth like a drunken snake. Dog had followed him from the encampment, and Preacher said to the big cur in a low voice, "Find him, Dog. Find the jasper who took those shots at me."

Dog bounded off, nose to the ground. He soon vanished in the desolate terrain, but Preacher knew he would still be close by.

In addition to his senses, Preacher also paid close attention to his instincts. His gut told him that he was being watched before his eyes spotted a tiny red flash on the ridge that loomed to his left. He knew it was the rising sun reflecting off metal, and the most likely metal to be up there in those trees was the barrel of a gun. Preacher rolled out of the saddle as a rifle boomed.

The ball sizzled through the air just above Horse's back and whined off a rock. Preacher landed on his feet, yelled, "Horse! Go!" and scrambled toward a boulder that would give him some cover. Horse galloped ahead, out of the line of fire.

Preacher knelt behind the boulder and laid the barrel of his rifle on top of it. He knew where the shot had come from, so he cocked the rifle, lined his sights on the spot, and squeezed the trigger. The rifle roared and belched a cloud of grayish-black powder smoke as it kicked against Preacher's shoulder. The hidden killer was well protected by trees and scattered rocks, but a lucky shot was always possible. Even if he didn't hit the bushwhacker, Preacher figured his shot came close enough to make the bastard duck.

As he began to reload, Preacher heard a sudden outburst of growling and snarling up there on the ridge, followed by an alarmed yell and then a howl of pain. Dog had found the bushwhacker and was introducing himself. Preacher finished ramming home a fresh charge in the rifle. Then he darted out from behind the boulder and his long legs carried him toward the slope at a dead run.

He heard a pistol crack and worried that Dog had been shot. The snarling and barking continued, though, as did the frenzied yells. Preacher started up the ridge, heading for the trees where the rifleman was concealed. They were about fifty yards away. The slope was steep enough so that even with Preacher's strength and conditioning, his heart was pounding by the time he got there.

As he came into the trees, Preacher spotted a buckskin-clad figure struggling with Dog. The big cur had the man's left arm in his mouth and was savaging it, but the man managed to grope at his belt with his right hand and pulled a big hunting knife. The blade rose, ready to strike at the dog.

"Hey!" Preacher yelled.

Taken by surprise, the bushwhacker twisted toward him. Preacher had time to realize with a shock, just before he pulled the trigger, that he was looking at the little trapper called Stump, not Luther Snell. Then the rifle blasted and Stump was thrown backward as the heavy lead ball smashed into him. The knife flew from his fingers as he fell.

"Dog!" Preacher called commandingly as he ran forward. "Dog, back off!"

The wolflike creature obeyed the command, letting go of Stump's arm and backing away, although he continued to growl. Preacher pulled one of his pistols as he approached the fallen Stump. The gun was double-shotted, with a heavy charge of powder, and if Stump tried any tricks, Preacher would blast a hole clean through him.

Stump was in no shape to attempt any trickery. Preacher's shot had hit him high on the right side of the chest. As Stump's chest rose and fell, Preacher heard the faint whistling sound that meant the rifle ball had penetrated a lung. Blood bubbled frothily from Stump's mouth. The little trapper didn't have long to live.

Preacher dropped to a knee beside the wounded man and said, "Stump, what the hell were you thinkin', potshottin' at me that way? You and me always got along all right."

Stump stared up at him through pain-glazed eyes. "You mean . . . you made fun o' me . . . and I never did nothin' . . . about it."

"Aw, hell, Stump," Preacher said, upset that some joshing had led to this. "It didn't mean nothin'."

"Not to you . . . maybe. I . . . hated you . . . for it."

Preacher hadn't known. He shook his head, sorry for the part he had played in all this. But then he stiffened and those feelings were forgotten as Stump continued to gasp out words accompanied by more blood.

"That's why I . . . went along with Snell . . . He said we'd . . . get even with you."

"What did you do, Stump?" Preacher demanded through gritted teeth. "What did Snell do?"

"Him and me and . . . some other fellas . . . called you out of your tent . . . clouted you over the head . . . then Snell and the rest of us . . . went inside . . . to take turns . . . with your squaw . . ."

Stump closed his eyes and a shudder ran through him. For a second Preacher thought he was gone. But then Stump forced his eyes open again and licked some of the blood off his lips. Looking up at Preacher, he rasped, "It was Snell . . . he's the one who started . . . hittin' and kickin' her . . . nobody else really planned on . . . hurtin' her."

"But you stood by and let it happen," Preacher said accusingly. "I'll bet some of you even helped him."

Stump didn't deny it. He just said, "I never meant to . . . hurt nobody . . . but I knew you . . . wouldn't believe that, Preacher. Snell wanted me to . . . come with him and the others . . . and go after those pilgrims . . . but I had to . . . try to get rid of you . . . first."

Preacher tensed even more as he listened to Stump gasping out the words. He didn't care that much anymore about the little trapper trying to ambush him. Something else Stump had said had caught his attention. He leaned closer and asked sharply, "What pilgrims are you talkin' about? Willard Carling and his bunch?"

"Y-yeah. Snell said . . . Carling's rich . . . said we could grab him and . . . make him pay to be let loose."

"Damn it! You're sayin' he means to kidnap Carling?"

"And . . . and the others."

That meant some of the other Easterners might be killed, and Preacher had no doubt that Snell planned to rape Faith Carling and maybe kill her. Preacher's jaw tightened with rage at the thought of it.

"How many men does he have with him?"

"Dunno . . . eight or ten."

That was enough to overpower Rip Giddens and the handful of other frontiersmen who had signed on to accompany Willard Carling's expedition. Rip and the others would probably be killed outright. Preacher didn't know who all had thrown in with Snell, but if they were going after the expedition, they had to be as bad as Snell was.

And he was the only one who knew about this, he realized, the only one who had any chance of warning the party of Easterners.

"I'm sorry about this, Stump, but I got to leave you here," Preacher said as he started to get to his feet.

Stump stopped him by summoning up the strength to reach out and grab his sleeve. "Leave me here . . . to die alone . . . you mean."

"You brung it on yourself," Preacher said bluntly. "Shootin' at me was one thing. Missin' that many times was your real mistake."

Stump didn't seem to hear him, though. The little man let go of Preacher's sleeve and fell back with a rattling sigh. His staring eyes glazed over the rest of the way.

Preacher didn't take the time to bury him. He hurried back down the hill, called Horse and Dog to him, and mounted up to head back to the valley where the Rendezvous had taken place, moving as fast as he could ride.

Chapter Nine

Unfortunately, Preacher's pursuit of Stump had taken him in the opposite direction from the way Willard Carling's party had traveled when they left the valley. By the time Preacher got back to the site of the encampment, almost everybody was gone. Only a few trappers remained. Carling and the others had long since moved out of sight. They would be miles away by now.

One of the men who hadn't left yet was friends with both Preacher and Rip Giddens. Preacher rode over to the man and said, "Howdy, Wingate."

"Howdy yourself, Preacher," the tall, red-bearded Wingate replied. "Say, did you hear some shootin' a while ago, just 'fore you took off like a bat out o' Hades?"

"Those shots were aimed at me," Preacher explained. "I went after the fella who fired them."

"Luther Snell?" Wingate guessed.

Preacher shook his head. "Stump."

That news shocked Wingate. "Stump? I didn't think that sawed-off little runt would have the gumption to ambush you, Preacher."

"Stump was a lot more bitter and angry than any of us realized."

Wingate grunted. "Yeah, I reckon so. You catch up to him?"

"I did," Preacher replied grimly.

"Well, then, I reckon ol' Stump won't be comin' to any more Rendezvous. Too bad. But he had it comin' for tryin' to bushwhack you like that."

"That's not all he did. Before he died, he admitted that he'd been with Snell and some others when they attacked Mountain Mist and killed her."

Wingate let out a whistle. "I never did quite believe Snell when he said he didn't have nothin' to do with that. You goin' after him and the others, Preacher?"

"Damn right, but that ain't all of it. Snell's got his sights set on that bunch o' pilgrims. He wants to kidnap that artist fella, Carling, and make him pay a big ransom to get free. Lord knows what he and his pards will do to the rest of the bunch."

Wingate's bearded features hardened at that revelation. "You need some help dealin' with this?"

"I think it's sort of my snake to stomp," Preacher said. "But I appreciate the offer, Wingate. When you were talkin' to Rip over the past few days, did he happen to say where all he planned to take those folks?"

"They were headin' north, toward Baldpate," Wingate said, naming a mountain that bore an uncanny resemblance to the hairless head of a man. "I don't know for sure where else they were goin'. Rip said somethin' about Seven Smokes, I think."

That was a valley about twenty miles distant where seven hot springs were located. Steam rose from the springs most of the time, but because the steam looked like smoke, the place had gotten the misleading name Seven Smokes. It made sense that Rip might take the expedition there. That sort of spectacular scenery was just the sort of thing that Willard Carling wanted to immortalize on canvas.

"Oh, yeah," Wingate went on, "he said they might try to visit ol' Hairface's band, too."

Hairface was a chief of the Teton Sioux who was reasonably friendly toward white men. The chief had some white blood himself, enough so that a little beard stubble had sprouted on his cheeks when he was a young man, giving him his name. The beard never grew enough that it needed to be shaved, just enough to make Hairface stand out from his fellow Sioux. Hairface's father, Preacher recalled, had been one of the first white trappers in these mountains, a citizen of a long-since-vanished settlement called New Hope.

"I'm obliged for the help, Wingate," Preacher said as he lifted his reins. "Reckon I'd better get started after Carling's bunch. I want to catch up to 'em before Snell and his pards do."

"That may be hard," Wingate said with a frown. "They've all got a head start on you."

Preacher nodded. "I know. That's why I've got to make up some ground." He lifted a hand in farewell as he turned Horse. "So long, Wingate."

Without looking back, he headed north, hoping that as one man on a good mount, he could move faster than either of the groups he was following.

Rip Giddens was a hardheaded, practical man, or at least he liked to think of himself that way. But like most men, he had his superstitious side, too, and as the group that he led rode toward Baldpate, he had a vague sensation somewhere deep within him that things might not work out just as he had planned. The Rendezvous they had left early that morning had been an eventful one, but not all of those events had been good. Far from it, in fact.

Twisting in his saddle, Rip looked behind him at the riders strung out along the trail. Willard Carling came first, with an eager expression on his face. His head turned ceaselessly from side to side as his eyes darted everywhere, trying to take in everything at once. Carling was nearly always cheerful and enthusiastic, with a friendly smile on his face for everyone. Not much of a man, maybe, but he had a good heart and could paint up a storm. His biggest problem was that he usually thought the best of everyone and didn't seem to realize that there were some pretty sorry sons of bitches in the world.

That couldn't be said of Jasper Hodge. The journalist had a certain cynicism and world-weariness about him. Just the opposite of Willard Carling, Hodge was probably too quick to think the worst of folks. He complained more than Carling did, too.

But not as much as the next rider in line, Carling's sister Faith. She had made it perfectly clear on numerous occasions that she didn't really want to be here. She had been perfectly happy back in Boston and had had no real desire to visit the frontier, despite her claims of being a poet and seeking inspiration in nature. The only reason she had accompanied her brother to the frontier was because he had insisted that she come along. Rip knew from talking to Carling that he and Faith were orphans, the only ones left in their family. Carling had inherited quite a bit of money from his father, who had been a wealthy banker in Boston, and that windfall had allowed him to pursue his dream of painting without having to worry about working for a living. Faith, though, being a woman, existed mainly on the kindness of her brother, and so she had agreed to come along on the expedition to keep him happy. Carling was generally considerate of other folks, but he seemed to have a blind spot that kept him from seeing that his sister wasn't happy.

That left Chester Sinclair, and Rip wasn't quite sure what to make of him. Sinclair was big and strong, but he let people push him around anyway. Carling wasn't necessarily mean to him, but he ordered Sinclair around like a slave. Rip understood that if you worked for a fella, you were supposed to do what he told you, but he wasn't sure he would have been able to put up with some of the things that Sinclair did. And it wasn't just Carling who bossed him. Hodge did, too, and Faith was probably the worst of the bunch when it came to taking advantage of Sinclair's accommodating nature. The fella had probably grown up poor, Rip reflected, and so he accepted without complaint whatever burdens were heaped on his head by those he considered his betters.

The Easterners were followed by Sparrow and the men Rip had hired to come along and help him guide and guard the pilgrims and keep up with their supplies and packhorses. Switchfoot had gotten his name because he was such a good dancer, able to keep his feet moving so fast it was hard for the eye to follow them. Rip didn't know why Hammerhead Jones was called that, unless it was because he had such a hard skull. There was nothing distinctive about Ed and Tom Ballinger except the fact that they were both tall and extremely skinny. Rip wasn't sure if both of them together weighed as much as he did. But that didn't mean they weren't tough as whang leather and damn near tireless. They could work all day without seeming to feel it.

They were all good fellas, tough fighters, men who would do to ride the river with, Rip thought. They ought to be able to handle just about anything that might come up.

But for some reason, he was still worried. He kept his rifle lying across the saddle in front of him, and his eyes roved constantly, on the lookout for any sign of trouble.

Everything seemed peaceful, though, when he called a halt at midday in a high mountain meadow that was practically bursting with wildflowers. Carling exclaimed happily over how beautiful the scene was. "I simply have to get this on canvas," he declared.

Rip frowned a little. "Well, I was sort of plannin' on us movin' on north all afternoon and gettin' close to Baldpate." He lifted an arm and pointed. "You can sort of see it there, in the distance, but it'll look a heap more impressive when we get closer to it."

"Yes, yes, I'm sure this mountain you're talking about will be very majestic," Carling said with a hint of impatience in his voice. "But we're surrounded by such splendor here that I just can't let this opportunity go to waste."

"Well, all right," Rip agreed reluctantly. "I reckon you're the boss."

"That's right, I am, and we can camp here tonight if we need to, can't we?"

Rip looked around. "It ain't a very good place to camp. There ain't no water, and we're sort of out in the open. There's no place to fort up in case of trouble."

"Oh, what sort of trouble could there be? A place so lovely could only be inhabited by friendly souls!"

Rip sighed. Carling had a hell of a lot to learn about the frontier, and Rip could only hope that the artist wouldn't have to learn it the hard way.

Sparrow got started preparing a cold lunch from food she had brought along from the Rendezvous, while Chester Sinclair set up an easel and canvas and then got out Carling's paints and brushes. Faith and Hodge contented themselves by strolling around the meadow looking at the flowers and talking. Rip's eyes narrowed as he saw the way Sinclair glanced at the two of them. He recalled the way Sinclair had jumped Preacher the night before. Sinclair was sweet on Faith despite the way she sometimes treated him, Rip thought, and that could cause problems. He took note of the dark look that passed across Sinclair's face as he heard Faith and Hodge laughing together.

Don't borrow trouble, Rip told himself. Just wait for it and deal with it when it comes.

He told Switchfoot, Jones, and the Ballingers to spread out around the meadow with their rifles and keep an eye on things while Carling was painting.

"What are you gonna do, Rip?" Switchfoot asked.

"Thought I'd scout on up the trail a ways. I don't know if Mr. Carling is gonna let us go on today or not, but if he does, I want to be sure where we're goin'."

He mounted up and rode north, keeping the main range of peaks on his left. Some smaller mountains rose to the right, but the course Rip followed was fairly level.

After a while the trail had curved around enough so that he could no longer see the meadow where the rest of the party was stopped. That didn't worry him. He would hear the shooting if any trouble broke out. As he watched a herd of moose go trotting past in the distance and an eagle wheeled overhead against the deep blue sky, he thought that Carling was right about one thing—this was really pretty country.

That beauty could hold plenty of danger, though, and Rip's instincts were still trying to warn him about something. As he came to a small creek lined with aspens and cottonwoods and clumps of thick brush on its banks, he reined in and frowned. His horse lowered its head to drink, then suddenly jerked back up. The horse realized that something was wrong, too. Rip started to lift his rifle and look around, even though he didn't know what he was looking for.

A shape hurtled out of the brush along the creek bank and launched itself through the air at Rip. He twisted in the saddle and tried to bring the rifle to bear, and as he did so he caught a glimpse of buckskins and raven-black hair plastered down with bear grease and streaks of bright paint on a red face. Then the young Indian warrior crashed into him, knocking the rifle aside before Rip could pull the trigger. The collision sent Rip toppling out of the saddle.

He hit the ground hard and lost his grip on the rifle. Even though he was half-stunned, he knew he couldn't afford to just lie there with a kill-crazy Indian on top of him. The Indian lifted a tomahawk, ready to smash it down on Rip's skull. Rip's hand shot up and grabbed the warrior's wrist, stopping the tomahawk as it began its downward stroke. With his back arching, Rip heaved up off the ground and flung the Indian aside. The warrior was smaller and lighter and was no match for Rip's greater strength. He rolled across the creek bank and fell into the water.

Rip surged to his feet and lunged for the rifle he had dropped. Before he could reach it, several more buckskin-clad warriors charged out of the brush. Rip roared angrily as they closed in on him. He knew his chances of getting out of this ambush alive were slim, but right now all he wanted to do was get his hands on a couple of them, crack their heads together, and maybe choke the life out of another one or two of the warriors.

He didn't get that opportunity. Something crashed into the back of his head, and blackness exploded through his consciousness, wiping it out and carrying him away into an endless dark void.

Chapter Ten

Chester Sinclair stood back and watched as Willard Carling painted. The brush in Carling's hand moved in swift, sure strokes, going from palette to canvas and back again as Carling hummed softly to himself under his breath. Sinclair was somewhat in awe of Carling's talent. The fact that somebody could daub paint on a canvas and actually make it look like something was akin to magic as far as Sinclair was concerned. That ability was beyond his comprehension.

The same thing was true of Faith Carling's skill with words. Sinclair wasn't even that good at talking. He got tongue-tied easily, especially around Faith. How she could select the right words and put them together in the proper order to create beautiful poems was beyond him. Sinclair could read and write, but he figured he couldn't have put a decent-sounding sentence on paper to save his life.

And Faith was beautiful as well as being smart and talented. She was way too good for the likes of him. Sinclair told himself that sternly every time he allowed his mind to drift and started thinking about what it would be like if he were Faith's beau. Sometimes, he even dared to ponder what it would be like if they were married. . . .

He found himself looking at her now, as she strolled

around the meadow with Jasper Hodge. Sinclair's jaw tightened in anger and resentment. He didn't like Hodge. The journalist was too arrogant, too sure of his own intelligence and good looks. Sinclair would have liked to take him down a notch or two. . . .

But of course that would never happen. No one could ever say that Chester Sinclair didn't know his place. The son of a father who had worked in a shipyard and a mother who had been a servant in a wealthy Beacon Hill household, Sinclair knew that his destiny was to play a subservient role in the affairs of others who were richer and better than he was. That meant he would never be around Faith Carling in any capacity other than that of her brother's employee. Certainly, he had no right to entertain any romantic thoughts whatsoever about her.

"What do you think, Chester?" Carling asked as he stepped back a pace and cocked his head to the side as he studied the painting.

Sinclair knew that Carling wasn't really interested in his opinion. Asking for it was just something Carling did, an excuse for a momentary pause while Carling himself decided what he thought of the work so far. Sinclair answered anyway, as he always did, saying, "I think it looks wonderful, sir."

In truth, the painting really *was* good. In a relatively few brush strokes, Carling had captured the sweep and variety of colors in the flower-bedecked meadow, and the snowcapped mountains rising in the background added a touch of perspective and majesty to the scene.

"It still needs work," Carling said, and he stepped closer to the easel and poised his brush over the palette again, selecting which color he would use next.

Sinclair heard Faith's merry laugh and turned his head to look at her and Jasper Hodge as they walked along together about a hundred yards away. Although they were far enough from everyone else so that their conversation was private, they weren't totally alone. Sinclair spotted one of the men Rip Giddens had hired to come along with them, the one called Hammerhead Jones. He was leaning against a tree trunk at the edge of the meadow, his rifle at his side. Giddens had placed the men at various spots around the meadow to act as sentries. Seeing Jones there, not far from Faith and Hodge, made Sinclair frown. Not for the first time, he wished that Carling had left Faith back in Boston. He'd had no right to subject his sister to the rigors of the frontier. Sinclair was convinced it was dangerous out here—even though they hadn't encountered any sort of real peril so far, only minor annoyances.

He was gazing narrow-eyed at Faith and Hodge when movement beyond them caught his eye. Jones must have noticed the same thing, because he suddenly straightened from his casual pose and caught up his rifle as he stared in the same direction Sinclair was looking.

Several buckskin-clad figures had emerged from some trees and were coming toward Faith and Hodge. The two of them had their backs to the strangers. A ball of cold fear exploded in Sinclair's stomach as he recognized the men as Indians. They broke into a run, charging silently toward Faith and Hodge, who were unaware of their danger.

"Miss Carling!" Sinclair shouted. "Look out!"

At the same moment, Jones yelled, "Injuns! Run, you damn fools!" He brought his rifle to his shoulder and fired.

The shouted warnings and the blast of the rifle got the attention of Faith and Hodge, all right. Faith jerked her head around and looked behind her, and a scream ripped out from her as she saw the warriors with their painted faces rushing toward her and the journalist. Hodge let out a startled yell, too, and grabbed Faith's hand. He broke into a run, dragging her with him.

Jones's shot must have missed, because none of the Indians broke stride. Sinclair dashed over to his horse and reached into a saddlebag where a couple of pistols were kept. He pulled the guns out one at a time and then spun around again, ready to race to Faith's aid. As he broke into a run, he cocked the guns.

He had only gone a couple of steps when he tripped and fell. Both pistols discharged as he struck the ground, and the roar of the exploding powder was deafening to Sinclair.

Worse still, he was now unarmed unless he wanted to use the empty pistols as clubs. He scrambled back to his feet and looked around wildly, hoping that the Indians hadn't caught up to Faith and Hodge yet.

They hadn't. Terror had lent wings to the feet of both of them. They sprinted across the meadow toward the spot where the horses had been halted. Their pursuers were closing the gap behind them, though. Sinclair stared in horror as the Indians began to shout and brandish tomahawks.

More help was on the way. Switchfoot and the Ballinger brothers were running in from other parts of the meadow. Switchfoot paused long enough to fire his rifle, and his aim must have been more accurate than Jones's because one of the Indians stumbled. The warrior didn't go down, though, just clapped a hand to a grazed arm for a second and then charged forward again, still shouting war cries.

"Oh, my God!" Willard Carling said as he dropped his palette and brush. "Savages!"

This was all wrong, Sinclair thought. While Giddens had warned them that not all of the Indians out here on the frontier were friendly toward whites, he had promised that he would avoid the areas where the more hostile tribes were known to roam. For that matter, where *was* Giddens? He had said that he was going off to scout, but he should have been back by now.

This was no time for pondering such questions, Sinclair realized. Still gripping the empty pistols tightly, he ran to meet Faith and Hodge. He wasn't going to let anything happen to Faith if he could prevent it. He would sell his life dearly to protect hers.

"Keep running!" he called to them as they came closer. "Hurry! Hurry!"

They hurried, all right. They sprinted right past him. Sinclair skidded to a stop, planting his feet and bracing himself for the inevitable assault.

One of the warriors lunged out in front of his companions and came straight at Sinclair, his paint-streaked face contorted in a scream of hate. He swung the tomahawk in his hand at Sinclair's head.

Sinclair ducked, only to discover that was exactly what the Indian wanted him to do. The warrior's knee rose sharply and drove into Sinclair's jaw. The blow staggered Sinclair and sent him falling to one knee. The tomahawk whipped at his head again, but this time the blow was no feint. It was intended to crush his skull and dash his brains out.

He jerked up the pistol in his left hand and felt the impact shiver up his arm as he blocked the tomahawk with the barrel of the gun. At the same time he rammed the barrel of the other pistol into the Indian's belly as hard as he could. The warrior grunted in pain and doubled over. Sinclair swung the left-hand gun against his head. The weapon landed with a dull thud. The Indian pitched to the ground.

Sinclair started to rise to his feet, but one of the warriors tackled him before he had a chance to straighten. He went over backward. The Indian crouched on top of him, howling out his hatred, tomahawk poised to sweep down and end Sinclair's life.

A rifle boomed somewhere, and the warrior was driven backward by a ball that struck him in the left shoulder. Something hot and wet splattered across Sinclair's face, and it was a second before he realized that it was blood from the Indian's wound. Feeling sick, he rolled away from the wounded man and came up on hands and knees. Somehow he had managed to hang on to both of the pistols.

When he lifted his head and looked around, he saw one of the Ballinger brothers—he had never been able to tell Tom from Ed—locked in a desperate struggle with one of the remaining Indians. The other brother was trying to reload his rifle. Sinclair realized that it had been Ballinger's shot that had saved his life.

To his horror, he wasn't able to repay the favor. One of the remaining warriors leaped at the man, whirling his tomahawk, and with a ghastly thud it crashed against Ballinger's head. Ballinger went down, blood streaming from the wound.

Sinclair threw himself at the warrior who had just struck down one of the brothers. The Indian tried to whirl to meet this new threat, but he wasn't in time to stop a pistol from crashing against his skull. The warrior went down, and Sinclair hoped with a newfound savagery of his own that the red-skinned bastard was dead.

Stumbling a little, he turned to see what was going on. The other Ballinger brother was down, and Sinclair's stunned eyes saw more of the painted figures in buckskin emerging from the woods. Six, eight . . . no, more than that, a veritable horde of savages, sweeping down on the hapless party of whites. Sinclair jerked his head around, trying to locate Faith. He spotted her near the horses, still screaming, while her brother and Jasper Hodge fumbled ineffectually with pistols. Switch-foot and Hammerhead Jones had retreated, too, and were grabbing the reins of the packhorses. They wanted to get out of here, and Sinclair didn't blame them.

"Run!" he shouted at the other men. "Take Miss Carling and go! I'll hold off the Indians—"

He didn't get any farther because someone tackled him from behind. He tried to catch his balance but failed. As he fell to the ground with the stink of bear grease in his nostrils from the attacker who clung to his back, he thought that he had only seconds to live. The Indian would probably jerk his head back and cut his throat.

Sinclair twisted his body desperately, unwilling to just lie there and be slaughtered like a pig. He was bigger than all the Indians, but their wiry strength was a match for his more plodding musculature. He felt more than one set of hands clawing at him, trying to hold him down on the ground. He drove an elbow into the stomach of one of his enemies, slashed at another with one of the pistols, and felt the barrel rip across flesh. The war cries filled his ears, which already rang maddeningly from all the shooting.

Even over that racket, he seemed to hear Faith's screams, which grew more terrified by the second. Whether he imagined her shrieks or really heard them, he didn't know, but his fear for her sent fresh strength into his muscles. With a bellow of rage, he threw off his attackers and surged to his feet, ready to do battle no matter what the odds.

One of the Indians swung a tomahawk at him. He twisted out of the way but couldn't avoid the blow completely. The flat of the flint head struck his left shoulder with such force that his entire arm went numb and pain shot through his side. He dropped the gun in that hand.

From the other side, a warrior crashed a fist into Sinclair's jaw. He struck back with the gun in his right hand, swinging it in a backhanded blow that sent the Indian tumbling on the ground.

There were just too many of them. They were all around him now, his vision filling with lithe, buckskin-clad bodies and painted faces. Hard fists hammered him to the ground. He tried to get up, but his strength deserted him. Raging inwardly because he had failed Faith, he struggled to get up until repeated blows to the head left him dazed and unable to move. He lay there, pinned down by the weight of several warriors.

Time passed, but Sinclair had no idea how much of it had gone by before he was finally lifted to his feet by his captors. Dizzy and sick, he would have fallen again if not for the cruelly tight grips they had on him. He felt like sobbing as he saw that the others had been taken prisoner, too, even the Ballinger brother who had been wounded. The man wasn't dead, though, Sinclair saw to his surprise. All of the whites were still alive, just helpless prisoners of these savages.

The four guides were bloody and battered from the fight. Faith, Carling, and Hodge appeared to be unharmed, but they were pale and wide-eyed with fear, especially Faith, who seemed to be on the verge of hysterics. Sinclair hoped she would control the reaction. She didn't want to do anything that would provoke their captors even more.

The Indians chattered excitedly among themselves in their own language. Sinclair had no idea what they were saying, but they seemed to be happy about all the supplies they found on the packhorses. They were less impressed with Willard

Carling's paints and canvases, which they tossed aside as if the items were worthless.

"Here now!" Carling objected. "Be careful with those!"

"You'd better not anger them any more than they already are, Willard," Hodge advised. "Who knows what these murderous savages will do?"

Faith let out a little sniffling sob. Sinclair's heart went out to her, and the rage he felt inside toward the Indians grew stronger. He was too beaten up to do anything about it, though.

Several more Indians came up, dragging someone with them. Sinclair wasn't too surprised when this unconscious prisoner was dumped on the ground and he saw that it was Rip Giddens. They must have jumped Giddens first while he was out scouting, then backtracked him here to the meadow.

Odd how such a beautiful place had so quickly become a scene of fear and horror.

The Indians gathered up all the horses. The still-senseless Giddens was tossed roughly over the back of one of the animals. The prisoners were grouped together and prodded into motion. Sinclair had no idea where the Indians were taking them, but he supposed they ought to be grateful that they hadn't all been murdered outright.

Unless, of course, the savages were taking them somewhere to torture them to death.

That thought made a shudder go through Sinclair, but he managed to keep putting one foot in front of the other. He fought down his own fear and told himself that as long as they were alive, they had a chance. They would have to wait for a good opportunity to escape, and if one came along, they would have to seize it. In the meantime, he would try to recover as much as he could from the thrashing he had received, so that he would be in good enough shape to fight if he got the chance.

Their survival was up to them now, he thought. No one was going to come to help them. He wished Giddens had gotten some more men to come with them, maybe even that ruffian

Preacher. But Preacher was doubtless miles away by now, not giving them another thought.

One thing was certain, Sinclair vowed grimly. If the savages tried to hurt Faith Carling, they would have to come through him first. He would die before he would let them harm her.

Of course, that might be exactly what they had in mind. . . .

Chapter Eleven

Horse responded gallantly anytime Preacher asked him for his best efforts, and today was no exception. Preacher kept moving at a fast pace all morning as he tried to cut the gap between himself and the two groups he was after.

He would catch up with Snell and the other men who were bent on kidnapping Willard Carling first, and as he rode Preacher asked himself whether he wanted to try to deal with them right away, or get around them without them knowing it and hurry on to warn Rip Giddens and the Easterners that they were in danger. The ten-or-twelve-to-one odds that he would face if he took on Snell's bunch didn't bother him all that much. He had faced high odds in battle before and come through all right.

But anything could happen in a fight, and if he jumped Snell and the other men first, and they got lucky enough to kill him, then no one would be left to warn Rip. Somewhat reluctantly, Preacher decided that the best thing to do would be to avoid Snell's gang and try to catch up to the group of pilgrims.

In order to do that, and to save himself some time, he figured to take some shortcuts that he knew of. Rip probably knew about them, too, but he wouldn't take inexperienced travelers over any of the trails Preacher had in mind. The trails were too rough for that. If Rip was headed first for Baldpate, as Wingate had said, then he would follow the nice, easy route that curved along north at the foot of the mountains. Snell would probably take the same trail, since he didn't know anyone was aware of his plans and wouldn't be in any particular hurry to catch up.

So Preacher took to the high country, sending Horse up slopes that most mounts wouldn't have been able to negotiate. The rangy Horse was almost as nimble as a mountain goat, though. Preacher pointed Horse in the right direction and let him pick the best path. Dog bounded along from rock to rock behind them.

They climbed steadily but angled northward at the same time. Midday found them on a narrow, twisting ledge that followed the face of a cliff. Preacher's left shoulder almost brushed the sheer stone wall beside him, while his right foot in the stirrup hung over a drop of several hundred feet. It was enough to make a man a mite nervous, and he would've been if he hadn't been on the sure-footed Horse. Dog padded behind him, not quite as exuberant now. From time to time the big cur glanced over at the void and whined.

"Don't worry," Preacher told him. "There's only another mile or so o' this."

Eventually, the ledge led back down to lower ground, but they were still hundreds of feet higher than the trail down below. Preacher dismounted on a boulder-littered shoulder to let Horse have a breather. He took his rifle and went over to the edge of the slope. Jagged juts of rock rose and fell below him, sweeping all the way down to the valley between the mountain ranges. As he stood there, Preacher stiffened at the sound of distant gunshots. They came from several miles to the north, he judged. His lips drew back from his teeth in a grimace. Had Snell already caught up to the Easterners?

Preacher was about to whirl around and hurry back to mount up, even though he had intended to give Horse more time to rest. But as he turned, movement caught his eye, and he stopped to peer down into the valley. A good half mile away, and several hundred feet below him, riders had come into view, also heading north. They were sort of bunched up, but Preacher thought there were about a dozen of them. He went over to Horse and dug a spyglass out of his saddlebags. Returning to the edge of the shoulder, he dropped to a knee behind a boulder and opened the spyglass. He rested the thin tube on the rock and put his eye to the end of it.

The spyglass was powerful enough so that the faces of the riders below seemed to spring up at him. He recognized the ugly, bearded features of Luther Snell right away. Preacher's eyes went from face to face as he noted the identities of the men riding with Snell.

Euchre, Hardcastle, Vickery, Abner and Patch Dimock— who were cousins, not brothers—Collins, Mitchum, Singletree, and Baldy . . . Preacher knew each and every one of them, and what he knew about them wasn't good. Euchre, Hardcastle, and the Dimocks had been partners with Snell for a long time, and they weren't any better than he was. Vickery, Collins, and Mitchum had been friends of Stump, and probably wondered why the little trapper hadn't joined the group. Singletree and Baldy were loners, but they were willing to throw in with other fellas if the pickings were good enough. All of them worked as trappers, but all of them had unsavory reputations and were said to have been in trouble with the law before coming west to the mountains.

Preacher wasn't one to hold a man's past against him. The frontier changed some fellas, gave them a sense of freedom and perspective in their lives and turned them into pretty good folks. But most men who were no good in Philadelphia or St. Louis or Cairo, Illinois, were still no good when they reached the Rockies, and Preacher had a feeling that was true of the men he was looking at now.

He closed the spyglass and turned around to sit with his back propped against the boulder. If Snell and the rest of his bunch were still this far south, he asked himself, then who had been doing that shooting to the north?

Had Rip and his charges run into some other kind of trouble?

Preacher frowned darkly at the thought. He was facing enough problems already, trying to get Rip and the others out of the danger they didn't even know they were in. Now he had to worry that something else might have happened to them.

After a moment, he stood up and went back to Horse, staying low so there wouldn't be any chance of Snell or the others spotting him. He stowed the spyglass away and then led Horse as far back on the shoulder of rugged ground as he could before mounting up again. For a minute there, as he had peered through the glass at Snell, he had thought about how easy it would be to line up a rifle shot and blow the bastard right out of his saddle. The range was long, but Preacher had made shots like that before and was confident that he could do it again. He knew now that Snell was responsible for Mountain Mist's death. He had been convinced of it before, but now he had heard the truth from the dying Stump and there was no longer any doubt. Snell deserved to die.

But killing him would alert the others, and there was no guarantee that they would abandon their plan and turn back if Snell was dead. They might have come after Preacher, too, and tried to kill him. He couldn't afford to risk that.

Not until he found out for sure what, if anything, had happened to Rip Giddens and the group of pilgrims in his charge.

Preacher rode on, being careful not to let himself be spied by the group of men riding on the trail below. He moved as fast as he could and still be cautious. Gradually, he worked his way down out of the mountains, and when he came out on the level ground at their base, he looked back to the south and saw no sign of Snell and the others. He was far enough ahead of them now that he didn't have to worry about them spotting him.

He turned Horse to the north and heeled him into a ground-eating trot. Dog ranged ahead, flushing out ground squirrels and birds.

Preacher judged that he ought to be getting pretty close to the spot where the shooting had taken place. Sure enough, as he entered a broad meadow covered with wildflowers, something out of place caught his eye. Things were scattered around in the middle of the meadow. He couldn't tell what they were at first, but as he came closer he recognized the rectangles as Willard Carling's canvases. Some were blank, but others had works in progress on them, including the portrait of Preacher that Carling had started back at the Rendezvous.

From the looks of the canvases, somebody had tossed them around haphazardly. Jars of paint were scattered across the ground, too, some of them broken but most of them intact. Brushes had been thrown down as well.

Preacher knew good and well that Carling never would have treated his precious supplies like that, and neither would any of the other members of his party. Dismounting to study the ground closer, Preacher found several tracks left by feet clad in moccasins. Those prints could have been made by Rip Giddens or some of the other guides, Preacher thought—but they could have been made by Indians, too. The way the canvases had been thrown around as if they were worthless made Preacher think that Indians were to blame for whatever had happened here. The paintings wouldn't have meant anything to them.

Dog trotted around sniffing at everything he could find, but after a moment he stopped and began to whine as he looked intently at something on the ground. Preacher went over to him and found that the big cur was standing over a stain on the grass where something dark had been splashed. Preacher rubbed his fingers on the stain and then looked at his fingertips.

"Yeah, it's blood, all right," he said heavily to Dog, "and pretty recent, too."

That didn't bode well, but at least there were no bodies lying around. Everything he had seen painted a pretty clear picture in Preacher's mind. The Easterners and their guides had been stopped here for some reason when Indians had jumped them. There had been a fight, and at least one person was hurt fairly badly, to judge from the amount of blood that had been spilled on the ground. But there was a chance, at least, that no one had been killed.

That meant Rip, Carling, and the others had all been taken prisoner.

Preacher glanced toward the south. Snell and the rest of those ruthless, money-hungry bastards were coming up behind him, and up ahead somewhere was a band of Indians on the warpath. Hard to believe that old Hairface's bunch would do a thing like this. The Teton Sioux had always been friendly to whites, at least compared to tribes like the Crow and the Blackfoot.

First things first, Preacher told himself. He had to catch up to the Indians, find out what sort of shape the captives were in, and rescue them if he could. Then he would deal with the threat that Snell's gang represented. Of course, it was possible that Snell and the others would run afoul of hostile Indians, too. That would take care of part of Preacher's problem. But he wasn't going to count on that.

"Come on, Dog," he said as he swung up into the saddle. "We'll see what we can do to help them pilgrims."

It wasn't really his problem, but he wasn't the sort of man to turn his back on folks in trouble. Anyway, Rip was his friend, and to a lesser extent, so were Switchfoot, Jones, and the Ballingers. If the Indians had killed any of them, Preacher wasn't going to be happy.

"Wh-what are they going to do to us?" Faith asked, her voice choked by sobs as she stumbled along between her brother and Jasper Hodge. From time to time one of the men had to reach out and grasp her arm to steady her. Chester Sinclair came along behind them, still unsteady on his feet.

"I think this is all just a misunderstanding," Willard Carling said. The edge of terror and desperation in his voice made it clear that he *hoped* it was all a misunderstanding. "We mean these people no harm, and they have no reason to harm us."

"They don't need a reason," Hodge said bitterly. "They're savages. They scalp and kill white men just for the fun of it."

Faith sobbed again. She didn't want to be scalped or killed. She didn't want to be here. More than anything else right now, she wished she was back in the family home in Boston, on Beacon Hill overlooking the Charles River, safe and secure. She wished she had never agreed to accompany Willard on this mad journey into the wilderness. This journey from which none of them were going to return alive . . .

The savages surrounded them, trotting along tirelessly and not allowing the prisoners to slow down, either. Faith wished she could ride, but the Indians weren't allowing any of the prisoners to get near the horses.

Sinclair stumbled and nearly fell. One of the Indians yelled at him, strange, guttural words that Faith didn't understand, and struck him on the back with the flat of a tomahawk. These savages weren't even human, Faith thought. Their jabbering was like that of animals, not rational human beings.

Perhaps once they got to wherever the Indians called home, someone there would speak English. Faith could only hope that would be the case. If it was, they could explain that they were friendly and had come west to visit and write and paint, not to harm anyone. What threat could she and her brother, or for that matter, Hodge and Sinclair, represent to anyone? There had to be a way to make their captors understand that.

Why hadn't those frontiersmen Willard had hired killed the Indians, or run them off, or *something*? That was what Willard had paid the men for, after all—to protect them. And they had failed miserably. It had been left to the hapless Chester Sinclair to do most of the fighting.

Faith turned her head and looked over her shoulder at Sinclair. Big, dumb Chester—that was the way she had always thought of him. But today he had fought like a demon. Unfortunately, he had been no match for all those Indians.

"We're . . . we're stopping!" Carling gasped. "Thank God! They're going to let us rest at last."

"I don't think that's all they have in mind," Hodge said

ominously, and when Faith looked around again, she saw one of the red brutes stalking straight toward her, a grin on his ugly face. He stopped in front of her and reached up to touch her hair. The look in his eyes was unmistakably one of lust.

Faith screamed and fainted dead away.

Chapter Twelve

Sinclair's head still throbbed and he felt dizzy from time to time, but all that vanished in an instant as he saw the Indian accosting Faith Carling. His aches and pains were burned away by the flare of righteous anger that went through him. His hands clenched into fists, and he was about to step forward when Faith let out a shriek and then swooned.

Her brother caught her as she fell. Since she was as tall as Carling and almost as heavy, he was nearly knocked off his feet by the sudden weight. As he staggered and tried to hold her up, Sinclair moved threateningly toward the savage who had caused the violent reaction in Faith.

Before he could get there, one of the other Indians caught hold of the first one's arm and spoke sharply to him in their indecipherable tongue. The two red men traded hostile gazes for a moment, and Sinclair realized there was bad blood between them. The second Indian was scolding the first one for causing Faith to faint. Their eyes held each other in a level stare for several seconds; then the first Indian shrugged and turned away. The second one, who was evidently the leader of this group of warriors, snapped at his men, and they prepared to get moving again. The Indian gestured curtly at Faith, and then lowered his hand to the tomahawk tucked behind the rawhide belt around his waist. It was as if he was saying that if she couldn't keep up, he would dispose of her, Sinclair thought.

Carling obviously got the same impression, because he said quickly, "Don't worry, we'll bring her along. It'll be just fine. Chester, give me a hand here."

"Let me just take her," Sinclair said.

"You can't carry her by yourself. You're in no shape to do that."

"I'll be fine," Sinclair insisted. He put an arm around Faith's shoulders and then bent to slip his other arm behind her knees. When he straightened, he was carrying her like she was a child. His muscles felt the strain and his head throbbed worse for a moment, but he didn't care.

Despite the circumstances, he took a certain joy in the fact that at long last, Faith Carling was in his arms. And it never would have happened if they hadn't been attacked by these savages.

The group got moving again. Sinclair staggered along, carrying Faith. They were moving steadily toward the mountain Rip Giddens had told them about, the peak called Baldpate. Sinclair could see it better now, and he had to admit that it actually *did* look like an old man's hairless head.

Less than half an hour after Faith's swoon, she regained her senses. Her eyelids fluttered open, and she stared up at Sinclair in shock. "What . . . what's going on?" she gasped. "Chester, why are you carrying me?"

Carling answered before Sinclair could. "You fainted, dear. Passed out cold."

"That Indian," Faith choked out. "That awful Indian. Did . . . did he . . ."

"None of them touched you," Sinclair told her. "You're safe."

"But . . . you're carrying me."

"They made us keep moving. I had no choice. And I certainly meant no disrespect, Miss Faith."

Jasper Hodge put in, "Their head man acted like he was going to kill you if we didn't bring you along."

Faith's eyes widened as she stared at Sinclair. "Then you saved my life," she said.

He felt embarrassed. While the idea that she might feel gratitude toward him was appealing, it also made him a bit uncomfortable for some reason. He wanted her to like him, but for himself, not because she felt obligated in some fashion.

"I . . . I just did what I thought best," he managed to say.

"You can put me down now," she said crisply.

The statement took him by surprise. "Excuse me?"

"I said you can put me down. If I'm not injured, then I'm perfectly capable of walking. It's hardly proper for you to be carrying me like this, Chester. My God, you're like a bridegroom carrying his bride over the threshold."

Now *that* was an even more appealing idea, but there wasn't time for it to linger in Sinclair's mind because Faith continued. "Besides, it's not fair to make you carry me. You were badly beaten by those savages."

"I'm fine," he insisted gruffly.

"No, you're not. Now put me down."

Sinclair had no choice but to stop for a second and lower her so that her feet were on the ground again. One of the Indians brandished a tomahawk at them and spoke harshly. Faith began to walk alongside the other prisoners.

She looked around and asked, "Where are we?"

"Still going north," Carling replied. "Toward that mountain up there, the one that Mr. Giddens told us about."

As if he knew that he was being talked about, Rip Giddens suddenly let out a groan and raised his head. He was still slung over the back of one of the horses. Now that he was conscious again, the Indians halted briefly and dragged him off the animal, dumping him unceremoniously on the ground. The leader stood over him and harangued him in a loud, angry voice.

"I'm gettin' up, I'm gettin' up," Giddens muttered. "Keep your shirt on, Badger."

Carling stared at the frontiersman as Giddens struggled to his feet. "You speak their language?" he said in amazement. "You know this man?"

"I savvy enough of it to get the idea of what he's talkin' about," Giddens said. "And his name is Bites Like a Badger, but most folks just call him Badger." Giddens scrubbed his hands over his face and winced at the pain in his head. "He's a sub-chief of the Teton Sioux."

Badger spoke again, the words coming swift and harsh from his mouth.

Giddens grunted. "He understands a little of our tongue, too, enough for him to know that I just called him a sub-chief. He tells me that ain't the case no more. He's the chief o' his band of Tetons. Seems ol' Hairface is dead. Took sick and died of a fever one moon ago. One month, we'd call it."

"This Hairface . . . you said he was a *friendly* Indian."

"Yep." Giddens nodded. "And Badger ain't."

Carling's eyes widened. "Then he and his people . . . they're our enemies now?"

"You could say that. Even among the tribes that get along with us pretty well, there are always some hotheads who want war with the whites." Giddens gingerly fingered a lump on his head and grimaced. "Hairface always kept that bunch under control in his band. Badger here ain't near as sympathetic to us. He'll let the ones who hate whites do pretty much whatever they want."

Faith said, "They're going to kill us, aren't they? They're taking us back to their town or village or whatever you call it, and they're going to torture us and kill us." Her voice shook with fear.

Sinclair wanted to put his arm around her and assure her that he would never let anything like that happen to her, that he would protect her and everything would be all right.

But he knew that might not be the case, and he knew as well that Faith might not want his reassurances. It was obvious she still thought of him as a servant, and perhaps as a fellow prisoner, but nothing else.

And it seemed that he had larger worries than her lack of romantic interest in him, because Giddens nodded and said solemnly to Faith, "I reckon that's what they have in mind all right, miss. Unless we can get away from 'em somehow, I doubt if any of us will live to see the sun come up tomorrow mornin'."

"What the hell happened here?" Luther Snell said as he looked around the meadow at the scattered canvases, paints, and brushes. "That prissy little bastard wouldn't've left all this paintin' gear behind."

"Blood on the grass over here," Singletree called. Snell stalked over to join him in looking down at the dark stains.

Patch Dimock said, "Must've been Injuns, the way those paintin's are slung around. They wouldn't have had no interest in such-like."

His cousin said, "Injuns don't like paintin's to start with. Some of 'em think you steal a man's soul if you paint his picture."

Snell ground his teeth together and muttered curses. "Of all the damned bad luck! We go after Carling to make ourselves rich, and a bunch o' stinkin' red heathens carry him off!"

"How do you know they didn't kill him?" asked Baldy. He was older than the others, a lanky man who had been in these mountains for more than twenty years, and some said that the decades of isolation had left him touched in the head. Snell knew that Baldy might seem a little slow sometimes, but he was still pretty cunning.

"There's blood, but no bodies," Snell pointed out. "If the Injuns had killed Carling, or any of the rest of that bunch, they would've left the bodies."

Vickery nodded. "Yeah, that's right. They've taken 'em prisoner, sure as hell."

"What are we gonna do now?" Baldy asked.

"Go after 'em and get Carling back, of course!" Snell declared.

Vickery rubbed his rawboned chin. "I ain't so sure if I want to get mixed up in that, Snell. I agreed to come along with you mainly because Stump did, and if you look around, you'll see that Stump ain't here. And I sure as hell didn't sign on to do no Injun fightin'."

Snell felt rage building up inside him, but he made an effort to tamp it down. "Look, I don't know what happened to Stump," he said. "We waited for him as long as we could, but he didn't show up. Now, maybe he's comin' along behind us and will catch up 'fore the day's over."

"Yeah, and maybe he decided it was a mistake throwin' in with you, especially after what happened to that Injun woman of Preacher's."

Snell glowered at Vickery. "We all agreed not to say no more about that."

"Whether we talk about it or not don't have anything to do with whether or not it happened," Vickery replied with a shrug. "We know it did, Preacher knows it did, and sooner or later he's gonna come after us whether he's got any proof or not. You don't know Preacher like I do, Snell. *And* you still ain't answered what I said about havin' to fight Injuns."

"Damn it, ain't you ever had to fight those red devils before?" Snell sputtered. "Why're you makin' such a fuss about it now?"

"I never went out of my way to fight 'em," Vickery said. "And I ain't gonna do it now, either." He reached for his horse's reins. "I'm done, Snell. I got better things to do than throw my life away on some crazy scheme of yours."

As Vickery got ready to mount up and ride away, Snell struggled to retain control over his temper. He wanted to yank out one of his pistols and blow a hole in the ornery son of a bitch. Chances were, though, that if he did that it would just turn some of the others against him, too. He couldn't kill all of them.

But he couldn't let Vickery take off by his lonesome, either. That might start an exodus among the group, and before he knew it, Snell thought, he'd be alone. He didn't want that.

Thinking quickly, he said, "So, you figure you're a match for Preacher, do you?"

Vickery paused with one foot in a stirrup and looked around to frown at Snell. "What do you mean by that?"

"I mean you're ridin' off alone. When Preacher comes to settle the score with you for that squaw of his, you'll have to deal with him by yourself."

Vickery's frown deepened. "You said he couldn't do anything because he didn't have proof."

"And you just said that he would, whether he had proof or not," Snell pointed out. "Make up your blasted mind, Vickery. But remember this . . . if Preacher *does* hunt you down, how would you rather meet him? Alone, or with a bunch of good men backin' you up?"

Collins said, "There's an old saying about hanging together or hanging separately. Even though it's doubtful any of us would ever hang for what we did, the sentiment still applies here."

Collins was the one with the most education in the bunch, so Snell was glad that he had spoken up. Vickery took his foot back out of the stirrup and stood next to his horse for a long moment, rubbing his jaw as he thought over everything that had been discussed. Finally, he said, "I reckon you're right, Collins, and you, too, Snell. I may not like it, but we're sort of all in this together, ain't we?"

"Damn right we are," Snell said. "All ten of us. We're gonna get Carling back from those Injuns and make him promise to pay us a heap of money if we get him back to civilization safe and sound. He'll do it, too, if he knows what's good for him. And then we can afford to do anything else we want to. We can split up and never come back to these mountains, and Preacher will never find us. *That's* the way to deal with Preacher."

Singletree said, "I'd rather just kill him."

"If he comes after us," Snell promised, "that's sure as hell exactly what we'll do." He lifted his horse's reins. "Now mount up, boys. We got us some Injuns to catch."

Chapter Thirteen

To Preacher's keen eyes, the trail left by the Indians and their captives was fairly easy to follow. The Indians probably didn't know that anyone was after them, so they didn't hurry or try to conceal the signs they left behind. The group moved steadily toward Baldpate.

By late afternoon, Preacher figured he was closing in on them. Once again, he angled Horse into the foothills along the base of the mountain range. He couldn't just ride up behind the Indians. They would see him coming if he tried to do that. He had to approach in a more stealthy fashion, preferably after night had fallen.

He just hoped that the prisoners would be all right for that long.

He hadn't found any bodies as he followed the Indians, which was a good sign. It told him that no one had been so badly wounded during the struggle earlier in the day that they had died along the way to wherever it was the Indians were going.

Preacher wasn't sure what that destination was. The village of Hairface's people was in this direction, some miles east of Baldpate, about halfway between there and the valley of the Seven Smokes. Preacher still had his doubts about Hairface leading an attack on the Easterners and their guides, though. That just didn't fit in with what he knew about the Teton Sioux chief.

But the answers would come when he caught up with the Indians, he told himself. Maybe they were a raiding party of Crow or Blackfoot, although this was a mite far south and west for either of those tribes to be raiding. But they had been known to range pretty far at times, especially when they were in a hostile mood and looking for trouble.

"I know you're gettin' tired, Horse," Preacher said to his mount, "but you'll get a chance to rest after a while." He glanced at the sky and saw that the sun was lowering toward the peaks in the west. There was another hour or so of daylight left, he estimated. His belly growled. The day had been a long one, and all he'd had to eat since breakfast was some jerky he had gnawed on while he was in the saddle. He couldn't stop now, though, not when he was this close to catching up.

From the top of a wooded hill, he spotted his quarry a short time later. The Indians had brought along all the horses they had captured, but no one was riding. The prisoners were being forced to walk. Preacher made a quick count of the captives, even though that was somewhat difficult to do because the warriors had them surrounded to make sure none of them tried to escape. Preacher came up with ten and felt relief go through him. Four Easterners, Rip Giddens and the four men he had hired, plus Sparrow made ten. Just as he had thought, nobody had been killed during the fighting, but several of the captives were stumbling along as if they were hurt.

Preacher dug out his spyglass to get a better look at them. Of the four pilgrims from Boston, Chester Sinclair was the only one who seemed to have taken much of a beating. His face was bruised and had dried blood on it from several cuts. The guides were in worse shape, which came as no surprise to Preacher because he knew that all of them would have fought to protect their charges. One of the Ballinger brothers had a lot of dried blood on his head and face and was very unsteady on his feet. He was being helped along by the other Ballinger and Hammerhead Jones. Preacher figured the injured man had been clouted on the head with a tomahawk. Such wounds always bled like blazes, even when they weren't fatal.

Sparrow was all right and didn't appear to have been harmed at all. She just looked scared, was all. As well she might, since Indians on the warpath had even less liking for those of their own race who helped the whites than they did for the whites themselves.

Preacher moved the spyglass and studied the warriors who had seized the pilgrims and their guides. From the decorations on their buckskins and the markings on their faces, he identified them as Teton Sioux. A frown creased his forehead. It looked like he had been wrong about Hairface after all. Maybe something had happened to turn the normally friendly chief against the whites.

Then he looked at the warrior who was striding out in front of the others and his jaw tightened in recognition. The leader of this war party wasn't Hairface.

"Damn," Preacher said. "Bites Like a Badger."

He'd had run-ins with Badger before. Badger didn't like him and the feeling was mutual. The sub-chief and a few young bucks had once jumped Preacher while he was running his trap lines. Shots had been traded. A ball from Preacher's rifle had burned a scar across Badger's cheek and taken off a tiny bit of his ear. Hurt like hell, but not serious.

Badger took it serious, though, and had hated Preacher ever since. Things had gotten even worse between them when Hairface had apologized later to Preacher for Badger and the other warriors attacking him. That had damaged Badger's pride, which was much worse than losing a piece of ear.

Seeing Badger in charge of this war party told Preacher several things. Since Badger had been Hairface's primary sub-chief, it told Preacher that something must have happened to Hairface. Badger was running things now, and that didn't bode well for the trappers who made their livings in these mountains. It also told Preacher that he wouldn't be able to just waltz into the Tetons' camp and talk the Indians out of their prisoners. Now it was more important than ever that he rescue them, and as soon as possible because there was no way of knowing what Badger had in mind to do with them. The only thing Preacher was sure of was that it wouldn't be anything good.

He closed the spyglass and tucked it away in his saddle-bags. "Come on, Horse," he said as he lifted the reins. "We've still got a ways to go."

Keeping to the high ground, Preacher rode on toward Bald-pate, which loomed larger and larger to his left. He knew that the Indians wouldn't be able to reach their village before darkness fell. They would have to stop and make camp for the night and then travel on to their village the next day.

Sometime during those hours of darkness, Preacher intended to steal into their camp and free the prisoners, hopefully without the Tetons even being aware of what had happened.

The Indians would find out about it eventually, though, and when they did, Preacher and the others would have to run for their lives. Their best hope would be to find a place where they could fort up and wait out the trouble. The Tetons would give up eventually, especially if it looked like it was going to cost them more lives than they were willing to spend to recapture the whites. Badger might hate Preacher, but he was a canny enough leader to know that he couldn't push things too far without risking having his followers turn on him.

As the ball of the sun began to dip below the mountains a while later, Preacher was hidden in a thick stand of trees about five hundred yards from the spot where the Indians had stopped beside a small stream. They would spend the night here, where there was fresh water. Unfortunately, there weren't many trees around the spot they had chosen for their campsite, so Preacher wouldn't have much cover as he approached.

Dog sat beside him as he studied the terrain between his position and the place where the Tetons and their prisoners had stopped for the night. The big cur growled and whined softly. Preacher put an arm around Dog's muscular, thickly furred neck and said quietly, "Yeah, I know. I'm as anxious to get amongst them savages and raise some hell as you are, old fella. But gettin' those blasted pilgrims outta there safe and sound has to come first."

The prisoners had all sat down wearily on the ground as soon as their captors allowed them to. They had to be exhausted and scared, especially the ones from back East who weren't used to being forced to trot along ceaselessly for more than half a day. As Preacher watched, Badger came over to the prisoners and angrily kicked Sinclair, Carling, and Hodge back to their feet. Preacher could hear him yelling at them, but at this distance he couldn't make out the words.

The Easterners obviously didn't understand what Badger was saying, either. They started to mill around aimlessly, and that just made the chief angrier.

Rip Giddens pushed himself to his feet and spoke to them, then to Badger, and then again to the three Bostonians. He was translating, Preacher realized, or at least trying to. Preacher recalled that Rip spoke a little Sioux, and he could also communicate in the sign language that was nearly universal among the tribes west of the Mississippi. With Rip helping them to understand what Badger wanted of them, the three Easterners began gathering wood for a fire. Several of the warriors watched them at all times.

Once the campfire was going, the warriors began to prepare their supper. They made no move to feed the prisoners. It would be a hungry night for them, and a cold one, too, because even though this spring day had been warm, the nights at this time of year were still mighty chilly most of the time.

Preacher knelt in the trees as the last of the sunlight faded. He wanted to wait until it got good and dark before he tried anything. With the odds against him, he needed every possible advantage he could find.

And even that might not be enough. . . .

* * *

"When are they going to kill us?" Faith asked, only a slight tremor in her voice betraying just how frightened she truly was.

Rip Giddens scratched at his blond beard. "Well, I might've been wrong about us bein' dead by mornin'," he said. "From the looks o' things, they don't plan on killin' us tonight. They're takin' us back to their village. Whatever they do to us, that's where they'll do it, so the whole band can see what's happenin'."

Faith shuddered. "In other words, they want to entertain their women and children with our horrible deaths."

Rip shrugged and said, "We ain't there yet. There's no tellin' what might happen before we get there."

"But there's no one to help us," Jasper Hodge said miserably. "Absolutely no one."

The prisoners sat huddled together. Half-a-dozen warriors stood around them, guarding them. Faith had no doubt that if she or any of the others tried to get away, they would be killed mercilessly. The savages had plenty of captives to torture when they got to wherever they were going; they could kill one or two without really losing much.

The fact that she was able to think like that, to wrap her brain around such barbaric concepts, was a stunning example of just how much had changed for her since she left Boston. Since this very morning, as a matter of fact, although their previous experiences at the Rendezvous had begun to make her realize just what a different world this frontier was from the settled civilization she had always known back East. In Boston, death was something that arrived in an orderly, expected fashion, at home in one's own bed with one's friends and relatives gathered about. Out here on the frontier, though, death could arrive at any time, with no warning, a howling fury that ripped life away with no thought or consideration at all.

The badly wounded Ballinger brother let out a loud groan. He was lying down with his gory head in his brother's lap. The terrible wound in his scalp had been bleeding from time to time all day, and the poor man seemed to be out of his senses. He groaned again, and then his arms and legs began to jerk spasmodically. His brother cried out, "Ed! Ed, damn it, don't you die!" He leaned over and gripped the injured man by the shoulders.

More blood welled from the wound. The Indians watched impassively as the man continued to flail around. Faith had to look away, unable to stand the terrible sight any longer. But she heard Rip Giddens say quietly, "There's nothin' you can do for him, Tom. His skull's probably all busted up from bein' hit with that tomahawk."

"But he can't die!" Tom Ballinger said. "He just can't!"

No matter how much he wanted it to be otherwise, though, the damage had been done. Faith heard a hideous, rattling gurgle that she knew was Ed Ballinger's final breath. His brother began cursing in a low, intense voice.

"Might as well lay him down," Giddens said. "Maybe the Injuns will let us bury him—"

With a howl that expressed his own emotional anger, Tom Ballinger sprang to his feet and lunged at the nearest of the Indians, his hands hooked in front of him like claws, ready to rend and tear whatever he could get hold of.

"No, you fool!" Giddens yelled. "Somebody stop him!"

Faith had to turn and look then. She saw Chester Sinclair tackle Tom Ballinger and knock him off his feet before the grief-crazed man could reach the warrior he was about to attack. The Indian had already raised his tomahawk and was ready to dash Ballinger's brains out, but he lowered the weapon as Sinclair climbed on top of the frenziedly struggling Ballinger and held him down. After a moment, Ballinger stopped fighting and went limp, sobbing wretchedly as he lay on the ground.

"Good job, Sinclair," Giddens said. "I reckon you saved his life."

"Maybe," Sinclair said as he pushed himself up, keeping a wary eye on Ballinger just in case the man tried something else. "But saved him for what?"

That was the question none of them could answer.

Chapter Fourteen

The stars were out, glittering like jewels against the night sky, before Preacher made his move.

Horse's reins were tied to a sapling, but loosely so that he could jerk them free if it became necessary. In a firm whisper, Preacher told Dog to stay. The big wolflike creature whined softly about it, but did as he was told. A loud whistle from Preacher would bring both the animals racing to his side if he needed them.

He left his rifle behind, too. If he had to do any fighting in the Indian camp, it would be close work, the sort of killing best done with pistols or a knife. Preacher hoped it wouldn't come to that, although he thought it likely he would have to slit the throat of a sentry or two.

He took off his broad-brimmed hat and hung it on the saddle with his rifle. Then he moved toward the Indian camp, crouching low and taking his time about it. When he was still three hundred yards away, he dropped to his belly and began crawling through the buffalo grass.

His progress was slow but steady. The night had already turned cold, and the air was crisp. Sounds traveled well in it, which was why he tried not to make any. Every few minutes, he stopped to listen. The camp was quiet except for some snoring, but he knew better than to think that sound meant all the warriors were asleep. Badger would have left at least one man awake to stand guard.

When Preacher judged that he was close because he could hear the tiny gurgling of the creek, he lifted his head. He could see dark shapes sprawled on the ground. Exhaustion had claimed the prisoners. Most of the warriors were asleep, too, but he spotted faint movement in the shadow cast by a tree on the creek bank. The sentry was there, unable to remain completely motionless during the long hours of the night.

That restlessness, slight though it might be, was going to cost the warrior his life.

Preacher lowered his head and began crawling again. He circled wide so that he could get behind the Indian who was standing guard. Preacher had studied the campsite and not seen any signs of anyone else being awake. That was good. Maybe he'd have to kill only one man.

Preacher had closed to within a few feet of the sentry, and was about to make his move when he suddenly heard Faith Carling's voice. He froze where he was and listened, thinking that she was probably talking to her brother or one of the other pilgrims. No one answered her, though, and after a few minutes Preacher realized from the tone of Faith's voice that she was talking in her sleep, mumbling and muttering, her words incomprehensible except for the occasional "No" and "Don't."

She was probably dreaming about being captured by the Indians, Preacher thought. For Faith—and for just about anybody else, he reckoned—that would be a nightmare.

He stayed where he was and hoped that she would settle down soon. If she raised too much of a ruckus, she would wake up the rest of the war party, and Lord only knows how long it would be before they went back to sleep. To Preacher's great relief, Faith's rambling speech soon trailed off and then stopped. He was close enough to hear her breathing. It subsided into a steady rhythm again, telling him that she was sleeping soundly once more.

He gave it a few more minutes, just to be sure, then resumed his approach to the lone sentry. When he was close enough, Preacher drew his knife silently from its sheath and then rose to his feet without making a sound. His left arm shot out and looped around the warrior's throat, jerking back and clamping down across the Indian's throat like a bar of iron. That prevented the warrior from crying out or even grunting in pain as Preacher's other hand drove the blade of the hunting knife deep in his back. Preacher felt the steel scrape on bone for a second; then it slid on through the ribs and into the luckless sentry's heart. The man stiffened in Preacher's grasp, arching his back from the sudden, unexpected burst of agony that must have gone through him.

For good measure, Preacher pulled the knife out and then cut the Indian's throat, feeling the hot gush of blood on his arm. There was only a limited amount of blood, though, an indication that the man's heart had already stopped beating.

Quietly and carefully, Preacher lowered the corpse to the ground. Now came a much harder job—waking up the prisoners and getting them to sneak out of here without rousing the rest of the Sioux.

If there had been any way to stage a distraction of some sort, Preacher would have done so. Unfortunately, out here in the open terrain like this, there wasn't much he could do to divert attention elsewhere. He had to rely totally on stealth, his own and that of the captives, and while he trusted himself to be able to move quietly, he wasn't so sure about them.

But he had no choice, so he dropped back to the ground and eased forward on his belly, moving only a few inches at a time and stopping often to make sure the Indians were still sleeping.

The moon had not risen yet, but the starlight was strong enough so that he was able to make out which of the dark shapes on the ground belonged to Rip Giddens. Rip was bigger than anyone else in the party, even Chester Sinclair. Preacher eased up alongside the sleeping man. He put his hand over Rip's mouth and brought it down quickly, shutting off the big frontiersman's air. At the same time, he put his mouth next to Rip's ear and hissed, "It's Preacher!" His voice was so quiet that it couldn't have been heard more a foot away.

Rip jerked a little as he woke, but he didn't try to cry out or get up. Preacher continued in a faint whisper, "Don't move just yet."

Rip gave a minuscule nod to show that he understood. Preacher took his hand away from Rip's mouth. Rip turned his head a little so that his lips were next to Preacher's ear as he whispered, "Got any help?"

"No, just me. Wake up the other fellas, but be as quiet as you can about it. I'll rouse the pilgrims. We're gonna crawl outta here."

Rip nodded again. He rolled slowly and silently onto his side, then on over so that he lay on his belly like Preacher. They went in different directions, crawling toward the other sleeping forms.

Instinct made Preacher head for Sinclair first. If all hell broke loose, he wanted Sinclair awake and aware of what was going on, so the man could take part in the fighting. He followed the same procedure he had employed with Rip Giddens, crawling up next to Sinclair and then getting ready to clamp a hand over his mouth.

Sinclair shifted suddenly. Preacher thought Sinclair was moving around in his sleep, but without any warning, he grabbed Preacher's wrist and shouted, "You won't kill me in my sleep, you damned red savage!"

Instantly, the whole camp was aroused, the warriors springing to their feet and calling questions to each other. Preacher cursed, knowing that Sinclair had seen him creeping closer and taken him for one of the Indians. With his plan to sneak the captives out of the camp ruined, now there was only one thing Preacher could do.

Hit the Indians hard and fast.

He uncoiled from the ground, pulling both pistols from

behind his belt as he did so. "Run!" he bellowed at the top of his lungs. "Rip, get everybody the hell outta here!"

The Tetons were startled and confused, but they knew something was wrong. Their harsh shouts filled the air. As several of them lunged toward Preacher, he leveled the pistols at them and pulled the triggers. The guns roared and bucked in his hands as their heavy charges of powder exploded. Both pistols were double-shotted. The deadly lead balls thudded into flesh, and three of the charging warriors went down. Preacher didn't know how bad they were hit, whether they were killed or just wounded, and he didn't have time to check. He leaped forward, landing among the Indians and slashing right and left, using the empty guns as clubs.

Rip and the other three frontiersmen leaped up and joined in the fray, fighting desperately with their bare hands as they grappled with their captors. The Easterners sat up, roused from their sleep by the commotion, but they didn't take part in the battle. They probably weren't exactly sure what was going on.

Preacher had known as he slipped into the camp that the odds were mighty long against him being able to pull off this daring maneuver. He had needed a lot of luck—a year's worth of luck—and he hadn't gotten it. Now all he and the others could do was fight.

Several more warriors fell to the crushing blows that he landed with the pistols, but then someone leaped on his back and knocked him forward, onto his knees. The Indian who had jumped him howled angrily in his ear.

Preacher dropped the guns and reached up and back to tangle the fingers of both hands in the warrior's long hair. Even though the hair was slick with bear grease, Preacher managed to hang onto it as he bent forward even more and hauled hard with both hands. The warrior's howl of anger became a screech of pain as he flew over Preacher's head, flipped over in the air, and came crashing down on his back.

As Preacher surged to his feet, he pulled his knife from its sheath. Whirling around, he slashed at one of the Tetons and made the man jump back to avoid the blade. Starlight glittered on steel as Preacher twisted and went after another man, driving him back as well. None of the warriors wanted to get too close to him. He backed away from them, and as he did so he realized that Rip and the others were closing ranks, too, all of them coming together around the four pilgrims from Boston.

Unfortunately, even with the damage they had done, they were still heavily outnumbered. The war party had had at least thirty men in it, and although several of them were down, injured or worse, more than twenty warriors still surrounded the five frontiersmen. The only weapon the defenders had among them was Preacher's knife.

"Sorry, Preacher," Rip Giddens said in the tense silence that fell over the standoff. "I don't know how come you to follow us, but I reckon you should've stayed somewheres else."

"Preacher!"

The surprised exclamation came from one of the Indians. He stepped forward, tomahawk clutched in his hand, and in the starlight Preacher recognized the ugly features of Bites Like a Badger.

"You!" Badger spat in his own language.

A tight smile played over Preacher's lean face. "Yeah, it's me, all right, Badger," he replied in the Sioux tongue. "Didn't figure on seeing me again, did you?"

Badger's breath hissed between clenched teeth. "I hoped that I would," he said. "I prayed to the Great Spirit that I would have another chance to kill you, white man!"

Preacher moved the knife in his hand back and forth, taunting the chief. "Here I am," he said. "Come on if you feel lucky, Badger."

For a long moment, Badger didn't say anything. Then he grunted contemptuously and said, "Not here, not now. When we return to the village of my people, so that all may see."

"Problem is, I ain't goin' to the village of your people, and neither are these folks. They don't mean you any harm, so you're gonna let 'em go."

In a worried, quavery voice, Willard Carling asked, "What are they saying? What's going to happen to us?"

Before anybody could answer him, Badger smiled, which just made him uglier in Preacher's opinion. He snapped a guttural order.

"Take them! But do not kill Preacher!"

The Indians closed in. Faith let out a terrified scream. That galvanized Chester Sinclair into action at last. The big man leaped into the middle of the warriors and began flailing his fists at them in malletlike blows. Preacher, Rip, and the other frontiersmen were right behind him, yelling as they carried the attack to their would-be captors.

That move took the Indians a little by surprise, but its effectiveness vanished swiftly as they were overwhelmed by the sheer weight of numbers that the warriors had on their side. A tomahawk knocked the knife out of Preacher's hand, and once it was gone, fully half a dozen of the Tetons piled on him, grabbing him and forcing him to the ground. One by one the other men were pinned down as well.

"Tie them all," Badger ordered. "Make sure Preacher, especially, cannot move."

Within minutes, Preacher was hogtied. The bonds were so tight that he couldn't even wiggle his fingers, let alone have any hope of getting free. The other prisoners were tied up as well, even Sparrow. She bore up under that stoically, but Faith sobbed as rawhide thongs were pulled painfully tight around her wrists and ankles.

Badger loomed over Preacher and said with a sneer, "Now we see what your brave words amount to, Preacher. Nothing! You are my prisoner, and soon my people will see you die!"

Preacher didn't reply. There was nothing to say.

But he hadn't given up hope, and as he lay there with his arms and legs slowly growing numb from the tightness of his bonds, he vowed to himself that he would not only find a way out of this for himself, but also that he would rescue the other prisoners as well. As long as he was alive, there was always a chance. . . .

And there was no way of knowing when Fate might intervene and change everything.

Luther Snell fidgeted tensely as he waited for Baldy to come back from scouting up ahead. Snell had heard the shots and the angry yells, maybe half a mile away, but he didn't know what had happened. Maybe the Indians had nabbed Baldy. Maybe the old bastard had told the savages about Snell and the others, and any minute the murdering red heathens would fall on them and wipe them out.

But then Baldy came trotting out of the shadows and hissed, "Don't shoot! It's me!"

"What did you find out, you crazy old coot?" Snell demanded.

Baldy laughed. "You call me a crazy old coot, but who was it you sent slippin' up on them Injuns to see what they was doin'? Who was it, huh, Luther?"

With an effort, Snell hung on to his temper and said in a milder tone, "Just tell me what you found out, Baldy."

"Sure, sure. There was a fight."

"We know that. We heard the shots and the yellin'."

"I crawled up close enough to hear what was goin' on," Baldy continued. "Nobody knew I was there. Not the Injuns, not them prisoners, not even Preacher."

"Preacher!" The startled outburst came from several of the men at the same time.

Baldy chortled and nodded. "Yeah. Preacher. Best I could tell, he slipped in there and tried to get those pilgrims loose. But the Injuns woke up and there was a fight, and when it was over, they'd nabbed Preacher, too. Had him all trussed up like a pig goin' to market."

Snell raked fingers through his beard. "Damn it. I didn't figure on Preacher gettin' mixed up in this."

"None of us did," Hardcastle said.

Baldy said, "You shouldn't ought to have to worry about him. Badger's the leader o' that war party, and he hates

Preacher. Just give ol' Badger time, and he'll kill Preacher for us."

A grin spread across Snell's face. "You may be on to something there, old-timer."

"So what are we gonna do?" Vickery asked.

"We're gonna follow that war party and bide our time," Snell said. "We'll let those Injuns do our work for us and get rid o' Preacher. Then, when the time is right, we'll carry out the same plan we had before, to get Willard Carling in our hands and force him to pay us. We're still gonna be rich men. Nothing's changed . . . except that Preacher's gonna be dead."

Chapter Fifteen

Faith continued sobbing quietly until weariness overtook her and made her fall asleep again. That was a relief to Preacher, who didn't like lying there and listening to her cry. Every sob was yet another reminder that he had failed in what he'd set out to do.

He and Rip Giddens carried on a whispered conversation. The Indians didn't seem to mind. At least, they ignored the whispers and allowed them to continue.

"Why'd you follow us, Preacher?" Rip wanted to know.

Preacher could tell that the other men were listening and wanted to hear the answer to that question as well. He said, "Somebody took a shot at me this mornin', a while after y'all had pulled out."

"Who'd be a big enough damn fool to do that?"

"Stump," Preacher said.

That brought a startled exclamation from Rip. "Stump! What the hell did he want to do that for? He's always been a testy little bastard, but I didn't think he was crazy."

"He was afraid I'd find out that he was part of the bunch who attacked and killed Mountain Mist. He thought I'd come after him and settle the score, so he tried to get rid of me first."

"Lord," Rip said. "I didn't think Stump'd do a thing like that, either."

"I heard it from his own lips. He said it was Luther Snell's idea to rape Mountain Mist. I don't figure any of the others planned to kill her, though. That was mostly Snell's doin'. But the others sure as hell didn't try to stop him."

"Stump told you all this as he was dyin'?" Rip guessed shrewdly.

"Yeah. At least he had the decency to say he was sorry before he passed over the divide."

"Bein' sorry don't bring that poor gal back, or change the fact that he tried to kill you."

"No," Preacher agreed heavily, "it don't."

They fell silent for a moment as Rip digested what Preacher had told him, and then he pointed out, "That still don't explain why you followed us."

"Because Stump told me somethin' else. He said Snell had had another idea. Him and the other fellas who'd been with him were gonna trail you and these pilgrims and then jump you and kidnap Mr. Carling so they could hold him for ransom."

That prompted a squeak from Willard Carling. "They were going to kidnap *me*?"

Preacher nodded. He could still do that, even though he was tied up so tightly he couldn't really move otherwise. "That's right. They figured on makin' you pay them a bunch o' money to let you go."

"But . . . but I don't have a bunch of money! Not with me, anyway."

"They would have taken you back to Saint Looey, I reckon, and made you send a letter to your bank in Boston. They would've kept you locked up somewhere until you got a letter of credit back and withdrew the money from a bank in Saint Looey." Preacher paused. "Then they would have killed you so you couldn't tell anybody what they'd done."

"What about the rest of us?" Jasper Hodge asked.

"You would have been dead a long time before that," Preacher replied bluntly.

"My God, it's hard to believe that anyone could be so barbaric," Carling said.

Rip asked, "Was Stump supposed to be part o' that, too?"

"Yeah. But he wanted to get rid o' me, first." Preacher shook his head. "Didn't work out that way."

Silence fell again. It wasn't broken until Chester Sinclair asked, "What happens now?"

"They plan on takin' us to their village. Tied up like we are, I don't see any way we can stop 'em from doin' it."

"And then they'll kill us."

"That's what they got in mind, I reckon."

Sinclair let out a low groan filled with despair. "This is all my fault," he said in a choked voice. "If I hadn't shouted and woke them up when you were trying to free us, none of this would have happened."

"You can't know that," Preacher told him. "Something else could've gone wrong. The odds of gettin' away were against us to start with."

Sinclair didn't seem to hear him. "Miss Faith is going to die," he said hollowly, "and it's my fault." Suddenly, he reared up as much as he could, tied hand and foot the way he was, and shouted, "Let her go, you damned dirty savages! Let the woman go!"

"Sinclair!" Rip said sharply. "Sinclair, stop it!"

Sinclair ignored him. "Do you hear me, you heathens? Let her go!"

Several of the Indians leaped up and rushed over, Badger among them. Preacher couldn't do anything to stop it as the chief drew back his foot and unleashed a kick that smashed into Sinclair's face. The Easterner was driven back down. Badger kicked him again in the side, just for good measure, then again and again. Sinclair grunted in pain as the kicks thudded into his body.

Then Badger stepped back and said in his own language to Preacher, "Keep him quiet, or I will cut his tongue out."

"Bites Like a Badger is a brave man when his enemies are

bound," Preacher said dryly. He had hopes of goading the chief into ordering that he be untied.

Badger stiffened in anger, but he didn't rise to the bait. He just growled, "Remember what I said, Preacher."

As Badger and the other Indians turned away to go back to their sleep, Carling asked, "What did he say?"

"He told me that if Sinclair starts yellin' again, he'll cut out his tongue."

Carling shuddered. "Would he really do that?"

"Damn right he would. Don't doubt it for a second."

Hodge muttered, "Dear Lord, what sort of mad universe have we fallen into? How can such things happen?"

Preacher didn't bother telling him that it was liable to get worse before it got better.

The night was a long, miserable, pure-dee uncomfortable one. Preacher dozed a little, but not enough to do much good. He was still bone-weary when the sky began to lighten with the approach of dawn the next morning.

The Indians rose early and ate breakfast, but again, they didn't feed the prisoners. Preacher's belly was empty, causing a gnawing sensation in his midsection. He was sure the other prisoners felt the same way. The fact that they weren't being fed was a good indication of what their captors had in mind for them. Why waste good food on somebody who was going to be dead soon?

Faith started whimpering as soon as she woke up. Carling hitched himself over beside her and said, "Don't worry, dear. I'm sure everything is going to be all right."

"N-no, it won't!" she blubbered through her tears. "They're going to kill us all, and there's nothing we can do to stop them! And . . . and I can't feel my hands and feet anymore!"

"I don't imagine any of us can, since we're all tied so tightly."

Sinclair rolled over so he could look at Faith. "I'm sorry, miss," he said. "It's my fault—"

"Oh, shut up!" she snapped at him. "Whining about whose fault it is won't change anything."

Sinclair looked hurt by her sharp words, but he fell silent.

Faith began crying even louder as Bites Like a Badger approached her with a knife in his hand. She tried to scoot away from him, but was unable to move. Wearing a disdainful look on his face, Badger stooped and used the knife to cut the bonds around Faith's ankles. The rawhide thongs fell away as they were severed, allowing blood to rush back into Faith's feet. She gasped in relief that she hadn't been murdered, then winced as the blood returning to her lower extremities brought pain with it.

Badger went around the group, cutting the bonds on everyone's ankles. When he came to Preacher and the other frontiersmen, several warriors stood over them with tomahawks poised to strike, just in case any of the prisoners tried to lash out at the chief with their feet.

Pins and needles jabbed fiercely at Preacher's feet as the feeling came back into them. He endured the pain stoically, knowing that it would go away after a few minutes. It was almost gone by the time he was lifted onto his feet by a couple of the Indians.

Badger returned his knife to its sheath and grunted. "Now we go," he said, in English this time. He turned and stalked away.

All the prisoners had been hauled upright roughly. Now they were prodded into motion. Surrounded by their captors, they stumbled forward, weak from exhaustion and hunger, most of them worried about what was going to happen next.

Preacher didn't waste time or energy worrying. He was still determined to get himself and the others out of this predicament if he could.

If he couldn't . . . well, worrying wasn't going to keep him alive.

Tom Ballinger was forced to leave the body of his brother Ed behind for the scavengers. Wild-eyed with grief, Tom cursed the Indians bitterly, and for a few moments Preacher thought he was going to put up a fight and force the warriors to kill him, too. But then he subsided into his sorrow and began trudging along with the others.

All morning long, the forced march continued. They didn't encounter anyone else. Preacher had thought that maybe one of the trappers who frequented these mountains would spot them and fetch some help, but it didn't appear that was going to happen. It was still up to him to get them out of this mess.

Around midday, the group reached the spot where Preacher expected to find the Teton Sioux village. This large, open plain next to a twisting, fast-flowing stream was where the Tetons had had their lodges when Hairface was the chief of this band. Preacher was certain of that, because he had visited the place several times and he never forgot somewhere once he had been there.

But now the village was gone and Badger kept his warriors and the prisoners moving as they headed east. They were going toward the valley of the Seven Smokes.

"Hey, Badger," Preacher called to the chief in the Sioux tongue. "What happened? Did you move the village after Hairface died?"

Badger stopped and swung around to glare at Preacher. The fact that he had halted made all the other warriors stop, too, and surrounded as they were, the prisoners had no choice but to follow suit.

"Hairface was not the only one killed by the fever," Badger replied with a scowl. "Several others in the village died as well. It was decided by the elders that this had become an evil place and that the people should leave it and seek out a new home. I had a vision in which a badger, my spirit animal, came to me and led me to the valley of the Seven Smokes. So that is where the people went and where they live now."

It was a pretty long speech, and in the Indian's language it was longer still. When Badger finally finished, Hodge asked Preacher, "What's he saying? Why did we stop?"

"We stopped because this is where their village used to be," Preacher explained, "and I asked him what happened to it. He said there was sickness here, so they decided to move. Their village is now in the valley of the Seven Smokes."

"Say!" Rip exclaimed. "We were plannin' on goin' there. You mean we would've run into this bunch even if they hadn't jumped us?"

Preacher nodded. "Sounds like it. This expedition was a mite cursed to start with."

"I wish now we'd never come," Willard Carling said. "I just wanted to paint the wilderness and the savages who live here. Now it doesn't seem worth it."

"Not worth our lives?" Faith said in scathing tones. "Imagine that!"

For the first time, Carling showed a touch of impatience toward his sister as he said, "I didn't know this was going to happen, Faith. I certainly didn't set out to be captured and mistreated and ultimately killed by heathens."

"Nobody's dead yet except poor Ed Ballinger," Preacher pointed out. "No point in givin' up now."

Jasper Hodge said bleakly, "It's hopeless and you know it, Preacher."

"I don't know nothin' of the sort. If folks were quick to give up, there wouldn't even be a country over here. We'd still be a colony, lettin' the British run things any way they wanted to, fair or not. If ol' Dan'l Boone gave up, he wouldn't have crossed the mountains back East and showed folks there was a whole heap o' new territory to explore out here. The Wilderness Road never would've been carved out. Lord, if people were to give up on doin' what's right just because everything ain't perfect right away . . . well, hell, what would be the point in ever tryin' to do anything?"

"Noble words," Hodge said bitterly, "but they won't stop these savages from killing us."

Preacher couldn't argue with that. Hodge was correct that words wouldn't save their lives. It would take action for that.

And Preacher was going to be ready for that action, as soon as he got the chance.

Chapter Sixteen

It was late afternoon before the group reached the valley of the Seven Smokes. Preacher smelled the place before he could see it. The hot springs that dotted the valley gave off a fire-and-brimstone smell. Farther north was an area where such hot springs were even more common, including some where boiling water shot out of the ground at intervals, rising in a towering plume. In other springs, mud bubbled and roiled. About twenty years earlier, the mountain man John Colter had visited that area and from the descriptions he brought back, some folks decided that the place sounded like the gateway to Hades. So they started calling it Colter's Hell.

Other folks just figured that John Colter was crazy and had imagined the whole thing.

Preacher knew better. He never met John Colter because the famous trapper and buckskinner had died before Preacher came west, but over his years in the mountains he had known other men who were acquainted with Colter, and their stories were enough to make Preacher believe that Colter wouldn't have lied about such a thing.

Not only that, but Preacher had been to the place known to some as Colter's Hell, and had seen for himself the bubbling mud pits and the majestic geysers erupting from the rocks. It was a well-known area now.

The valley of the Seven Smokes wasn't as impressive, but the hot springs located there gave off the same sort of sulphurous odor that the ones farther north did. Preacher wasn't surprised when the group of weary, starving prisoners were prodded over a pine-covered ridge and found themselves stumbling down into the valley.

"I . . . I don't know if I can go on," Faith gasped.

"It ain't much farther now," Preacher told her. "That's the valley where their village is located, right in front of us."

"When we get there, will they feed us?" Hodge asked. The prisoners had been allowed to drink at some of the streams they came to, but they hadn't had any food for more than a day and a half.

Preacher didn't answer Hodge's question. He didn't know if the Indians would feed them. That would depend on how long Badger planned to keep them alive.

The sun was almost down by the time they reached the Teton Sioux village. As usual, the gathering of tepees had been located on the bank of a stream that flowed fast and cold, fed not only by springs but also by snowmelt from the towering peaks that surrounded the valley. The creek was lined with aspens, cottonwoods, and willows, while pines grew thickly farther up the slopes. It was a beautiful place, marred only by the faint smell of sulphur in the air, and Preacher figured the Indians had gotten used to it and probably no longer even noticed it.

Dogs ran out from the village to greet the party with frenzied yapping. The sight of the curs made Preacher think about Dog, and about Horse as well. He knew that by now Horse would have pulled free from the sapling where his reins had been tied. There was a good chance both animals had followed him from the spot where he had been captured. Dog would never lose his scent, and the stallion would follow along wherever the big cur went. Preacher had been keeping an eye on their back trail, thinking he might catch a glimpse of them, but so far he hadn't seen either of the animals. Still, he believed there was a good chance that if he let out a shrill whistle, they would come a-runnin'.

He wouldn't do that, though, as long as he was a prisoner. He didn't want his friends to fall into the hands of the Indians.

Alerted by the barking, youngsters hurried out of the lodges, followed by their mothers and old men and women. The warriors who had been left behind by Badger to guard the village while the chief and the rest of the war party were away strode out as well, carrying bows and tomahawks. One of them clasped wrists with Badger in greeting and cast a satisfied look toward the prisoners. "You had good hunting, Bites Like a Badger," he said.

Badger nodded and turned to point at his prize captive. "The one called Preacher," he announced.

That caused a sensation in the village. All of the Indians had heard of Preacher, and many of them had seen him before when he visited this band while Hairface was still chief. Preacher watched them staring and exclaiming over the fact that he was a prisoner. He thought that a few of the Indians looked disturbed by that, and wondered if they were remembering that he and Hairface had been friends. He sensed that not everybody in this village supported Badger's decision to put on paint and go to war against the whites.

But no one spoke up in protest as the prisoners were herded into the village and taken to one of the tepees. They were shoved inside the conical hide dwelling, which was bare of furnishings. Not even a solitary buffalo robe lay on the ground. The only thing inside the tepee was a fire pit filled with cold ashes.

The prisoners sat down awkwardly, since their hands were still tied behind them. With nine of them crammed into the tepee, quarters were rather tight. This late in the day, it was dark and gloomy inside, adding to the mood of despair that gripped most of the prisoners.

Chester Sinclair wasn't ready to give up, though. He said quietly to Jasper Hodge, who was seated next to him, "Turn around a little, Mr. Hodge, and I'll see if I can reach your bonds and untie them. If just one of us can get loose, then he can free the others."

Hodge hesitated, but then said, "I suppose it can't hurt to try." He scooted around until he and Sinclair were sitting almost back-to-back. Sinclair strained blindly with his hands, and after a moment he said, "I've got them. Now, let's see if I can . . . uh, untie them . . ."

Sinclair was wasting his time, Preacher thought. Badger and his warriors weren't novices at this sort of thing. The rawhide bonds were tied tightly enough that Sinclair could work at them for days without loosening them. But Preacher didn't point out how futile the effort was, because at least it gave Sinclair and Hodge something to keep them busy, so they weren't thinking about the grisly fate that might well be in store for them.

After a while, Hodge asked, "How's it coming along, Chester? Are you making any progress?"

"Not . . . much," Sinclair admitted. "My fingers are . . . so numb . . . I can't really feel what I'm doing. But I'll . . . uh . . . keep trying."

Night continued to settle down over the valley of the Seven Smokes, and soon it was almost pitch black inside the tepee. Only a tiny sliver of light came through the narrow gap that was left when the flap of tanned hide was pulled closed over the entrance. That dim glow came from the light of fires in the village.

Preacher happened to be looking in the direction of the entrance when the light coming through the gap suddenly brightened and took on a flickering, reddish hue. Someone was approaching the tepee with a torch.

A moment later, the flap was thrust aside, and the glaring light from a burning brand spilled into the tepee. Badger stood there with a torch in one hand. He waved the other hand at the prisoners and said, "Bring them."

Badger stepped back to let his warriors enter the tepee.

One by one, Preacher and the other captives were dragged out and stood up.

"They're going to kill us now," Faith moaned. "I just know it."

Badger spoke to Preacher in the Sioux language. "Tell the fire-haired woman to still her flapping tongue."

"He says for you to be quiet, ma'am," Preacher told her, passing on the message.

"But they're going to *kill* us!" Faith wailed.

"Maybe not," Preacher said slowly. He sensed that something about the situation had changed. Badger didn't look nearly as happy as he should have if he was about to torture and murder some of the whites he hated so much.

The prisoners were taken to a large open area in the center of the village. A thick post about six feet tall, made from the trunk of a young pine, stood in the center of the clearing, where it had been driven solidly into the ground. Broken branches were piled around the base of the pole, and Preacher knew why they were there. Indians got a great deal of enjoyment out of tying a captive to a post like that, piling wood around his feet, and setting it on fire. Even the most stoic of prisoners would scream in agony when they felt themselves starting to cook in their own juices.

Preacher's mind went back to that time he had told Snell and his friends about, several years earlier, when he had faced a similar fate as the prisoner of Brown Owl's Blackfoot band. Just like now, he had been bound to a tree then, and the Indians hadn't quite decided *how* they were going to kill him, only that he should die, but chances were they would have burned him to death as these Tetons planned to do.

That's when he had taken his big gamble and had begun to preach, too.

A day later, his voice had been raspy and tortured from hours upon hours of talking without stopping. But at last the Blackfeet had let him go, thinking him touched by the Great Spirit, so that it would cause them to lose their medicine if they harmed him. He gained not only his life but a new name as well.

He honestly didn't believe that tactic would work again, but if things got down to the nub, he would try it. He wouldn't have anything to lose.

Things didn't go as Preacher anticipated, however. Badger pointed to Rip Giddens and uttered a curt command. Two warriors grabbed Rip's arms and manhandled him over to the post. Rip looked angry, but his rugged face didn't show any fear as his arms were first freed and then jerked cruelly behind his back and around the post, where his wrists were tied together again with rawhide thongs. Being bound like that forced him to stand up straight against the post.

"Damn it!" Preacher said to Badger. "Rip ain't done nothin' to you. You know he's always been a friend to your people, just like me!"

"No white man is a friend to the human beings," Badger said, reiterating each tribe's belief that *they* were the only true humans and that all other people, especially the whites, were inferior.

"You know that ain't true," Preacher said.

"What about all of the warriors you have killed?" Badger shot back at him.

"Never killed nobody who wasn't tryin' to kill me first, or who didn't have it comin' for some other reason," Preacher insisted.

"What about Walks With a Limp, Gray Sky, and Tall Like a Pine?" Badger asked. "You stole their lives from them last night."

Preacher knew the chief had to be talking about the warriors who had been killed when he tried to free the prisoners. He said, "They met their deaths in an honorable fight, as did one of our party, the brother of one of my friends. Both sides have suffered. This does not mean we cannot be friends again." He raised his voice so that it carried over the large gathering of Tetons around the clearing in the center of the village. "Hairface was my friend, and so were others who are still here. I wish no harm to your people, and neither do those who are with me. Release them and welcome us as guests, and let there be peace between us."

He could tell from the looks on the faces of some of the men that they would like nothing better than to call a truce and be friends again. But Badger was the chief here, and while he was not the absolute ruler of these people—he could be overruled by a council of elders and wise men—his wishes carried a great deal of weight. The others would go along with what Badger wanted for as long as they could.

Badger sneered. "You talk of peace, Preacher, you who are known by some as the Wolf Who Stalks in the Night, the slayer of human beings, the enemy of our people."

"I am not your enemy," Preacher said steadily. He had to keep pounding home that message, or at least trying to. He didn't know if it would do any good, though.

"Some among us have said that," Badger admitted grudgingly. "That is why it has been decided not to kill you first." The chief lifted his arm and leveled it at Rip. "That is why this man will die first . . ."

Preacher's breath hissed between his teeth. He couldn't stand by and let Rip die.

"Unless you agree to what I propose," Badger went on.

That perked up Preacher's interest in a hurry. Was Badger about to offer him a way out of this mess?

"What do you wish of me?" he asked.

Badger's ugly smile reappeared on his scarred face. "More than once you have dared me to fight you, Preacher. If you agree, you are about to receive what you desire. You and I will do battle . . . to the death."

Chapter Seventeen

Preacher's keen brain grasped instantly what Badger probably had in mind, but before he could make sure, Faith let out a moan and asked hysterically, "What are the two of you saying? What's he going to do? Is he going to kill poor Mr. Giddens?"

Preacher turned his head to look at her and snapped, "Shut up." In a slightly milder tone, he went on. "Don't interfere, ma'am. These folks don't like it when a woman butts in while men are talkin'."

"Well!" Faith sniffed, able to take offense even though she was terrified. She added coldly, "Pardon me."

Preacher ignored her and turned his attention back to Badger. He said, "If I fight you, will you let the others go and cause them no harm?"

"You *will* fight me," Badger said, "and I make no promise about these others. But you will have a chance to do battle for your life."

Preacher shook his head. "No deal. I won't make a bargain like that."

Badger pointed at Rip again. "You would rather stand by and watch your friend die screaming in the flames?"

"Don't listen to him, Preacher!" Rip called out suddenly,

having understood enough of the exchange between Preacher and Badger to know what was going on. "I don't give a damn what he does to me. Make him promise to spare the others before you agree to anything."

"You may as well kill me now while my hands are tied, Bites Like a Badger," Preacher said to the chief. "You have no honor, anyway."

Badger's face darkened with anger. "For a white man to accuse one of the true people of having no honor is foolish! Everyone knows it is the white men who have no honor!"

Preacher shrugged. "Whatever you say." With a motion of his head, he indicated the others of the band. "But your people hear, and they know the truth."

Badger looked around as several of the warriors muttered under their breaths. He was the leader of a divided tribe, some of whom followed him, while others still held to the beliefs of Hairface. With a look on his face that told Preacher he knew he was boxed in, Badger said, "I agree. We will fight, and if you defeat me you and these others will go free. They will come to no harm from the Teton Sioux."

"Your word on that?"

Badger nodded. "My word, Preacher."

"All right, then," Preacher said. He turned so that he could hold his hands out behind him. "Cut me loose, and let me get some feelin' back in my hands."

Badger drew his knife, but paused before he slashed the bonds around Preacher's wrists. "There is one more condition," he said.

"What's that?"

"You must give me *your* word that you will not speak as you did in the village of the Blackfeet, when it was thought that the Great Spirit had touched you."

"Don't want me to go to preachin', eh?" The mountain man chuckled. "All right, Badger, you got my word on that, too."

As the chief sawed through the rawhide strips, he said, "You have not asked what will happen to these others if you lose."

Preacher felt the bonds fall free. He brought his arms in front of him again, and it was a blessed relief to be able to do so, even though the muscles were stiff and his numb hands soon felt like they were on fire as the blood flowed into them again. He grinned tightly and told Badger, "I don't intend to lose."

Badger scowled at him and said, "Just so you know, they will all follow you into death. But they will die quickly, rather than slowly and painfully. This I will do to honor a fallen enemy." He turned to one of the other warriors and held out his hand. The man drew his knife and put the handle in Badger's palm. Badger threw the knife at the ground, so that the blade buried itself in the earth next to Preacher's right foot. As Badger backed off several steps, he went on. "Pick it up whenever you are ready to die, Preacher."

"Be careful, Preacher," Switchfoot called. "That redskin's prob'ly a tricky sumbitch."

Jasper Hodge asked, "What's going on here? Why did he turn Preacher loose?"

"Take it easy, mister," Hammerhead Jones told him. "Preacher's gonna fight ol' Badger, for all our lives."

Willard Carling said, "Is this true, Preacher? You're going to do battle with that savage, with our fates riding on the outcome?"

"Yep," Preacher said as he continued rubbing his hands together, getting as much feeling back in them as he could before he had to pick up the knife and face Badger.

"But . . . but you're exhausted! You haven't eaten in ages, and you probably didn't sleep much last night."

"True on both counts," Preacher said with a faint smile.

"How can you hope to defeat him?"

"Easy. I don't have any choice." Preacher bent his knees and reached down to grasp the handle of the knife. As he straightened, he pulled the blade from the dirt. He wiped it on the leg of his buckskin trousers and nodded to the chief. "All right, Badger. You've got it to do."

With the ugly grin on his face again, Badger stalked forward, his knife held low and ready to strike viciously. Preacher didn't know why some folks seemed to think that Indians never showed any emotion. Badger was grinning like a possum in a persimmon tree.

Preacher moved forward to meet him. The onlookers stepped back a little, clearing an area for the two men to fight. They formed a large circle, with the post where Rip Giddens was tied to one side of it. The other prisoners huddled together near the post.

"I will enjoy peeling the hide off you, one agonizing strip at a time," Badger taunted.

Preacher sounded almost bored as he said, "You gonna fight or just try to talk me to death?"

Badger stopped grinning and snarled instead as he flung himself forward and slashed at Preacher with the knife in his hand.

Preacher wasn't there anymore, though, having twisted aside. He stuck out a foot, hoping that he could trip Badger as the chief's momentum carried him forward, but Badger nimbly avoided Preacher's leg and swung the knife in a back-handed strike that Preacher barely avoided. As it was, the point of Badger's blade caught for a second in Preacher's shirt and ripped it.

Preacher launched an attack of his own, slashing at Badger and forcing the chief to step back while he was already off balance. As Preacher had hoped, Badger's feet got tangled up with each other and he went down, falling over backward. Preacher dived after him, but Badger rolled desperately to the side. Preacher hit the ground instead.

Badger kicked out, his moccasin-shod foot crashing into Preacher's side. Preacher felt pain shoot through him and hoped that the kick hadn't broken a rib. He rolled the other way, putting a little distance between himself and Badger. As he came up on hands and knees and then surged to his feet, he saw that Badger was scrambling up, too. Both men reached their feet at the same time and attacked each other simultaneously. Sparks flew from steel as their knife blades rang together.

Preacher feinted, and when Badger twisted to meet it, Preacher swung his left fist in a blow that crashed against Badger's jaw. Indians were skillful wrestlers but they weren't much on bare-knuckle brawling, so the punch took Badger by surprise and landed solidly. He flew backward and sat down hard, skidding a few feet on his rump. But he flipped over lithely and came up again as Preacher rushed in, trying to seize the momentary advantage. Instead, Preacher had to stop short and throw himself backward to avoid being disemboweled by a sweeping upward stroke of Badger's knife.

On and on the two men battled, first one gaining a slight edge, then the other. Preacher drew first blood, leaving a bloody gash on Badger's right forearm. The cut wasn't deep enough to disable the chief, though, or even to slow him down very much. In fact, less than a minute later the tip of Badger's blade traced a fiery line across Preacher's side, and this time it cut more than buckskin. Preacher felt the warm flow of blood on his skin.

As the long minutes wore on, both men began to bleed in several more places. None of the wounds were serious enough to stop the fight, though. It appeared that nothing would do that short of death for one or both of the combatants.

Preacher's pulse hammered heavily in his head. Most of his attention was focused on his opponent, naturally enough, so he was only vaguely aware of the tense audience all around him and Badger. The Tetons didn't call out encouragement to their chief, but rather watched the fight in rapt silence.

That wasn't the case with the prisoners. Carling and Hodge both shouted advice and warnings to Preacher, although he ignored them. Faith cried out in alarm every time it looked like Preacher was about to be defeated. Of course, she was thinking more about what would happen to her if he lost, rather than about him, but Preacher didn't expect any more than that from the spoiled Eastern girl.

Rip and the other mountain men watched in silence, like the Indians. They knew just as well as the Tetons did how deadly serious this was. If the fight had been a brawl between two friends, they would have been whoopin' and hollerin' and enjoying the entertainment. The stakes in this battle were too high for such boisterousness.

Preacher's weariness began to tell on him. He called on his reserves of strength and stamina and kept moving as fast as when the fight had started. Sooner or later, though, his body was liable to betray him. All it would take was a momentary lapse, and then he would die and so would the other prisoners.

But Badger was tired, too, and Preacher could see that in the chief's eyes. He pressed the attack, hoping that Badger would be the first one to slip.

Instead, as Preacher lunged in, his foot came down on a small branch that had been kicked out from the pile around the base of the post where Rip was tied. The branch rolled under him, and suddenly Preacher felt himself losing his balance as he leaned far to one side. Unable to catch himself, he went down hard. At the same time, Badger swung his leg in a kick that caught Preacher on the wrist. The knife went spinning out of his hand.

Badger cried out in triumph as he threw himself on Preacher and the knife in his hand swept downward. Preacher writhed and flung a hand up just in time to catch hold of Badger's wrist and stop the killing stroke. The tip of the blade was barely an inch from Preacher's chest. Both men grunted from the strain as Badger tried to drive the knife into Preacher's body and Preacher struggled to keep him from doing it.

Suddenly, Preacher smashed his other hand against Badger's ear. That caused Badger to let up a little on the knife, and Preacher was able to twist the blade aside from his body. At the same time Preacher brought a knee up into Badger's belly. That shook the chief even more. Preacher hauled hard on Badger's arm and threw him aside. He rolled after Badger and wound up on the chief's back, an arm looped around his neck from behind. Preacher's other hand still had hold of Badger's knife wrist. Now the chief didn't have any leverage or any way to get at Preacher with the knife. Preacher increased the pressure on the arm around Badger's neck.

Badger began to flail and kick desperately as Preacher steadily, inexorably, choked the life out of him. Preacher dug his knee into the small of Badger's back and levered himself upward, maintaining his grip on the chief's neck so that Badger was forced to bend backward. Preacher knew that if he kept this up, the only question was whether Badger would choke to death before Preacher snapped his spine.

Badger let go of the knife and tried to bring his hand around so that he could claw at Preacher. Preacher held firm. Now that he had Badger in this death-grip, nothing was going to force him to let go.

Nothing except—himself.

Abruptly, Preacher released his hold and stood up, stepping back so that Badger was left lying on the ground, gasping for breath and looking a little like a fish that has been pulled out of a stream and dropped on the bank.

"Oh, my God!" Carling exclaimed in alarm. "What's he doing? Why didn't he go ahead and kill the Indian?"

"Hang on," Rip advised. "I reckon Preacher knows what he's doin'."

Preacher heard that, and he sure as hell hoped Rip was right. He hoped that he *did* know what he was doing.

Silence hung over the Teton village, a portentous silence broken only by Badger's rasping breaths. After a minute or so, Badger rolled awkwardly onto his back and then sat up, glaring murderously at Preacher. He rubbed his throat and husked, "Why do you not kill me? Why do you rob me of an honorable death?"

"Because there ain't anything honorable about any man dyin' when he don't have to." Preacher raised his voice so that all the Indians could hear him. "Your chief has fought well. He is a fine enemy, but I would have him for a finer friend, as Hairface was my friend." He waved a hand toward the prisoners. "These people and I mean you no harm. We come to the valley of the Seven Smokes in peace. Free them, and songs will be sung of the generosity of the true people. Welcome them as guests, and they will leave as friends, forever and ever."

There were mutters of agreement from some of the warriors, enough so that Badger couldn't fail to notice them. Still rubbing his throat, he said to Preacher, "Our fight was to be to the death. You would break your word?"

"Your life is mine," Preacher said. "It is up to me what to do with it . . . and I return it to you." He shrugged. "Perhaps I will kill you another day, Bites Like a Badger . . . but I don't think this will ever happen."

Badger continued to scowl, but finally he nodded in acceptance. He climbed to his feet, angrily waving away offers of help from some of his followers. He glared at Preacher and said loudly, "No one may kill this man but me, and I cannot kill him now without dishonoring myself. So he and his friends are free and may remain here with us as our guests for as long as they wish." He folded his arms across his chest. "So speaks Bites Like a Badger."

Rip Giddens and the other frontiersmen grinned with relief, although Preacher remained suitably solemn as he stepped forward and extended a hand to Badger. The chief didn't hesitate as he clasped Preacher's wrist.

"What . . . what does it all mean?" Willard Carling asked in astonishment.

"It means they ain't gonna kill us after all," Rip said as one of the warriors moved to cut him loose from the post. "It means we're gonna live . . . thanks to Preacher."

Luther Snell wiggled backward in the tall grass, moving carefully so as not to disturb it any more than he had to. Baldy was beside him, also withdrawing slowly and cautiously from their reconnaissance of the Teton Sioux village. The two men had crept close enough to the village so that they had been able to witness the brutal combat between Preacher and Bites

Like a Badger, and they had also heard what was said after that fight was over.

When they were far enough away that it was safe for them to stand up, they did so and hurried back to where they had left the rest of the group. "What'd you find out?" Euchre asked as Snell and Baldy trotted up to their hiding place in a clump of aspen.

Snell was seething inside from what he had seen. The anger erupted from him now as he said, "*Damn* that Preacher!"

"What did he do?" Vickery asked.

"He went and made *friends* with those damn redskins, even Badger!"

"You mean they ain't gonna kill him?"

"Nope," Baldy said. "Him and Badger are almost blood brothers now . . . even though I got the idea that Badger still don't like him very much."

"Badger can't hate him any more'n I do," Snell said. He wiped the back of a hand across his mouth and grimaced. "But those pilgrims ain't prisoners no more. They're guests of the Tetons now. It's gonna be harder than ever to get our hands on them."

"Oh, hell," Collins said. "Let's just give it up."

"I'm not givin' *nothin'* up!" Snell blazed. "We're still gonna be rich, and Preacher's still gonna die." He spat. "Hell, it's better this way."

"How do you figure that?" Vickery asked.

Snell summoned up an evil smile. "Because this way, I still get to enjoy killin' Preacher myself."

Chapter Eighteen

Now that Preacher and the others were guests of Badger's people, rather than captives, everything was different. Badger barked orders, and within minutes of friendship being declared, all the bonds had been cut and the former prisoners were freed. They were ushered into one of the other lodges, but this time several squaws escorted them there instead of tomahawk-toting warriors.

This lodge was larger and already had a fire burning in its fire pit. Thick, comfortable buffalo robes were scattered around on the ground. One of the women said to Preacher, "Wait here. We will bring food."

When they were left alone, Willard Carling rubbed his wrists where the tight rawhide thongs had chafed them and said, "I can't believe it. We're not going to die."

Faith looked at Preacher with newfound respect in her eyes. "You saved us," she said. "If you hadn't fought that savage and won, they would have killed all of us."

"Maybe," Preacher said with a shrug. "I'm the one Badger really had a grudge against. He might've been satisfied with killin' me and maybe Rip and Switchfoot and Hammerhead and Tom. But he might've let you folks live and made slaves out of you."

"Slaves?" Carling said. "How terrible! I didn't know Indians had slaves. I thought only illiterate Southerners kept other human beings in bondage."

Preacher grunted. "The tribes been makin' war and takin' slaves from each other as long as anybody's lived on this continent. And it sure as hell didn't start with them. All the Africans who've been brought over here were captured and sold to the blackbirders by other Africans. They've been enslavin' each other for thousands of years. Slavery goes all the way back to the Bible and probably before. It's easy for you folks from back East and up North to think that you're better'n folks down South because you don't own slaves, but somewhere in your family's past, odds are *they* did. And if they didn't, then some o' them *were* slaves. Or both. Only way to wipe it out is to wipe out the human race."

"You can't be saying that you approve of such things," Jasper Hodge said.

"Knowin' that something exists and approvin' of it are two different things."

Hodge and Carling might have continued the discussion, but at that moment Chester Sinclair burst out with uncharacteristic vehemence. "My God! We barely escaped a terrible death just a few minutes ago, and you're arguing philosophy and the human condition! Shouldn't we just be grateful that we're still alive?"

"I'm grateful," Preacher said. He winced a little as he lifted a hand to his side where Badger's knife had gashed him. "I'm also still bleedin' a little, I think."

Faith took a step toward him. "Let me take a look at it," she said quickly. "Maybe I can help."

"No, ma'am, that's all right. I'm bettin' that Rip or one of these other ol' boys has experience at patchin' up knife wounds. And squaws are mighty good at fixin' up poultices and things like that. I'll be fine, ma'am."

"I insist," Faith said. "Take your shirt off."

Preacher glanced at Sinclair and saw that the man was scowling again, evidently having already forgotten his own advice about just being happy to be alive. Preacher hadn't forgotten that Sinclair was sweet on Faith, and he didn't want the woman making a fuss over him and causing trouble between him and Sinclair. From what he had seen so far, he liked Sinclair the best of the four pilgrims, despite the man's apparent lack of self-confidence.

Faith wasn't going to be denied, though, so Preacher gave in and peeled his buckskin shirt over his head, wincing again as the blood that had already started to dry on the wound pulled free. It was an ugly gash about four inches long.

"That really ought to have stitches," Faith said with a worried frown on her face.

"Stitchin' up a wound out here is a tricky business," Preacher told her. "Sometimes you wind up just makin' it worse. Best thing you can do for a scratch like this is put a poultice on it and then bind it up as tight as you can."

"Where do I get this . . . this poultice?"

"Like I said, one o' the squaws can gather some moss and herbs and make one up."

Faith looked reluctant to turn Preacher's care over to the Indian women, but she didn't have much choice in the matter. A few minutes later, the squaws returned with a large pot of stew. The former prisoners crowded around it. The savory aroma emanating from the pot made all of them realize just how long it had been since they had eaten.

"Where are the bowls and spoons?" Faith asked.

One of the squaws handed out wooden bowls. "No spoons," Rip told Faith. "You just dip your bowl in the pot and then eat with your fingers."

Faith made a face. "How is one supposed to eat stew with one's fingers?"

"One picks out the pieces o' meat and onion and Injun taters and then drinks what's left," Rip explained with only a hint of dry humor.

Meanwhile, Preacher spoke to one of the squaws and showed her the gash in his side. She agreed to bring him a poultice to put on the wound and left the lodge to tend to it.

Everyone dug in, dipping their bowls in the stew pot as Rip had said. "Don't eat too fast," Preacher warned them. "Your bellies have been empty for a good long while, and they won't take kindly to it if you put too much food in there too fast."

A short time later, the Indian woman returned with the poultice, a mass of moss and mud and herbs. Faith wrinkled her nose in distaste at the smell that came from it.

Preacher didn't mind the smell, because he knew the poultice would help heal the gash in his side. The squaw plastered it onto the wound, then wrapped strips of rawhide around Preacher's torso and tied them tightly in place.

"Doin' it this way will leave less of a scar than if somebody tried to sew it up," Preacher said.

"It takes an incredible amount of knowledge just to survive out here, doesn't it?" Carling asked.

"Yeah, but folks learn."

"Either that, or they die," Switchfoot added.

When the meal was over and Preacher's wound had been tended to, the frontiersmen stretched out on the buffalo robes. Warm from the fire, and with their bellies full again, they would be asleep within minutes.

Faith looked around and frowned. "Where am I supposed to sleep?" she wanted to know. "There's no privacy."

She hadn't been worried about privacy the night before, when she was trussed up and thrown down on the ground as a captive, Preacher thought. He didn't point that out, though.

Chester Sinclair picked up one of the robes and carried it over to the rear wall of the lodge, where he spread it out carefully. "You can sleep here, Miss Faith," he told her. "No one will bother you." He left unspoken the pledge that he would see to that, but it was easy enough to read on his face.

"That robe sort of . . . smells a bit, doesn't it?"

"You'll get used to it," Preacher assured her. "And it's soft enough you won't really care."

"I suppose." Faith sighed and went over to the robe. She lowered herself stiffly onto it and stretched out, turning her back to the others in the tepee.

It wasn't long at all before several of them were snoring. As tired and beat-up as Preacher was, though, he still didn't go to sleep right away. As the fire burned down to embers and its light dimmed, he thought about everything that had happened since he rode into the Rendezvous several days earlier. Life had taken some . . . interesting . . . twists and turns since then.

He still missed Mountain Mist, more than he would have thought likely, in fact, considering that they hadn't been together all that long. And he was a mite sorry that he had been forced to kill Stump. The little trapper hadn't been a bad sort, really. He had just let his resentment and anger get the best of him, and done some things that there was no turning back from. Preacher regretted, as well, that his old friend Hairface had gone over the divide. But he had a new "friend" in Bites Like a Badger, he supposed.

He asked himself if he could really trust Badger. He knew that having extended the hospitality of the village, Badger wouldn't go back on his word. But if their paths crossed again somewhere else, away from the village . . . well, Preacher didn't know what would happen then, but he was pretty sure he would keep a damned close eye on ol' Badger.

Finally, he dozed off, allowing the bone-deep weariness that gripped him to carry him away into a dreamless oblivion.

Preacher was stiff and sore when he woke up the next morning, but that came as no surprise. He figured that Badger was hurting just as bad, and that thought put a faint smile on his rugged face. Everyone else seemed to still be asleep, so he got up quietly and slipped out of the lodge without disturbing them.

The Teton village was coming to life in the dawn. Women had gotten up and stirred the cooking fires until flames leaped up merrily. Dogs trotted here and there on the usual mysterious canine errands. Even this early, a few kids were playing. And while most of the warriors were still asleep, a few of them were out and about, too, carrying weapons and alertly watching the countryside around the village.

Preacher stretched some of the stiffness out of his muscles and then ambled over to one of the warriors, a middle-aged man he recognized from previous visits whose name was Panther Leaping.

"Panther," Preacher greeted the man. "May this day be a good one."

"A good day to die?" Panther Leaping asked with a quirk of an eyebrow.

"If the spirits will it so," Preacher replied. "Why are you watchful on such a fine morning?"

"Because the filthy, dung-eating Crow would like nothing better than to ruin it."

The warrior's emphatic answer made Preacher's eyebrows rise. "There is trouble between the Crow and the Teton Sioux?" he asked. "I had not heard about it."

"There is always trouble between the dung-eaters and the real human beings. The Crow have killed our warriors and stolen our women and horses."

"This is sort of far south for them to be raidin', ain't it?" Preacher asked.

"Tell that to Silver Bear. He is their chief now and seeks war not only against the Teton Sioux, but also the Ogallala and the Hunkpapa and the Miniconjou, as well as the Cheyenne and the Arapaho."

"Sounds to me like he don't get along with much of anybody," Preacher commented.

Panther Leaping lowered his voice to a confidential tone and said, "This is why so many of the older warriors among the people do not want Bites Like a Badger to pursue war against the whites. We should be getting ready to fight the Crow instead. That fight is coming, whether we want it or not."

"It will be a good fight," Preacher said. "But the true people will defeat the dung-eaters."

He didn't know if that was what would happen or not. Despite their degraded reputation among the other tribes, the

Crow were fierce fighters and could be counted on to give any enemies quite a tussle. But since Preacher was a guest in the village of the Teton Sioux, he was polite enough to declare that they would win if it came down to a battle.

"That is why we watch," Panther Leaping said. "Treacherous dogs that they are, the Crow might attempt to strike us unaware. So we watch for them, night and day."

The entrance flap on the lodge where the pilgrims slept was pushed back then, drawing Preacher's attention. He looked around to see Chester Sinclair emerge from the tepee. The big Easterner stretched, yawned, and looked around. Spotting Preacher and Panther Leaping, he walked toward them.

"Is everything all right this morning, Preacher?" he asked.

"Fine enough," Preacher replied. "We're alive, ain't we?"

Sinclair grinned. "I can't argue with that."

"You look almost happy, Sinclair," Preacher said.

"I am. I slept extraordinarily well. This high country air . . . it's like nectar to a man's lungs."

The way Preacher saw it, a man could drown in nectar just like he could in water, but he knew what Sinclair meant.

"How's your wound?" Sinclair went on.

"A mite stiff, but I'm fine," Preacher replied. "I slept pretty good, too. That and some vittles sure as hell make a difference in the way a man feels."

Willard Carling crawled out of the lodge in time to hear Preacher's last comment. "Amen to that," he exclaimed as he got to his feet. He came over to join the others and continued. "Preacher, I know you speak the language of these people. Could you ask them a question for me?"

"I'll try," Preacher said.

"I'd like to have my paints and my canvases back," Carling said. "Do you think the chief would send someone back to where they were left, so they could be fetched here?"

Chapter Nineteen

The question took Preacher by surprise. He frowned at Carling.

"I mean, if it's not too much trouble," the artist went on quickly. "Really, though, they had no right to discard our possessions like that."

"Out here a man's generally got whatever rights he makes for himself, and what he can hold on to," Preacher said. "But I reckon I can understand why you feel that way. You came to the frontier to paint, after all, and you can't do that without paints and canvases."

"Exactly! Thank you for understanding, Preacher. Now, if you'll just tell, what's his name, Bites Like a Badger . . ."

Preacher wasn't sure how Badger would react to the request, but he supposed it wouldn't do any harm to ask.

"Come on," he said to Carling. "We'll go see if we can find him."

He nodded farewell to Panther Leaping and led Carling toward Badger's lodge, which was one of the largest in the village and was located near the center of the gathering. When they got there, Preacher called out, "Bites Like a Badger! I would have words with you."

Badger must have been awake already, because the entrance

flap on the tepee was thrust back only seconds after Preacher spoke. The chief stepped out, crossed his arms over his chest, and regarded Preacher and Carling in a carefully neutral manner. Preacher thought he still saw some dislike in Badger's eyes, though.

"Preacher is in pain this morning?" Badger asked.

"No more so than Bites Like a Badger," Preacher replied. Neither of them was going to admit that they had gotten the hell beaten out of them by the other the night before.

"What is it you wish?"

Preacher waved a hand toward Carling. "My friend would speak to you."

"He speaks the language of the true people?"

"No, but I will translate his words for him."

Badger nodded and said to Carling, "Speak, white man."

"What did he say?" Carling asked with a frown.

"Tell him what you want," Preacher said.

"Me?" Carling held a hand to his chest. "But . . . but I thought you would—"

"Out here a man speaks for himself. Badger understands a little of what you say, but I'll put it in his people's tongue, too, so there won't be any misunderstandings."

"Well . . . if you're sure . . ."

"Go ahead," Preacher said firmly.

Carling swallowed. "Well, ah, Chief . . . I was wondering . . . if perhaps you could . . . could send someone to get my paints and brushes and canvases . . . that is, if it's not too much trouble and if you don't mind . . ."

"Beggin's not the way to go about it," Preacher interrupted. "Say what you mean. Tell him straight out."

Carling looked skeptical and a little frightened. "You're sure?"

Preacher nodded. He said quickly to Badger in the Sioux tongue, "Carling has expressed his respect for Bites Like a Badger and the true people. Now he will tell you what he wants." He glanced at Carling and added in English, "Spit it out."

"All right." Carling straightened and crossed his own arms

as he leveled his gaze at Badger. "You and your warriors took my paints and canvases and brushes. I want them back. I need them to paint. I want you to send men to get them and bring them back to me."

Preacher translated, making the speech a bit more flowery in the Indian fashion. Badger glared and demanded, "Does this foolish little man not know that I still hold his life in my hands?"

"Among his own people he is a great man, a shaman of sorts. He demands the return of what is rightfully his, and if he is truly a guest in this village, you will be a good chief and honor his demand."

"I could strike him down right now," Badger growled.

"You could kill him," Preacher acknowledged, "but if you do it will be a defeat for you, because it will forever be a stain on your honor. You have given your word that no harm will come to him and the others."

Badger shrugged at that reminder. "I will not harm him. And I will send a small party of warriors to bring his belongings, strange though they may be, to the village. But only if he pledges not to use them to harm any of my people."

"He means no harm to your people and wishes them only well."

Badger nodded reluctantly. "It is agreed." He paused, then added, "The little man possesses more courage than I thought, to speak to me the way he did."

"He possesses more courage than even he knows," Preacher said.

Carling had waited as long as he was going to. He asked, "Well? What did he say?"

Preacher turned toward him. "Badger will send men to fetch your gear. It ought to be here by nightfall, or maybe tomorrow morning, at the latest."

"That's wonderful! Should I, ah, thank him?"

"That'd be a good idea."

"How do I go about it?"

"Just speak your piece and maybe nod a little."

"All right." Carling faced Badger and said, "Thank you, Chief. You are a fine man, and I will paint your portrait first, before anyone else in your village."

Preacher translated, "He promises to honor you with his medicine as soon as his paints and brushes and canvases are returned to him."

Badger grunted and returned Carling's nod.

Preacher touched the artist's arm. "Come on. Let's go back to the lodge with the others. Even though the Tetons have promised us their hospitality, it wouldn't be a good idea to go wanderin' around too much, especially by your lonesome."

"Don't worry about that," Carling said. "I don't intend to stray far from your side, Preacher!"

By the time Preacher and Carling got back to the lodge, the others were awake. Faith rushed up to her brother and threw her arms around him. "My God, Willard!" she exclaimed. "Chester told me you went off to confront that awful Indian! Have you lost your mind? He could have killed you! And all over some stupid paints and canvases!"

Carling stiffened and pulled back from her a little. "Stupid paints and canvases?" he repeated. "I don't talk that way about your poetry, Faith."

She fluttered a hand. "Oh, you know I didn't mean anything by it. I just meant you shouldn't be risking your life like that."

"I wasn't risking my life. I was simply letting the chief know that he had no right to throw away my property, and that I wanted it back." There was a note of pride in Carling's voice as he added, "And he agreed with me, too."

Faith's eyebrows arched. "He did?"

"He most certainly did. He promised that he would send some of his warriors to retrieve my gear. Didn't he, Preacher?"

"Yep," Preacher drawled. "You stood up for what was right, Mr. Carling."

"Please, call me Willard. After all, we're fellow frontiersmen now, eh?"

Preacher wouldn't have gone quite that far, but he didn't see any point in hurting Carling's feelings. He said, "Sure, Willard."

Jasper Hodge looked around at the village and said, "Well, now that we're here, what are we going to do?"

"I'm going to wait until I get my paints and canvases back," Carling said, "and then I intend to spend at least a week painting."

Faith sighed. "I suppose I could try to compose some verses about the way these savages live. It's hardly a fit subject for something as beautiful as poetry, but an artist works with the materials at hand." She turned to Preacher. "What about you?"

"I figured I'd rest up and let these scrapes and bruises I got heal. After that, I don't know." Preacher's eyes narrowed. "Snell's still out there somewhere. He'll be a threat to you folks as long as him and his bunch are around. Besides, I got a score to settle with him, so I may just go lookin' for him instead o' waitin' for him to come to me."

"You mean you're going to try to kill him?"

"He's got it comin'," Preacher said simply.

"Perhaps," Hodge said, "but no one declared you judge, jury, and executioner, Preacher."

Preacher laughed humorlessly. "The nearest judge and jury are back in Saint Looey, Hodge. That's as far in this direction as the law has gotten. Out here, justice comes from the barrel of a gun."

"That's not justice. That's anarchy."

"That's the frontier. Sooner you learn that, the better."

Hodge shook his head. "I'm a civilized man. I'll never believe the same way you do, Preacher."

Preacher shrugged. "I don't recollect sayin' that I cared one way or the other whether you believed like me."

Hodge flushed with anger, but he didn't say anything else. The squaws who had been given the task of caring for the guests arrived with food for breakfast, and everyone sat down cross-legged on the ground to eat, even Faith. She complained some about having to eat with her fingers, but not as much as the night before. Maybe eventually, she would adjust to life on the frontier—but Preacher wasn't going to hold his breath waiting for that to happen.

After the meal, the frontiersmen found places to stretch out and get another nap. They had sleep to catch up on, and like most men who were accustomed to living in rugged and often dangerous conditions, they slept like logs whenever they had the chance to do so safely.

Preacher stayed awake, though, because he wasn't convinced that they were safe yet. Instinct gnawed at the back of his brain, trying to warn him that trouble still loomed on the horizon. He knew better than to disregard a hunch like that.

But as the day wore on, it certainly seemed like the rest of their visit to the Teton Sioux village was going to be peaceful. While Preacher kept an eye on them to make sure they didn't get in trouble, Willard Carling and Jasper Hodge roamed around a bit, looking at everything with great interest. Hodge even took a pad of paper and a pencil from inside his coat and made notes about everything he saw.

"Material for the book I plan to write," he explained when he saw Preacher looking at him with a puzzled frown. "This volume will make me a famous historian and naturalist."

Preacher nodded. Hodge was an ambitious man. Fame called out to him, singing a siren song.

Preacher, on the other hand, had more fame in these mountains than he really wanted. A reputation as a tough, dangerous man sometimes came in handy, because folks thought twice about messing with somebody like that. But being well known also attracted trouble at times, because there was always somebody who thought they were tougher than he was and wanted to take him down a peg.

Faith Carling's writing equipment had been lost when she was taken captive with the others, but she borrowed some paper and an extra pencil from Hodge. Using a flat rock for a writing table, she began to compose a poem. Chester Sinclair hung around where she was, obviously trying not to be too obvious about his feelings for her—and failing. Faith ignored him, though.

During the afternoon, Rip Giddens sought out Preacher and engaged him in a low-voiced conversation. "You trust ol' Badger, Preacher?" Rip asked.

"Not completely," Preacher replied bluntly. "He'll keep his word as long as we're here in the village, but that's all I'm sure of."

"We can't stay here forever," Rip said. "Sooner or later we'll have to leave."

Preacher nodded. "Yep. That may be what Badger's waitin' for. He's just bidin' his time now. Of course, the Crows could change all that."

"How do you figure?" Rip asked sharply, clearly interested by Preacher's reference to the other Indian tribe.

"Accordin' to what Panther Leapin' told me, the Crows been raidin' down here lately," Preacher explained. "Panther figures it's only a matter of time until they launch a real attack on the Tetons."

Rip let out a low whistle. "Crows hate just about ever'body, and just about ever'body hates them. But they're dangerous, Preacher, no doubt about that."

Preacher nodded and said, "If they go to war, then Badger will have his hands full with that, and he likely won't have the time or inclination to bother with us no more."

"Yeah," Rip said as he rubbed his jaw in thought. "There's one mighty big problem with that, though."

"Yeah," Preacher agreed with a faint smile, his tone tinged with irony. "Bein' in the middle of a war between two Indian tribes ain't exactly the safest place in the world, now is it?"

Chapter Twenty

Like most of the men who came to the Rocky Mountains in search of beaver pelts, the red-bearded trapper called Wingate was happy being by himself. He could go for weeks, even months, without seeing any other white men, and he didn't particularly care whether or not he saw any red men, as long as the ones he saw weren't hostile. With his horse and a pack mule, he rode through the majestic scenery, and was glad to be alive and free and out in the open where he could enjoy all the sights and sounds.

He got a mite nervous, though, when he realized that somebody was following him.

All morning, his instincts had been worrying him, so along about noontime, he found a place in some thick woods where he could leave his horse and mule, and then taking his rifle, with which he was an excellent shot, he climbed to the top of a rocky spur and settled down behind some boulders to watch for whoever was dogging his trail.

He didn't have long to wait. Within fifteen minutes, he began to hear the sound of hoofbeats—a lot of hoofbeats. A large group of riders was coming toward him. They weren't moving all that fast, though. Wingate revised his assumption that whoever these gents were, they had been following him.

Maybe they just happened to be going the same direction he was, which was generally north and west.

The frontiersman's eyes narrowed in surprise as he saw the first of the riders come into view, moving at a deliberate pace around a large cluster of boulders. They were white men, wearing red-and-blue uniforms and black shakos. Sunlight reflected off the rifles they carried and the brass buttons and insignia on their uniforms. The man in the lead wore a saber belted around his waist and had a little fancier uniform than the others. Wingate supposed he was the officer in charge.

What the hell were a bunch of soldiers doing out here? From time to time, the Army sent an expedition to the frontier, but so far nearly all of the exploration and settling done west of the Mississippi had been by civilians, either individuals or fellas who worked for private companies.

The men Wingate was looking at now were definitely soldiers, though. Nobody else would parade around in get-ups like that.

He counted them as they came around the rocks. Fifteen men, counting the officer. Several of them were leading packhorses.

Wingate frowned. He supposed the soldiers had a right to be here; after all, ever since the Louisiana Purchase, this territory had been part of the United States. But it was damned odd to see soldiers wandering around in the mountains, especially on their own. Wingate would have expected to see a civilian guide or two with them.

Were they lost? They acted like they knew where they were going, but Wingate knew that when it came to the Army, that didn't really mean anything. Soldier boys could march right off a cliff and act like they knew where they were going.

He waited until they were closer, then, acting on an impulse, he stood up and held his rifle over his head. "Hey!" he shouted. "Hey, down there!"

Instantly, the soldiers reined their horses to a halt, and several of them raised their rifles and pointed them at Wingate before the officer twisted around in the saddle and called for them to hold their fire and lower their weapons.

Then he turned back toward Wingate and shouted, "Hello, my good man!"

Wingate didn't much cotton being called anybody's good man in that tone of voice, but he chalked it up to ignorance on the part of the officer and told himself to be tolerant. He called, "What're you fellas doin' out here? You lost?"

"Could you come down here, so we won't have to shout?" the officer asked.

Wingate shrugged. "Stay there! I'll be along in a minute."

He climbed down from the rocky prominence, fetched his horse and mule, and led them out of the trees toward the group of soldiers. As he came closer, Wingate saw that the officer was a young man in his twenties, with a little mustache that curled up on each end. Having served in the War of 1812, the trapper was a little familiar with military ranks and thought the insignia on the officer's uniform meant that he was a lieutenant. Probably fresh out of West Point and on his first assignment. His superiors probably hadn't been too smart, sending him out into the wilderness like this.

"Howdy, Lieutenant," Wingate greeted the man.

The officer swung down from his military saddle and offered his hand. As Wingate took it, the man said, "I'm Lieutenant Royce Corrigan, sir, at your service."

"Wingate's the name," the trapper introduced himself.

"You wouldn't happen to be a guide, would you?" Corrigan asked. "I'm afraid we lost ours a few days ago. An unfortunate encounter with a, uh, grizzly bear."

"You mean a griz got him?" Wingate shook his head. "That ain't a good way to go, bein' mauled by one o' them monsters. I reckon the griz et the poor bastard, too?"

"Well, uh, no. We shot the creature. Killed it. But not in time to save poor Stevens."

Wingate drew a sharp breath. "That wouldn't be Blacktooth Stevens you're talkin' about, would it?"

"Actually, yes. Did you know him?"

"Met him at Rendezvous a few times. Damn. So ol'

Blacktooth's gone under, has he? Shame. Did you skin out that bear and save the meat and the hide?"

Corrigan frowned. "No. Should we have?"

"You left the carcass to rot?" Wingate sounded scandalized. "Ol' Blacktooth'd be upset with you for lettin' it go to waste that way."

"Yes, well, we didn't know any better," Corrigan said, clearly a little irritated by Wingate's criticism. "You didn't answer my question about whether or not you're a guide."

"I'm a trapper. But I reckon if you fellas need some help gettin' to where you're goin', I could lend you a hand."

"That would be splendid. I can pay you the money that I had paid to Mr. Stevens. We recovered it from his, ah, body before we buried him."

"That'll be fine. Where you headed?"

"Well, actually, I'm not sure. You see, we're looking for a party of travelers who came out here recently. They were supposed to visit a trappers' Rendezvous and then continue their expedition through the mountains."

Wingate grunted in surprise. "You wouldn't be talkin' about a bunch o' pilgrims from back East, would you? A little painter fella and his sister, and a couple o' other gents?"

"That's them!" Corrigan said excitedly. "Mr. Willard Carling's party. Do you know where they are?"

"I could prob'ly find 'em. I saw them at the Rendezvous, and I know which general direction they were headin'."

"That's wonderful. You're a godsend, Mr. Wingate."

"First time anybody's ever called me *that*," Wingate said with a chuckle. "It's important that you find those pilgrims, is it?"

"Important? I should say so. It's a matter of an absolute fortune!"

The warriors Badger had sent to retrieve Willard Carling's belongings returned to the village that evening, bringing with them all the canvases, brushes, and pots of paint that hadn't been broken, along with one easel. Carling almost cried with relief when he saw them.

"Now I can get to work again," he said. "First thing in the morning, as soon as the light is good, I'll begin that portrait of the chief, as I promised."

"Gettin' him to stand still for you may not be easy," Preacher warned.

"Oh, I'm sure he'll cooperate. Who wouldn't want to have his portrait painted?"

Preacher just grunted. What Willard Carling didn't know about Indians would just about fill that big canyon down south a ways.

The night passed without incident. The Easterners seemed to be adjusting to the food and the sleeping arrangements. Chester Sinclair especially seemed to be taking to it. Preacher noticed that Sinclair had stopped shaving. Both Carling and Hodge used borrowed knives to scrape their beards off every day. Sinclair had some nice dark stubble going, though.

True to his word, first thing the next morning, Carling had Sinclair set up the easel and place a blank canvas on it. "I wish I hadn't lost some of my paints," the artist complained. "I know I'll have to make do, but it's still annoying." He smiled as an idea occurred to him. He turned to Preacher, saying, "There are drawings on the outside of these hide dwellings—"

"They're called tepees or lodges," Preacher said.

"Yes, yes, that doesn't matter. I remember also that when those savages captured us, they had colorful streaks on their faces. These Indians have their own paint!"

"Well, yeah," Preacher agreed. "They make different colors o' paint, mostly from berries and such."

"Could you get them to make some for me?"

Preacher thought it over and nodded. "Might be able to do that."

"Excellent! Now, if you'll just fetch the chief and let him know that I'm ready for him to pose . . ."

Preacher gave a little shake of his head and tried not to

sigh. Dealing with Willard Carling was a little like trying to deal with a headstrong child. It was easier to do what he wanted than to argue with him.

Might come a time, though, when Carling would get his rear end paddled, again just like a headstrong child.

Preacher went in search of Bites Like a Badger, and found the chief talking to some of the other warriors. As he came up, Preacher overheard enough of the conversation to know that Badger was sending the men out to scout, to make sure there was no Crow raiding party in the area. The warriors loped off on their errand, and Badger turned to Preacher, still wearing that neutral expression.

"What do you want?" Badger asked.

"Carling is ready to paint your portrait."

"What is this . . . portrait?"

"A picture of you," Preacher explained. "You stand still, and he paints what you look like."

"I paint myself," Badger said coldly, "and when I do, it is for war."

"No, that ain't what I mean. Come with me, and you'll see what I'm talkin' about."

Reluctantly, Badger went with Preacher, and as they came up to Carling, the artist greeted the chief effusively. "There you are!" Carling said. "Thank you for agreeing to pose for me. Now, if you'll just stand right over there . . ."

With Preacher translating, Carling got Badger posed like he wanted him. Badger wore his buckskins and a headband this morning, but not the feathered headdress that was his by right as the chief of this band. After a few moments, Carling said, "No, no, this just isn't right. It's like trying to paint a magnificent peacock without its plumage. Chief, you're going to have to get your headdress and put it on."

"Says he wants you to put on your war bonnet," Preacher drawled in translation.

"Does he wish to go to war with me?" Badger demanded.

"Nope, it's all for show. Better get your tomahawk and your

bow and a quiver of arrows while you're at it." Badger was armed only with a knife.

The chief scowled. "I do not like this pretending to go to war. It feels wrong to me."

"Sorry," Preacher said with a shrug. "He's your guest, though, so I reckon you've got to oblige him."

Indians seldom if ever cursed, and if they did, it was with words that they picked up from the whites. But as Badger started toward his lodge, he was muttering something in the Sioux tongue under his breath. Preacher figured it was a good thing he couldn't hear well enough to translate what Badger was saying.

"Oh, dear," Carling said as the chief stalked off. "He's not deserting us, is he?"

"He'll be back," Preacher assured the artist. "He's gettin' his war bonnet and some other gear, so he'll look savage enough to suit you."

Carling smiled. "That's splendid!"

Badger came back a short time later, suitably bedecked in war bonnet and a fancier set of buckskins with a lot of beaded decorations that must have taken his wives hours and hours of tedious, painstaking labor. He had a fringed quiver full of arrows slung on his back, a tomahawk with a feather tied to its handle tucked behind his rawhide belt, and a sturdy bow gripped in his hand. A couple of squaws followed behind him, smiling and occasionally giggling. They were probably the ones who had decorated his buckskins. Several other squaws and children trailed along, too, and some of the warriors came over to see what was going on as well.

Carling was impressed. "Now *that's* how a noble savage is supposed to look!" he said as he positioned Badger again and then picked up his brush. "Preacher, tell him to tip his head back a little and turn it to the left . . . that's it . . . he needs to put his left foot a little in front of the right . . . yes, just like that . . . Now, Chief, stare off into the distance and look as solemn as you can . . . perfect!"

The whole thing drew quite a crowd. Now only did the

Indians gather around to watch, but so did Rip Giddens and the other frontiersmen, along with Hodge, Sinclair, and Faith. Willard Carling seemed to like being the center of attention. He talked constantly as he worked, using a thin slice of wood as a makeshift palette.

Preacher had to admit that it was pretty impressive the way Carling could daub paint on the canvas and actually make it look like something. The drawings the Indians made on rocks and tepee walls were very simple, with the representations of humans and animals being nothing more than stick figures. Under Carling's skilled touch, though, the portrait of Bites Like a Badger that began to take shape really looked like the chief. It was amazingly lifelike, in fact, especially considering that Carling was nowhere near finished with it. The painting would still require a lot of details and fleshing out.

Like nearly everyone who lived on the frontier, Badger had experience at staying still. A lot of times a hunter might have to remain motionless for a long time before he got a good shot at his chosen prey. But even so, the chief began to get restless after a while. He said to Preacher through gritted teeth, "This mad white man needs to stop talking and finish what he is doing."

"He's workin' at it, don't worry. But it'll be a while yet before he's finished."

"I cannot stand here all day," Badger complained.

"Tell him he needs to stop talking," Carling called to Preacher. "His head's not quite right now."

"Maybe you'd better stop for a while," Preacher suggested. "You don't want him gettin' too impatient with you."

"But I've barely started!" Carling sighed dramatically. "Oh, very well. Since the chief is being gracious enough to extend his hospitality to us, I suppose I should honor his wishes. Anyway, I can work on the background while he's doing whatever it is that chiefs do."

"You can move now," Preacher told Badger.

"Thanks to the Great Spirit for that," Badger grumbled. He broke the pose, lowering his head and shaking it to loosen muscles that had grown stiff. Then he started walking toward Carling.

"What's he doing?" the artist said, visibly alarmed. "He can't look at the painting yet. It's not finished!"

"I reckon you'd better let him be the judge of what's proper and what ain't," Preacher advised.

"Very well. But be sure and tell him that it will look a lot better when it's done."

Carling stepped back as Badger circled around to the front of the easel and stared at the portrait. Carling had roughed in his figure, and it looked remarkably like the chief. For several long moments, Badger didn't take his eyes off the painting.

Then he turned toward Carling with a snarl on his face, jerked the tomahawk from behind his belt, and raised it over his head, ready to split the artist's head open.

Chapter Twenty-one

Carling let out a high-pitched scream of terror as Badger threatened him. Preacher stepped forward quickly, poised to grab the chief's wrist if the tomahawk started to fall.

"Stop him!" Carling cried. "He's going to kill me!"

"Settle down," Preacher growled at him. He could see now that while Badger was mighty upset, the chief had control of his temper and wasn't going to strike immediately. "What's wrong?" Preacher asked him in the Sioux tongue.

With his free hand, Badger pointed at the painting and said, "He has stolen my soul!"

"You knew he was paintin' your picture," Preacher pointed out. "Why are you so upset now, Badger?"

"I did not know it would look like that! That is me! He has stolen my soul!"

"Why is the chief so upset?" Carling practically moaned, unwitting echoing Preacher's question to Badger. "I told you to tell him that it'll be better when it's finished, Preacher!"

"That ain't the problem," Preacher said grimly. "It's too good now. He thinks you've taken his soul and put it on the canvas."

"Told you some o' them Injuns feel like that," Switchfoot put in.

"But . . . but what can I do?"

Preacher wasn't sure. This whole thing seemed sort of silly on the surface, but he knew that it was really deadly serious. To an Indian, there was nothing worse than interfering with his prospects for a happy afterlife. Without a soul, Badger couldn't go on to his just rewards when he died. He would wander the spirit world, aimless and miserable, for the rest of eternity. So to his way of thinking, Carling had done just about the worst thing possible.

Preacher didn't know what Badger had expected the portrait to be like, but it was too late to worry about that now. He said, "What will it take to make this right, Badger? The white man knows little of your ways and meant no harm."

Badger slowly lowered the tomahawk, but he was still clearly furious. "He must put my soul back in my body," he demanded.

"How does he go about that?" Preacher wanted to know.

"He must . . . he must . . ." Badger threw back his head and howled. "I do not know! My soul is gone, and I do not know how to get it back!"

Preacher turned to Carling and said, "Paint over it!"

"What? But that . . . that would destroy it! All my work would have been for nothing!"

"Better that than havin' Badger think you've stolen his soul," Preacher said. "If he keeps workin' himself up into a state, he's gonna forget that he promised you'd be safe here in the village."

"Are you sure that's the *only* thing I can do?"

"I ain't sure o' nothin', but it's worth a try." Preacher turned to Badger and went on. "He will put your soul back in your body. Return to where you stood before while he performs the ritual."

"I will have my soul again?"

"My word on it, Badger."

Badger brandished the tomahawk at Carling one last time and said, "Give me back my soul, white man!"

Carling didn't understand the words, but Badger's feelings were clear. Carling swallowed hard and said to Preacher, "Tell him not to worry, everything will be fine."

Badger posed again, and Carling got to work. He took white paint and brushed it onto the canvas with swift, broad strokes, spreading it until the portrait of Badger could no longer be seen. While he was doing that, Preacher said to the chief, "You should feel your soul coming back into your body now."

"Yes, I feel it," Badger said in obvious relief. "It is good to have a soul again."

What had taken Carling a couple of hours to paint required only a matter of minutes to cover up. When he was finished, he sighed dispiritedly and said, "All right, it's done. It's all ruined."

"But you're still alive," Preacher pointed out. He called Badger over, and the chief looked at the painted-over portrait for a long moment before he nodded solemnly.

"It is good," he said. With that, he glared one last time at Carling and then stalked off.

"Well!" Faith said. "What did he expect? Didn't he know that Willard was painting his picture?"

"Their ways and ours are so different sometimes that it's hard to know how they'll feel about something," Preacher explained. "I thought Badger understood what was going on, but I reckon he didn't."

"Can I paint *any* of them?" Carling asked. "Or will they all react like that?"

"Maybe you'd better stick to landscapes for a while," Preacher advised. "Might be safer."

"Very well. But perhaps you could talk to the Indians, Preacher, and find some of them who would be willing to pose for me . . . without threatening to kill me."

"I reckon I could do that."

Carling wiped sweat off his forehead. "I know artists are supposed to suffer for their art, but getting threatened with a tomahawk . . . that's ridiculous!"

Somewhat to Preacher's surprise, he found several of the warriors who were willing to pose for Carling without fear of having their souls stolen. It made more sense when he realized that they were all older men who had been friends with Hairface. Every-one in the village knew that Badger had been terribly upset when he saw Carling's portrait of him. Preacher supposed the warriors were trying to make a point by posing. It was the sort of subtle dig at Badger that had to have the chief seething.

Not surprisingly, after a few days, Badger came to Car-ling and made a long speech that had the artist baffled. "What's he saying?" Carling asked Preacher.

"Says he wants you to paint his picture," Preacher drawled as he tried not to grin.

"What? But I already painted his portrait, and he threat-ened to kill me because of it!"

"Yeah, but he sees you paintin' pictures of all them other warriors, and it's an insult to his honor that they look like they have more courage than he does. If they ain't scared o' losin' their souls, then he can't be, either."

Carling closed his eyes and pressed the fingertips of one hand to his temple. "This is something he really wants?" he asked without opening his eyes.

"It appears so," Preacher said.

"Very well, then." Carling summoned up a smile for Badger and went on. "I'd be glad to paint your portrait again, Chief. Just dress as you did the last time and come to see me whenever you're ready."

Preacher translated, and Badger nodded solemnly.

"I swear, I could stay out here a hundred years and never understand these people," Carling said in exasperation when Badger was gone.

"That's sort of the way I feel about folks who live back East in big cities," Preacher said.

The gash in Preacher's side was healing just fine. The poul-tice had done its job. He didn't think the scar would be too bad, but it didn't really matter since his body was already cov-ered with scars. The bruises he had received in the fight with Badger were fading, and the soreness in his muscles had just about gone away. He started thinking again about how he was going to resolve his unfinished business with Luther Snell and the other men responsible for the death of Mountain Mist.

Willard Carling seemed to be happy, humming to himself and talking as he painted all day. Jasper Hodge was also busy making notes and writing. Faith had given up on composing any poems, but seemed to be reasonably content watching her brother at his work. At least, she had stopped complaining quite so much.

But it was Chester Sinclair who was enjoying this sojourn in the Teton Sioux village the most. He had made friends with Panther Leaping, and the two of them could often be found deep in conversation, Sinclair speaking English and Panther expounding in Sioux. Somehow, though, each seemed to get the basic idea of what the other was saying, probably because Sinclair had picked up some of the Indian sign language.

His beard had grown more, and most of the time he wore a buckskin shirt that one of the squaws had given him. Preacher had noticed that squaw making eyes at Sinclair, but he seemed oblivious to her interest in him. He was still smitten with Faith Carling, and he was usually somewhere near her when he wasn't visiting with Panther.

One day, Preacher found the two men throwing tomahawks at a stump. Panther was trying to show Sinclair how to use the weapon. Sinclair was pretty clumsy at first, missing the stump entirely with his throws, but he got the hang of it fairly quickly. When he threw the tomahawk and the head of it stuck in the stump with a solid *thunk!* he grinned and looked around to see if anyone had witnessed the feat.

"Did you see that?" he asked Preacher.

"Sure did. That's pretty good, Chester."

"Panther Leaping is a good teacher," Sinclair said with a nod toward his newfound friend. "Do you think Faith would like to see me throw the tomahawk?"

"I wouldn't know," Preacher said dryly. "You'd have to ask her."

"I believe I will." He hurried off.

Preacher hoped that Sinclair wouldn't be too disappointed

in Faith's reaction. She didn't strike him as the sort of woman who'd be too impressed by the way a fella threw a tomahawk.

A shout suddenly caught his attention. He looked around and saw several warriors hurrying toward the northern edge of the village. Realizing that there was some sort of trouble looming, Preacher followed them, along with Rip Giddens. "Somethin's up, Preacher," Rip said, "and I got a hunch it ain't good."

"You an' me both, Rip," Preacher agreed.

They came up to a gathering of warriors, and saw that the men had formed a circle around a young brave who was panting heavily and bending over to rest his hands on his knees as he tried to catch his breath. The young man also had a bloody gash on his forehead. He had been in a fight, and then he had run a long way.

The warriors parted as Badger came up. The chief confronted the young man and asked harshly, "Long Grass, where are the other scouts?"

Long Grass was able to straighten up, but he was still breathing heavily. Blood dripped into his eyes from the wound on his forehead, but he ignored it.

"Dead," he said in reply to Badger's question. "We encountered a Crow war party. My companions fought bravely, but there were too many of the dung-eaters. They killed the others and almost killed me. I escaped to bring warning. Otherwise, I would have stayed and died with my Sioux brothers."

"The dung-eaters are coming here?" Badger asked sharply.

"They were headed in this direction when we met them."

"Where?"

"At the head of the valley of Seven Smokes," Long Grass said.

That wasn't good news, Preacher realized. The head of the valley wasn't far away, and the war party wouldn't be far behind the wounded scout.

"How many?" Badger asked.

"More than the five of us could have counted on all our hands and feet."

Rip said quietly to Preacher, "Lord, that's more'n a hundred Injuns!"

Preacher nodded, his face grim. "Yep. And they'll be painted for war."

At that moment, Long Grass let out a groan and collapsed. Preacher saw another terrible wound on the back of the young man's head that hadn't been visible to him until now. Long Grass shuddered and then heaved a loud, rattling sigh. Preacher recognized it as a death rattle, and knew that the young warrior had just gone over the divide.

Badger knelt beside Long Grass for a moment and rested a hand on the young man's shoulder. "Songs will be sung about your bravery," the chief promised. Then he straightened and began barking orders. The village would be under attack soon. There was no time to waste.

"What'll we do, Preacher?" Rip asked as the two of them hurried back to the lodge where the rest of the visitors were staying. "Reckon we ought to grab those pilgrims and light a shuck out o' here?"

Preacher shook his head. "Then we'd be on our own, and if the Crow overrun the village they might come on after us. We've got a better chance of stoppin' 'em here."

"You mean we're gonna fight on the side o' Badger and his people?"

"Don't see as we've got much choice. Anyway, we're their guests, and it's the honorable thing to do."

"I never figured to die helpin' one bunch o' redskins fight off another bunch o' redskins."

"Well, that's the thing about death," Preacher said. "When it's ready to come callin', it don't much care what anybody's been figurin' on."

Chapter Twenty-two

"What?" Willard Carling asked a few minutes later, his voice rising in surprise and fear. "We're going to fight Indians?"

"Crows," Preacher explained. "Most o' the other tribes call 'em dung-eaters and don't like them."

"That would explain the name," Jasper Hodge said.

Preacher ignored the journalist. "Their normal hunting grounds are north and east of here, but from what I've heard, they've been raidin' in this area for a while. Badger's had scouts out, watchin' for them, and a little while ago the Crows jumped one o' the scoutin' parties and wiped them out except for one warrior who made it back with a warnin'. Then he died, too."

Faith shuddered and said, "That's awful."

"But why do we have to fight?" Carling asked. "We don't have anything to do with hard feelings between the tribes."

"You accepted Badger's hospitality," Preacher pointed out.

"After he terrorized us and tried to kill us!"

Preacher shook his head. "Doesn't matter. These folks are our friends now, and we have to help them. Besides, I'd rather fight the Crow with Badger and his warriors on our side than have to take them on later by ourselves."

"That makes sense," Sinclair said. "Make our stand here where we have allies."

"Yep."

"Count me in. Just give me a gun and some ammunition. Panther gave me a tomahawk, too, if I have to use it."

Faith stared at him. "Chester, have you lost your mind? You're no Indian fighter. You're not a fighter of any kind."

"You may be wrong about that, Faith," Sinclair said, and even in these desperate circumstances, Preacher noticed that the man didn't call her *Miss* Faith anymore. Sinclair was making progress.

Too bad he might not live long enough to actually make her understand how he felt about her.

The frontiersmen's weapons had been returned to them after they became guests of the Indians, rather than prisoners. Preacher and Rip distributed extra pistols and powder and shot to Carling, Hodge, and Sinclair. Carling and Hodge looked uncertain what to do with the weapons, and Preacher wished they'd had time to practice with them. That luxury wasn't going to be afforded them, however.

"Ma'am, you and Sparrow get inside the lodge and stay there, no matter what you hear goin' on out here," Preacher told Faith.

"All right. But I still don't understand why we don't just try to get away."

As the two women went into the lodge, Sparrow looked around and caught Preacher's eye. She touched the knife she wore at her waist. Preacher knew what she meant—she would kill Faith and then herself before letting them fall into the hands of the Crows. Preacher nodded.

Then, as he turned to the other men, a shout went up from the edge of the village. "Here they come," Preacher said.

With the other men following him, he ran toward the sound of the alarm. Sinclair was almost eager to get in on the fighting, and Rip and the other frontiersmen didn't hang back, either. Carling and Hodge brought up the rear, and both of them looked like they would have preferred to retreat into the lodge with Faith and Sparrow. They trotted along after Preacher and the others, though.

Knowing that one of the scouts had gotten away, the Crow war party hadn't wasted any time getting here, and they hit the village hard and fast before the defenders had much time to prepare for an attack. Crow warriors, their faces painted, ran out of the trees at the edge of the village and were among the lodges almost instantly, screaming out their hatred for the Tetons. Instead of an orchestrated battle such as white men might have fought, this was a chaotic, hand-to-hand melee from the first moment of the attack.

Preacher had his rifle in his hands, so he used it first, picking out a Crow who was just now emerging from the trees and drawing a bead on him. The rifle roared and bucked against Preacher's shoulder as he pressed the trigger. The Crow warrior ran right into the heavy lead ball and died with a surprised look on his face as it smashed into his heart and flipped him backward.

Preacher dropped the empty rifle at his feet and yanked his pistols from behind his belt. He cocked them and lined them up on a knot of howling Crow raiders surging toward him. Smoke and flame belched from the muzzles of the pistols as they blasted their deadly, double-shotted loads into the attackers. Every ball found a different target. Four of the Indians went down, knocked off their feet by Preacher's lead.

With his guns empty, Preacher took the time to jam the pistols behind his belt again, then drew his knife and the tomahawk with which he had also armed himself. There was no shortage of enemies, so he plunged right in, hacking and slashing all around him.

Elsewhere in the fight, Chester Sinclair emptied his pistol as well, feeling an unexpected surge of savage exhilaration as he saw the ball rip into the throat of one of the raiders. Blood fountained from the Crow's neck as he clutched at the wound, fell to his knees, and then pitched forward on his face. Sinclair leaped over the still-twitching body and crashed the empty gun against the skull of another warrior. He was surprised to find that he could distinguish the Crows from the Tetons, even in this bloody chaos. He had been around Panther and the others in the village enough so that he could recognize the markings on their buckskins.

It helped that the Crows were painted for war, too.

Nothing was going to help Willard Carling and Jasper Hodge. Both men were terrified to the point of being panic-stricken. Given their druthers, they would have found a hole somewhere and crawled into it. But the Crow raiders didn't give them a chance to do that. One of the marauders ran straight at Carling, screaming at the top of his lungs and brandishing a tomahawk. Carling screamed back at him, jerked up the pistol in his hand, turned his head, closed his eyes, and pulled the trigger.

Nothing happened. He had forgotten to ear back the gun's hammer and cock it.

Carling kept screaming as a pistol roared close beside him. He didn't open his eyes until Hodge grabbed his shoulder and shook it.

"I shot him!" Hodge cried exultantly. "I actually shot that Indian!"

Carling looked around and saw the Crow writhing on the ground as blood welled from the wound in his chest. Hodge stood next to the artist, a grin on his face.

"You forgot to cock your gun," Hodge said.

"Like this?" Carling asked as he used both thumbs to pull back the hammer on the heavy flintlock pistol.

Then he glanced up and saw one of the raiders holding a bow with an arrow nocked and drawn back, ready to fire. The arrow was aimed right at the unsuspecting Hodge's back.

Carling shoved the journalist aside, thrust the pistol toward the Indian with the bow and arrow, and fired, yelling in pain as the recoil knocked the weapon from his hand. But luck guided the shot and the hastily fired ball struck the Crow in the forehead, shattering his skull and pulping his brain before it blew out the back of his head. He let go of the arrow, anyway. It cut through the air between Carling and Hodge and fell harmlessly to the ground.

Both men had managed to kill one of the enemy and saved each other's lives in the process, but now their guns were empty and it would take them several minutes to reload, since they'd had very little practice at that. Carling grabbed Hodge's arm and said, "Let's get out of here!"

They turned and ran deeper into the village, hoping that none of the raiders would follow them.

Preacher's tomahawk had laid out several of the Crows, splitting their skulls. Others had fallen to the cold, slashing steel of his knife. The bodies were piled up around his feet, and both of his hands were coated with the enemy's blood. His arms were splattered with gore up to the elbow. He struck in a steady rhythm, right and left, right and left, as the Crows tried to close in around him only to be hewn down like wheat. Arrows sliced through the air near Preacher's head. Some came close enough to rip at his buckskins and leave crimson streaks on his weathered hide. He ignored them and concentrated only on striking out at the howling, rage-twisted faces that seemed to swim toward him out of a bloody mist.

The other frontiersmen were fighting in much the same way, emptying their guns and then plunging into the fray with knives and tomahawks. Big Rip Giddens was giving almost as good an account of himself as Preacher, roaring lustily as he struck at the Crows and laid them out on the ground.

Not far from him, Tom Ballinger fought well, too, until one of the raiders ran a lance through his right thigh from behind. Tom yelled in pain as the leg crumpled underneath him. The Crow paused to try to yank the lance free, and that was his undoing. Tom twisted as he fell and swiped his knife across the Indian's throat. Blood gushed hotly on Tom's hand as the Crow gurgled and died. Tom sprawled on the ground with the lance still lodged in his flesh and began trying to crawl back into the battle.

Switchfoot and Hammerhead Jones fought back-to-back, each protecting the other, until an arrow skewered Switchfoot in the chest. He grunted in pain and stumbled forward. Realizing that Switchfoot had been hit, Hammerhead swung around and grabbed his friend before Switchfoot could fall.

"Lemme go," Switchfoot gasped. "I'm done for, Hammerhead."

"The hell with that," Hammerhead said. "We'll get you somewhere so you can sit down and we'll get that arrow out—"

Before he could do anything else to help Switchfoot, a Crow war ax crashed down on Hammerhead's skull. The legendary hardness of his head didn't protect him from the vicious blow, but even as the world was going black around him, he retained the strength to swing around and smash his tomahawk into the face of the raider who had struck him. The Indian fell back dead, his head cleaved practically in two by the blow.

Then with blood and gray matter oozing from his shattered skull, Hammerhead toppled to the ground next to the body of Switchfoot, who had already collapsed. The two friends died side by side.

The Tetons had been trying to stop the Crow raiders at the edge of the village, but there were too many of the invaders. They attacked on too broad a front for the defenders to stop them. From the corner of his eye, Preacher saw Crow warriors with painted faces rampaging into the village and penetrating to its interior. He thought about Faith and Sparrow cowering inside that lodge as he buried his tomahawk in the skull of an enemy and then jerked it free.

"Rip!" he shouted. "Fall back! Fall back!"

Rip Giddens did as Preacher said, continuing to fight as he retreated slowly toward the center of the village. Preacher did likewise. He glanced around for the others, saw the motionless forms of Switchfoot and Hammerhead lying on the ground. There was nothing he could do for them. Tom Ballinger had somehow gotten back to his feet, but he was severely hampered by the now-broken lance that impaled his thigh.

"Sinclair!" Preacher called. "Help Ballinger!"

Sinclair had just banged the heads of two of the Indians together, knocking them out. For a second, it seemed that Preacher's shouted command failed to penetrate his battle-fogged brain, but then he gave a little shake of his head and turned to grasp Tom Ballinger's arm. He half-dragged, half-carried the wounded man as they followed Preacher and Rip.

Preacher didn't see Willard Carling or Jasper Hodge anywhere. He hoped that the two Easterners hadn't been killed. Wherever they were, though, there was nothing Preacher could do to help them right now. They were on their own.

As a matter of fact, Carling and Hodge had made it almost all the way back to the lodge where Faith and Sparrow were hiding. Carling had failed to pick up his pistol when he dropped it, so the only weapon they had was the empty gun Hodge still carried. Carling said frantically, "Why don't you reload?"

Hodge pushed the pistol into Carling's hands. "Why don't *you* reload? You know as much about it as I do!"

As Carling trotted along, he fumbled with the powder horn and the shot pouch Preacher had given him. "Oh, I'm not cut out for this!" he moaned as he poured powder into the barrel of the pistol but then managed to spill some of it onto the ground. "I'm an artist, not a . . . a woodsman!"

"Well, I'm a writer!" Hodge shot back. "Do you think *I* know how to do anything useful?"

"Here, hold the gun while I pour some more powder in it."

Working together as they hurried along, they managed to get the pistol reloaded. Unfortunately, neither of them realized that Carling had dumped at least twice as much powder down the barrel as was needed. They rammed home two balls, double-shotting the gun as they had seen Preacher do with his pistols.

"There!" Carling exclaimed. "Isn't that our lodge?"

Hodge said, "I think so, but I'm not sure. All these tepees look alike to me!"

"I'm sure it is," Carling said. "I recognize the drawings on it. Let's see if Faith and Sparrow are still all right."

He jerked the entrance flap aside and started into the lodge, only to be confronted by a screaming-mad Sparrow, who lunged at him with her knife drawn back, ready to plunge the blade into Carling's body because she had mistaken him for one of the Crow raiders. Carling yelped and threw himself backward to avoid the attack, but he stumbled and tripped and fell to the ground, striking his head hard enough that he was knocked out.

Hodge cried, "Sparrow, wait! It's us!"

The Indian woman stopped, realized what she had done, and whirled around to retreat back into the lodge. Hodge thought for a second that she was running away from him, but then he glanced over his shoulder and saw half a dozen of the painted savages charging at him. He still had the pistol in his hands, so he jerked it up and fired.

The too-heavy charge of powder exploded with a huge roar and cracked the pistol's breech, even as the blast wrenched the gun out of Hodge's hands and threw him backward, singeing his eyebrows and blistering his face. The two balls loaded in the gun were propelled out with such force that they smashed completely through the body of one Crow warrior and buried themselves in the belly of another. Both raiders died almost instantly.

Hodge lay stunned on the ground, not far from the unconscious form of Willard Carling.

Even though two of the Crows were down, the other four were still on their feet. They headed for the lodge, thinking that the two white men must have been trying to protect someone inside it.

Faith had thrown herself facedown on one of the buffalo robes and burrowed into it as if she could somehow hide there. A tense-faced Sparrow knelt beside her, the knife raised to strike. Sparrow's gaze was fixed on the entrance to the lodge, and as the hide flap was suddenly wrenched aside and savage painted faces leered in at her, she cried out in horror and started to bring the knife down toward Faith's back. Sparrow intended to drive the blade into Faith's heart and then use it to cut her own throat before the Crows could reach her.

She didn't get the chance. One of the raiders had already spotted the white woman on the ground, and his arm flashed back and then forward as he threw his tomahawk. The perfectly balanced weapon revolved once as it flew through the air; then its head smacked into Sparrow's ample bosom and buried itself there. She cried out in pain and bent forward, dropping the knife before she could strike the mercy blow. Slowly, she toppled to the side, blood leaking from the wound.

The raiders charged into the lodge. A couple of them bent and grabbed Faith, jerking her to her feet. She screamed raggedly as she saw who had hold of her. One of the Indians slapped her hard, his hand cracking across her face. She sagged in their cruel grip, momentarily knocked senseless by the blow.

They dragged her out of the lodge.

Elsewhere, Chester Sinclair had realized that the Crow invaders were pouring into the village, and he was struck by an almost paralyzing fear for Faith's safety. He shook it off, knowing that he had to reach her side as quickly as he could. Still practically carrying Tom Ballinger, Sinclair hurried to catch up to Rip Giddens and thrust the wounded man into Rip's arms. "Here!" Sinclair said. "I've got to get to Faith!"

He sprinted off, leaving Rip and Preacher to help Ballinger.

Preacher might have gone after Sinclair, but at that moment, several Crow warriors came at them from the side. Since Rip was burdened with Ballinger, Preacher had to deal with the threat by himself. He stepped between Rip and the attackers, sunlight flickering on the head of his tomahawk and the blade of his knife as he waded into the Crows. A minute later, the three men were stretched out on the ground, quivering and jerking as their lifeblood gushed from the wounds Preacher's deadly weapons had given them.

Some of the lodges were on fire now, the blazes started by

the raiders. Sinclair dashed through the coiling smoke and got confused for a moment, unsure of where he was. But then he oriented himself and hurried on toward the lodge where he would find Faith and defend her to his dying breath, if need be.

The problem was, when he got there she was being dragged out of the lodge by several Crows. She was already their prisoner.

"No!" Sinclair bellowed as he threw himself at them. "Let go of her, you bastards!"

He swung his tomahawk so hard at one of the savages who got in his way that the head sheared through muscle and bone, almost decapitating the savage. But then it got stuck when Sinclair tried to wrench it free, and he lost precious seconds. In that time, several more Indians closed in around him. One of them swung a war ax against his head, luck making the flat of it strike Sinclair's skull instead of the edge. The blow knocked him to his knees, where someone kicked him in the back and sent him sprawling on the ground. The world spun dizzily around him, and he wasn't even aware of someone tapping him and shouting, "I claim him!" in the Crow tongue. He was pounded and kicked and pummeled into submission, but he wasn't killed.

It remained to be seen whether that was fortunate or not.

Preacher, Rip, and Ballinger continued battling their way toward the lodge. Preacher did the bulk of the fighting, but once Rip got his right arm around Ballinger, that freed up his left to swing a tomahawk. Ballinger used his right arm for the same purpose. Between them, they accounted for several of the savages.

The hellish racket that had filled the air ever since the attack started was beginning to subside some now. Hoarse screams of pain could still be heard coming from all over the village, mixed with the crackling of flames as lodges burned. But it was clear that the intensity of the attack was waning. The Crows had struck the blow that they intended and were now starting to retreat, taking prisoners and loot with them.

Carrying the blood-smeared knife and tomahawk, Preacher

trotted up to the lodge where he had left Faith and Sparrow. He spotted Willard Carling and Jasper Hodge lying on the ground and thought at first that the two Easterners were dead, but then he saw that they were beginning to stir as consciousness returned to them. He stopped and knelt beside them momentarily, searching for wounds. Hodge's face looked almost sunburned. Preacher couldn't figure that one out, but it seemed to be the only real injury the two men had suffered.

He left them lying there and stepped over to the tepee, thrusting the entrance flap aside. His rugged features hardened even more when he saw Sparrow lying there in a pool of blood, an ugly wound in her chest. She had been struck probably by a tomahawk, from the looks of the injury, but the weapon had been wrenched free and taken by the savage who had wielded it.

There was no sign of Faith Carling.

As Preacher let the flap fall closed and stepped back, Rip and Ballinger came up, moving awkwardly because Rip still had to support most of the other man's weight. "Where's Miss Carling?" Rip asked grimly. "Inside the lodge?" It was clear from his tone of voice that he expected her to be dead, and probably scalped.

Preacher shook his head. "She ain't here, but Sparrow's in there. Dead."

"Damn!" Rip's voice was bitter now. Like all the others, he had been fond of Sparrow.

"Let's see if these two know what happened." Preacher went over to Carling and Hodge, who were sitting up by now. Carling held his head in his hands, while Hodge looked around in confusion. "Willard, did you see your sister?" Preacher asked.

"What?" Carling winced as he spoke. "What did you say, Preacher?"

"Your sister, did you see her when you and Hodge got back here?"

"No. I . . . I started inside . . . and Sparrow, of all people, tried to stab me!"

She must have thought that he was one of the Crows, Preacher thought. Carling had probably neglected to call out and identify himself before entering the lodge.

"And then I seem to remember falling," Carling went on. "I . . . I believe I hit my head . . ." He probed his head and exclaimed in pain as he found a sore lump on the back of it. "Yes, I definitely hit my head. I must have knocked myself out when I fell."

"I think that's what happened," Hodge put in. "I know I saw Willard fall . . . and then some of the savages came at me. I still had a pistol, so I fired at them . . . I think it blew up. Anyway, that's the last thing I remember."

Pure dumb luck had saved their lives, Preacher realized. Both men had been knocked unconscious, and the raiders had taken them for dead. Carling and Hodge were extremely fortunate that the Crows hadn't taken the time to scalp them anyway, or riddle them with arrows.

Carling gripped Preacher's arm, not paying any attention to the blood splattered on it. "You asked about Faith," he said desperately. "Where is she, Preacher? What's happened to her?"

Preacher could only shake his head. "I don't know. It looks like the Crows may have carried her off."

"Oh, my God!" Carling raked his fingers through his hair. "You mean she's a prisoner again?"

Rip put in, "I don't see Chester around here, neither. You think the Crows got him, too, Preacher? I know he was headed this way."

The same thought had occurred to Preacher. Sinclair would have attacked against even overwhelming odds if he was fighting to save Faith. If he had been killed, his body would still be here, so that left only one reasonable explanation. For some reason, the Crows had taken Sinclair prisoner instead of killing him.

Now, once again, Sinclair and Faith were captives, in the hands of savages in a savage land.

Chapter Twenty-three

By the time the sun was lowering toward the peaks in the west, the Crows were gone, leaving death and destruction in their wake.

Screams of pain still rose from the devastated village, along with chants of mourning from the wives of warriors who had been killed. The women tore their dresses and beat themselves on the breast and rubbed ashes on their faces. They had plenty of ashes to choose from, since half of the lodges in the village had burned down.

There had been nearly a hundred warriors in the village, but many of them were now dead and others were badly wounded. Badger had survived, but all of the pride and arrogance was gone from his face. He was the chief of a defeated people. A dozen or more captives, mostly children and young women, had been taken away by the Crows. They would be turned into slaves by the hated dung-eaters. If more of Badger's warriors had survived, he might have gone after the Crows and tried to rescue the prisoners. As it was, though, he had barely enough men to mount a defense of the village if it was attacked again by other enemies.

Preacher searched the entire village, but didn't find Sinclair and Faith or their bodies. They were gone; there was no doubt about that. And the only place they could have gone was with the Crows.

Carling sat cross-legged on the ground, rocking back and forth and saying over and over, "What are we going to do? What are we going to do?" Hodge paced around ineffectually. Rip tended to the wound in Tom Ballinger's leg, finally getting the lance out of it and binding up the injury as best he could. Ballinger might live, but he would never be the same again and would probably have a bad limp the rest of his life. He would have to recover for quite a while before he could travel.

Preacher took stock of the situation and didn't like the conclusions he came up with. Someone had to go after the Crows and try to free Sinclair and Faith. At least, Rip was in pretty good shape, as was Preacher himself. But other than the two of them, the only ones available to join a rescue party appeared to be Willard Carling and Jasper Hodge, who were almost as big a danger to themselves as they were to the enemy.

Preacher walked up to Carling and said sharply, "Stop your moanin' and get on your feet."

Carling lifted his head and blinked at Preacher. "What?" He seemed to be half out of his mind with grief and worry.

"I said stand up," Preacher grated. "Hodge, stop that pacin'. We got plans to make."

"Plans?" the journalist repeated. "What sort of plans? What on earth can we do?"

"We can go after them damn Crows and get Miss Carling and Sinclair away from them."

Carling and Hodge stared at him for a long moment. Then Hodge said, "You've lost your mind. There are only four of us."

"There was only one o' me when I started after Badger's war party, figurin' on rescuin' you folks. I managed to do that."

"Only by getting captured yourself and almost dying in battle with that savage!"

"Best be careful about callin' Badger a savage," Preacher

warned. "We'll be countin' on him for a little help in the way o' supplies and arms and such-like."

"Why can't he and his men go rescue the prisoners?" Carling asked. "The Crows are *their* enemies, not ours."

"That ain't the way it works. Badger and his people have folks to lay to rest and a village to rebuild. He lost about half his warriors in that fight. He can't afford to lose any more."

"But the Crows lost men, too," Hodge pointed out. "Didn't you say that a lot of them were killed?"

"Yeah, maybe as many as thirty or forty," Preacher admitted. "It's hard to be sure because they carried most of the bodies off with 'em, rather than leavin' 'em behind to be mutilated. But there's still probably at least sixty warriors in that bunch. Badger could take every man he's got left and still be outnumbered."

"And yet you think the *four* of us would have a chance?" Hodge asked in amazement.

"What choice do we have, if we ever want to see Miss Faith and Sinclair again?"

Rip added, "And a handful o' men can sometimes do what a bunch can't . . . especially when one of 'em is Preacher."

Carling said quietly, "I could never live with myself if something terrible happened to Faith and I just stood by and let it take place. I have to try to save her." He looked at Preacher. "Thank you for helping me to see that."

Preacher saw something in Carling's eyes he hadn't seen there before—a hint of steely determination. It was only a hint, to be sure, but it was there.

"You can't be serious!" Hodge said. "Four men against sixty or more?"

"Five," a new voice said.

Preacher turned his head and saw Panther Leaping coming toward them. The middle-aged Teton Sioux warrior had picked up his share of bruises and scratches during the battle, but he appeared to be in reasonably good shape. And Preacher knew him to be a good fighting man.

"You know what we're talkin' about, Panther?" Preacher asked him in Sioux.

"Yes," Panther replied in English. "Chester taught me . . . some of your tongue. He was . . . good friend." The warrior clasped his hand into a fist and lightly struck his chest, signifying the unlikely but strong bond that had sprung up between him and the big Easterner.

Preacher nodded and said, "Five of us, then." He glanced at Hodge. "That is, if you're goin' along."

"Oh, you're not going to leave me here alone with these savages," Hodge replied quickly. "Make no mistake about that."

"We'll start first thing in the morning."

"Why not tonight?" Carling asked. "Now that we've made up our minds, why waste time?"

"Because it's late," Preacher explained. "It'll be night before much longer. We need to eat and rest, get a good night's sleep if we can. I've got a hunch that the Crows will be headin' back to their usual huntin' grounds as fast as possible, now that they've hit Badger's people so hard and taken some prisoners. We may have a long chase in front of us."

"Poor Faith," Carling murmured. "I'm sure every minute she's in the hands of those savages will be pure hell for her."

Faith didn't know how much longer she could keep going. She was exhausted, and having to help Sinclair along just added to her weariness. He was a big man and had quite a bit of weight leaning on her. She kept her right arm around his waist, and he had his left arm wrapped around her shoulders. It was much too intimate to be proper. . . .

Not that the savages who had taken them prisoner cared one whit about what was proper.

When they had dragged her out of the tepee after killing Sparrow—Faith had caught a terrifying glimpse of the Indian woman's crumpled body with the tomahawk buried in her chest—the first thing she had seen was Chester

Sinclair racing to her aid. At that moment, her heart had leaped with hope.

That hope had been dashed almost instantly as the Crow raiders swarmed over Sinclair, beating him to the ground and knocking him senseless. Faith had fully expected them to chop him into little pieces with their knives and tomahawks, but one of the savages had struck Sinclair with a stick that had a couple of feathers tied to it. A coup stick, that was what it was called, Faith remembered. She had heard Jasper Hodge talking about them as he imparted bits of knowledge he had picked up during his stay in the Teton Sioux village. Some Indians carried the sticks into battle, and it was a point of honor for them to use the coup stick to touch an enemy without killing him. Or something like that. Faith had no interest in the barbaric customs of these people.

But she had the impression that Sinclair's life had been saved by the Indian's action. That was why they had taken him prisoner instead of killing him on the spot. The Indian probably planned on making Sinclair a slave, as Faith recalled Preacher and the others discussing a few days earlier.

Sinclair was the only adult male who had been taken prisoner. The other captives were all women or children. And Sinclair was still too groggy to be able to do anything except stumble along with Faith's help. She hoped that all the blows to the head hadn't permanently impaired his faculties.

She knew she was going to need his help to survive this captivity.

The two of them were surrounded by the other prisoners, a couple of dozen in all. Faith estimated that the Crows numbered fifty or sixty, so there were plenty of them to surround the captives and prod them along. The warrior who had tapped Sinclair with the coup stick seemed to be the leader of the party. He was short but very muscular, and he strode along at the head of the column with an aggressive confidence that spoke of command. From time to time, he barked what sounded like orders at the other members of the war party.

An hour or so after leaving the village, the Indians and

their prisoners came to a small canyon. Faith was surprised to see a large number of horses gathered inside the canyon. She supposed the Crows had left their ponies there before going to attack the village. Now they mounted up, but the prisoners were not allowed to ride as the grueling trek continued. The Crows forced the captives to walk, poking at them with lances if they lagged or stumbled too much.

"Faith, I . . . I'm sorry," Sinclair gasped out as they struggled along. "I wanted so much to protect you, and instead I failed you."

"It's all right, Chester," she told him. "There was nothing you could do. There were just too many of the savages."

"I should have done *something*. . . ."

He sounded more coherent now, so she asked, "Can you walk by yourself? No offense, Chester, but you're a big man, and it's hard for me to help you along like this."

"My head's still pretty woozy, but let me give it a try." He took his arm from around her shoulders and straightened. Although he swayed a little, he managed to stay upright. "I can make it," he said stubbornly. "I'm sorry I've had to lean on you."

"It's all right," she said, and to her slight surprise, she meant it. She also found that she missed the feel of his arm around her. She thought about reaching for his hand and clasping it, but of course she couldn't do something that forward, even under these dire circumstances.

Sinclair seemed to grow a little steadier on his feet as they pressed on. It occurred to Faith that the prisoners were like a herd of cattle or sheep being driven by the mounted Indians around them. The chief, if that was who he was, still rode at the front of the group, and didn't call a halt to the forced march until the sun was almost down.

By that time, Faith was so tired she thought she couldn't go another step. The muscles in her legs felt like lead. She sank down onto the ground and moaned.

Sinclair knelt beside her and asked, "Is there anything I can do to help?"

"Not unless you can get me away from these savages," she

said. "And I don't think you can do that, Chester, outnumbered sixty to one as you are."

Sinclair frowned and looked around. "You never can tell what might happen. I'll keep my eyes open for a chance to escape."

"Oh, no!" she said. "You'll just get yourself killed. I don't want that."

"Are you saying that we should cooperate with them?"

"What other choice do we have?" Faith asked bleakly.

Sinclair sighed in grim acceptance of her words. He gazed off into the distance through narrowed eyes and said, "Maybe Preacher will come after us, the way he did before when we were captured by Bites Like a Badger."

"You're assuming that Preacher is even still alive."

"Of course he's alive." Sinclair sounded surprised that she would think otherwise. "He's too good a fighter to have been killed in battle."

"I don't know much about warfare, but I assume good fighters get killed in battle all the time. There must be good fighters on both sides, you know."

"I suppose you're right. Still, I'm not going to give up hope—"

Sinclair might have said more, but at that moment, several of the Crow raiders came up and shouted at the prisoners, prodding them onto their feet.

Faith moaned again and said, "I thought we had stopped for the night."

"I guess not." Sinclair came to his feet and reached down to extend his hand to her. "Come on. I'll help you up."

Faith hesitated. Then she took his hand and let him pull her upright.

She didn't let go of it, either, as the worn-out and dispirited group of prisoners began trudging northeast again, surrounded by their captors.

Chapter Twenty-four

The men lurking in the trees half a mile from the Teton Sioux village had listened to the screams and shots and other sounds of battle and not known exactly what was going on at first. Then, Luther Snell and Baldy had crept closer until they could see the desperate struggle taking place.

"I ain't sure, but I think them other Injuns is Crows," Baldy had said as he and Snell knelt among some tall reeds at the edge of the creek that meandered past the village, a quarter of a mile upstream. "Hard to tell for certain without gettin' closer, and I ain't in much of a mood to do that right now."

Snell grunted. "No, I don't reckon that'd be too healthy. What're Crows doin' down here? This ain't their normal stompin' grounds."

"No, but a Injun'll go a long way when he's in the mood for raidin' . . . and from the rumors I've heard, ol' Medicine Bull has been raisin' hell lately. Says he's gonna make this a bloody summer for all the enemies o' his people."

"Which is just about ever'body, when you're talkin' about them dung-eaters." Snell had nodded slowly. "I'll bet you're right, Baldy. I bet it's Medicine Bull an' his Crows raidin' that village. Question is, what're we gonna do about it?"

"Do about it?" Baldy snorted. "I dunno about you, Snell,

but I plan on keepin' myself well clear o' that village until it's all over. I may not have any hair to lose, but I'm still a mite partial to this old ass o' mine!"

"Carling's in there," Snell said, nodding toward the embattled village. "Without him, we can't get rich."

"Don't matter how rich you are when your scalp's decoratin' a Crow war lance. Anyway, there's not a damned thing we can do right now. We got to just wait until the fightin's over and hope that Carling lives through it all right."

"Yeah, I guess you're right," Snell said with a sigh. "I just wish we'd figured out a way to get our hands on that prissy little bastard before now."

For almost a week, the party of white men had been hiding out in the vicinity of the Teton Sioux village, keeping an eye on the place and making sure to stay out of the way of the scouts and hunting parties sent from the village into the surrounding area. Snell had used a spyglass to verify that Willard Carling was still in the village, along with the other pilgrims from back East, Rip Giddens and the other frontiersmen who had been hired as their guides—except for the late Ed Ballinger—and that damned Preacher. Carling and the others didn't seem to be prisoners anymore, though. As far as Snell could tell from watching them, they had the run of the village. Everything was friendly now. Carling was even painting portraits of some of the warriors.

Snell didn't know exactly how that had come about, but it sure put a crimp in his plans. He and the men with him couldn't just waltz into the middle of an Indian village and kidnap somebody. Even though Snell didn't like waiting for anything he wanted, he knew the smart thing in this case was to be patient. Carling and his companions would leave the village sooner or later . . . and when they did, Snell's men would jump them and take Carling prisoner.

The attack on the village had come out of the blue and taken Snell by surprise. It was an added complication they didn't need. But like Baldy said, there was nothing they could do about it but wait and see how things played out.

Snell just hated to think that he and the others had come all this way and spent all that time for nothing.

Once they had determined what was going on, Snell and Baldy returned to the temporary camp in the woods where the others waited. They had been shifting their camp every day to avoid discovery by scouts from the village, and the rest of the men were getting tired of it. Snell didn't want to lose them. He knew he needed some sort of a lucky break—and soon.

The attack on the village by Medicine Bull's Crows wasn't it.

When they got back, Vickery demanded, "What's goin' on over there, Snell? What's all the ruckus about?"

"That village is bein' raided by a war party from another tribe," Snell explained. "Baldy thinks it's Medicine Bull and his Crows."

"Damn it!" Vickery burst out. "That tears it, I reckon. No point in us hangin' around here now."

"Nothin's changed," Snell said in a hard voice.

"Nothin' except that there's no chance of us gettin' our hands on Carling now."

Snell shook his head stubbornly. "You don't know that."

"*You* don't know that he's gonna live through that fight."

"I don't know that he won't." Snell struggled to control his temper. "Look, chances are that Carling's hidin' somewhere until the battle's over. Did he seem to any of you fellas like the sort who'd take a hand in somebody else's fight?"

"Didn't seem like much of a fighter at all," Ab Dimock said. "Luther's right. When the trouble started, Carling prob'ly found hisself a hole, crawled into it, and pulled it in after him."

"Damn right," Snell said. "Which means that after the raid is over, it'll be easier than ever to get hold of Carling. He won't have as many Indians around him. And maybe some of the folks with him, like Preacher and Giddens, will get themselves killed. I don't see *them* lettin' a fight go by without takin' a hand in it."

Several of the men nodded and muttered agreement. Vickery was still stubborn, though. He said, "So you're tellin' us that we've got to just keep on waitin' like we been doin', Snell?"

"If you want to be rich like the rest of us, that's what you'll do."

"You been danglin' that carrot in front of our noses right along, but I don't feel any richer. Fact of the matter is, with us runnin' low on supplies, I'm startin' to get hungry, and that makes me feel downright poor."

"You can leave any time you want," Snell said coldly. "We've been all over that."

The two men glared at each other for a long moment, and then Vickery looked away and shrugged. "I've spent this much time on this harebrained scheme. I reckon I can waste a little more."

Snell nodded curtly. "We'll see how much of a waste it is when we're countin' that fortune in ransom money we get for Carling," he said confidently.

But after everything that had happened, he wished he felt as confident as he sounded.

By the next morning, things weren't much better in the village. The weeping and wailing and chanting for those who had died continued, as it would for some time. Wisps of smoke still rose from the ruins of some of the burned-out lodges. Grim-visaged warriors patrolled the area around the village just in case the raiders returned, although no one really believed that would happen.

Bites Like a Badger's scarred face was bleaker than ever as he listened to Preacher explain that he, Rip, Carling, Hodge, and Panther Leaping were going after the Crows.

"You have great courage," Badger said when Preacher was finished. "But you are fools."

"How do you reckon?" Preacher wanted to know.

"You are five against how many? Fifty warriors? Sixty?"

"Yeah, we'll be outnumbered," Preacher admitted. "But we can move fast, and we'll hit the Crows when and where they're not expectin' it. That'll give the prisoners a chance to get away."

"You seek to rescue only the fire-haired woman and the big white man," Badger accused. "You care nothing for the women and children of my people who were taken away by the dung-eaters."

"That ain't true. We'll do our best to free all the captives."

"I cannot prevent you from doing this, nor would I wish to if I could. What do you need from me?"

Preacher didn't heave a sigh of relief that Badger was going to cooperate, but he felt one inside. "We have guns," he said, "but we could use some extra powder and shot if you've got it." He knew the tribe didn't have an abundance of firearms, but they possessed some they had captured from whites over the years, or traded for with trappers in friendlier times.

"All that we have is yours," Badger said with a nod. "What else?"

"We want our horses back, and some spare horses in case some of the prisoners need to ride. Maybe some food so we won't have to stop and do any huntin'."

"Agreed."

"And a couple of good bows, along with arrows, for Rip and me," Preacher added. They might need to do some quiet killing, and arrows were good for that. Panther would take along his own bow and arrows, of course, and Preacher didn't see any point in trying to get any for Carling and Hodge, who would need a lot more time to master the weapon than Preacher had to spare.

"This will be done," Badger said.

"One more thing," Preacher went on. "Do you know who was in charge of that war party? I sort of like to know who my enemies are."

"I saw him with my own eyes," Badger said solemnly. "It was Medicine Bull, war chief of the dung-eaters." Badger grimaced. "I hate to call such a one by the honored name of chief."

Preacher rubbed his bearded jaw in thought. "Medicine Bull, eh? Our trails have never crossed before, but I've heard of him. He's supposed to be a mighty warrior."

"For a dung-eater," Badger said with a sneer.

Preacher let that pass without comment. He didn't care about the hostility between the Tetons and the Crows except as it affected his own problems. He said, "If Medicine Bull is as cagey as I've heard, it won't be easy gettin' those prisoners away from him."

"No. But if anyone can do it, Preacher . . . I believe it is you."

That sentiment surprised Preacher a little, and it surprised him even more that Badger had expressed it. That was a pretty good indication of just how shaken up the chief really was.

Preacher wanted to promise Badger that he would bring the captive Tetons home, but he wasn't in the habit of making promises he didn't know if he could keep. So he kept his mouth shut, nodded his thanks, and went to tell the others to get ready to go. They would be moving out on the trail of the raiders very soon.

Willard Carling wore a haggard look in this bloody dawn, and Preacher suspected he hadn't slept much the night before. Determination was still etched on Carling's face, though. Jasper Hodge just looked tired and scared.

Rip Giddens and Panther Leaping walked up to the lodge about the same time that Preacher did. "Well, it's done," Rip announced heavily. "I hope Switchfoot and Hammerhead don't mind bein' laid to rest on scaffolds, Sioux-fashion, instead o' bein' buried like white men."

"Both of them spent a lot of time with the Indians," Preacher said. "I don't reckon they'd be bothered by what you did."

"I didn't have a shovel, so I didn't have much choice. Panther and me built their scaffolds, wrapped 'em up good, and helped 'em on their way along the Great Sky Road. Like I said, it's done."

Preacher could tell that Rip blamed himself at least partially for the deaths of his friends. Rip was the one who had asked Switchfoot and Hammerhead to come along on the Carling expedition. But the two men had made up their own minds whether or not to accept the proposal, and they had done it knowing full well the dangers that might be involved. There were dangers involved with doing just about anything west of the Mississippi.

Someday, Preacher would point that out to Rip, but not

now. Now there just wasn't any time for such things. Instead, Preacher said, "Badger's givin' us our horses back, along with some extra mounts, powder an' shot, and some supplies. Plus those bows and arrows I told you about, Rip."

"Good," Rip said with a nod. "I'm ready when you are, Preacher."

"Soon as we've got everything together, we'll get started."

Jasper Hodge asked, "Are you *sure* about this, Preacher? I mean, I want to rescue Faith and Chester as much as anybody, but it just seems so futile to go up against such overwhelming odds."

Before Preacher could answer, Carling said, "You wouldn't feel that way if it was *you* in the hands of those savages, Jasper, instead of Chester Sinclair. If you were a captive, you'd be praying that someone would come and help you."

"I'm sure that's true," Hodge said with a scowl, "but it doesn't change the facts of the matter. There are only five of us. What chance do we have, really?"

"Folks didn't give ol' George Washington and the Continental Army much chance against the redcoats, neither," Preacher said. "And I know for a fact that most folks who saw the British marchin' up the delta toward New Orleans figured Andy Jackson and the rest of us boys were done for. But we weren't. We whipped those Englishers and sent 'em runnin' all the way back down the Mississipp' to the Gulf of Mexico."

"I still say it's different," Hodge responded sullenly. "But I'm not trying to back out. I said I'd go along with you, and I will. I just think it's a fool's errand, and we'll all wind up dead."

Preacher chuckled. "Badger just said pretty much the same thing to me. Congratulations, Hodge. You're thinkin' like a savage."

Hodge flushed, but didn't say anything else.

Within half an hour, the rescue party was ready to leave. The four white men swung up into their saddles while Panther Leaping climbed onto his sturdy Indian pony, which had only a blanket spread on its back. Another pony had been loaded with supplies. Panther would lead it, while the other four men each took the reins of an extra horse.

Preacher and Rip had the bows and the quivers full of arrows slung on their backs. Their rifles were held across the saddles in front of them. Preacher had salvaged the rifles that had belonged to Switchfoot and Hammerhead and given them to Carling and Hodge. Each man also carried a brace of pistols, a knife, and a tomahawk.

Tom Ballinger limped out of the lodge to bid them farewell and good luck on their mission. He had a crude crutch propped under his right arm, and a young Indian woman stood to his left and helped steady him.

"I wish I was goin' with you boys," Tom said. "I don't much cotton to stayin' here."

Preacher knew that although Tom had gotten over his brother Ed's death to a certain extent, Tom hadn't forgotten that Ed had been killed when Badger and the other members of the Teton war party had jumped them. Now he was going to have to stay here and recuperate while surrounded by the people he blamed for his brother's death.

"I wish you were comin' along, too, Tom," Preacher told him. "We could use another good man."

"Well, I'll be here when you get back with the prisoners," Tom said gruffly. "Good luck."

"And the same. Stay off that bad leg as much as you can."

Preacher leaned down from the saddle to shake hands with Tom, as did Rip. Then, with Preacher leading the way, the group of five would-be rescuers rode out of the village. Ballinger lifted a hand and waved awkwardly after them, even though they didn't look back.

The thought was strong in his mind that he would never see them again.

Chapter Twenty-five

Over the past few days, Wingate had gotten to know Lieutenant Royce Corrigan fairly well, because the young officer liked to talk. And as was common with a lot of young men, Corrigan liked to talk about himself. So Wingate had heard all about how Corrigan had grown up in a small town in upstate New York and had gotten into the military academy at West Point because his father had been a colonel in the Continental Army and had served with General George Washington during the Revolution. Just as Wingate had suspected, this assignment was the first one Corrigan had received since being commissioned as an officer. Why in the blue blazes somebody back East had thought it would be a good idea to put a wet-nosed youngster in charge of some troops and send them into the heart of the Rocky Mountains was a mystery to Wingate, but in his own relatively brief military experience he had learned that what the Army decided didn't necessarily have to make sense. Some fella in a fancy uniform said go, and the soldiers went. That was the way it had always been, all the way back to the Spartans in ancient Greece, and that was the way it would always be, Wingate supposed.

Corrigan didn't really try to find out anything about the man who was serving as their guide, and that was just fine with Wingate. Like most mountain men, he was just naturally close-mouthed around strangers.

The important thing was, they were closing in on the folks they were after. Wingate wasn't sure why Corrigan was looking for the members of Willard Carling's expedition—that was the one thing about which the lieutenant had been rather circumspect—but Wingate hoped to catch up to them soon.

They had followed the trail toward Baldpate, and there had been some bad moments when they came upon the scene of what had evidently been a battle between the Carling expedition and some Indians. Further on, they had found some remains that Wingate thought belonged to one of the Ballinger brothers. It was impossible to say which one, and Wingate wasn't completely sure that the body was that of either Tom or Ed, because varmints had been at it. But still, it was obvious that something bad had happened.

There were no other bodies, though, which meant the other members of the expedition had pushed on, either on their own—or as prisoners of the Indians. So the soldiers pushed on as well, with Wingate and Lieutenant Corrigan leading them. The trapper's keen eyes were able to pick up the trail left by those they were following. He recalled that Rip Giddens had said something about taking Carling to the valley of the Seven Smokes. It looked like that was where they were headed now. The question was whether or not the destination was their own choice, or if they were being forced there as captives.

When a few distant popping sounds came to Wingate's ears, the frontiersman called an abrupt halt. "Hear that?" he said to Corrigan. "Somebody's shootin'."

The young officer nodded. "I do hear it. Is it some sort of battle, do you think?"

The shots were sporadic. "Don't know," Wingate said. "Could be some hunters, I suppose. Can't really tell from the sound of what's goin' on."

After only a few minutes, the shooting stopped. Corrigan

said, "If it was a fight, it wasn't much of one. Everyone has already ceased fire."

Wingate thought about that, and didn't tell the lieutenant that plenty of epic battles had been fought in these mountains in which not a single shot had been fired. The Indians didn't have all that many guns. They fought with arrows, knives, and tomahawks, all of which didn't make much noise. But there was no point in alarming Corrigan until they knew for sure what had happened.

"Let's go find out," Wingate said.

Unfortunately, night fell before the soldiers could get very far, and they were forced to make camp. Wingate didn't like it. The shots he had heard made worry gnaw at him. But it would have been foolish to push on in the dark, and he knew it. Even the wet-behind-the-ears Lieutenant Corrigan knew that. So they waited until the next morning before resuming their journey through the mountains.

It was almost the middle of the day before they reached the valley of the Seven Smokes. Wingate had been here before and knew the area fairly well. He had already noticed that the Teton Sioux village of Hairface's people was no longer where it had been located before, and that was puzzling, not to mention a mite worrisome. Momentous things had been going on around here, but Wingate had no idea what they were.

Entering the valley from the south, Wingate, Corrigan, and the soldiers proceeded north, taking their time now and moving cautiously because they didn't know what they were going to run into. But even as alert as they were, they were startled when a group of about ten men suddenly stepped out of a thick growth of trees and pointed rifles at them. Some of the soldiers instinctively lifted their own weapons and leveled them. All it would have taken at that tense moment to unleash bloody chaos was for one man to get nervous enough to press the trigger.

But before that could happen, Lieutenant Corrigan called out, "Hold your fire! Damn it, hold your fire!"

Wingate's eyes widened in surprise as he stared at the men

who had them covered. They weren't strangers at all, he realized, and they weren't Indians. They were trappers Wingate
was acquainted with from Rendezvous in the past. He didn't
much like any of them, but at least there was no reason for
them to fight.

"Snell!" he said sharply. "Luther Snell! It's me, Wingate."

The stocky, bearded figure who seemed to be the leader of
the riflemen held up a hand and said to his companions,
"Take it easy, boys." A grin stretched across Snell's bearded
face. "Looks like we're all on the same side."

Wingate wasn't so sure about that. He recalled what
Preacher had told him about how Snell and the others had attacked and killed Mountain Mist, and also how Snell planned
to kidnap Willard Carling and hold him for ransom. He
opened his mouth to say something, but then thought better
of it. Snell's bunch was almost as big and well armed as this
troop of soldiers, and Wingate had no doubt that they would
fight if Corrigan tried to arrest them. Since they had seen evidence that Indians were on the warpath around here, maybe
it would be better to keep what he knew to himself, rather
than accusing Snell. If they found themselves fighting the
redskins, Snell and the others would be worthwhile allies.

And he could always tell Corrigan what he knew about
Snell later on, once things were safer, Wingate mused.

The lieutenant turned to Wingate and asked, "These men
are friends of yours?"

Wingate forced a smile onto his face and nodded. "They
sure are," he lied.

"Then maybe they can help us locate the Carling expedition."

Snell's bushy eyebrows rose in surprise. "You're lookin' for
that artist fella and his friends?" he asked quickly.

"That's right," Corrigan said. "Do you know where they are?"

"'Deed I do." Snell pointed toward the north. "They're a
couple miles in that direction, bein' held prisoner in a Sioux
village. And if you've come to rescue 'em, Lieutenant, you
better hurry, 'cause I think those savages are plannin' to kill
them most any time now!"

* * *

This was the stroke of luck he had been waiting for, Luther Snell told himself as he looked at the red-and-blue uniforms of the soldiers.

When he and the others had heard the riders coming, Snell's first thought was that a war party was about to stumble upon them. The men had grabbed their guns, ready to fight and sell their lives dearly if necessary.

Instead of enemies, the newcomers turned out to be potential allies, and a plan immediately suggested itself to Snell.

He had been worried all morning because he hadn't seen any sign of Willard Carling while he was spying on the Teton Sioux village. Nor did he see any of the other pilgrims, or Preacher and Rip Giddens. It was possible that all of them had been killed in the battle with the Crows the day before. The thought that he had come so close to the means of making himself rich, only to possibly lose it, was almost enough to drive Snell mad. He *had* to find out what had happened to Carling.

Of course, he couldn't just walk into the village and ask. He didn't trust the Indians, not for a second. But with the soldiers on his side, he and his men could hit the village hard and fast on horseback, wipe out the remaining warriors before they knew what was happening, and force some answers out of the survivors. He and the others would still be outnumbered by the remaining warriors in the village when they attacked, but with the element of surprise on their side, Snell was confident they would be victorious. That was why he talked fast and thought even faster, explaining to Wingate and the lieutenant in command of the patrol about how the Indians had captured Carling and the others and held them prisoner for almost a week. That wasn't exactly the truth, but Snell didn't care about the truth, only about getting what he wanted.

"My God!" the lieutenant exclaimed when he heard that

the prisoners were in danger. "We have to get in there and rescue them."

"Those Injuns'll put up a fight," Snell warned, "so you better go in shootin'."

"Hold on a minute," Wingate said. "How do you know they're about to kill the prisoners?"

Snell hesitated, but Baldy came up with an answer, picking up on what Snell was trying to accomplish. "They been chantin' all mornin', and I know a killin' chant when I hear one, Wingate. I've come damn near hearin' savages singin' a death song for me too many times not to recognize it."

"I *have* to rescue those captives if at all possible," Lieutenant Corrigan said. "I believe we should attack the village right away."

Snell wondered what was so all-fired important about the soldiers getting their hands on Carling and the others. That might present a problem later on. But for now, all he was really concerned with was making sure Carling was even still alive.

"Now you're talkin', Lieutenant," Snell said. "We'll lend you boys a hand." He turned to his men. "Get the horses. We're gonna teach those redskins a thing or two."

Wingate still looked a little doubtful, but he didn't make any objection as the combined force prepared to attack the village. Snell recalled that Wingate was friends with Preacher, so he didn't expect the red-bearded trapper to like him very much. Like everybody else who had been at that Rendezvous, Wingate knew about the bad blood between Preacher and Snell. But at the moment, Wingate believed that Preacher was a captive in the Sioux village, so he would be willing to take part in the effort to free him.

"Part of the village burned down yesterday," Snell said as the group of soldiers and trappers rode closer. "Don't know what happened; maybe one o' the cook fires got out of control. We saw the smoke and thought about tryin' to sneak in while that was goin' on to get the prisoners loose, but we figured there were too few of us to put up a good fight if they caught us."

"Well, you don't have to worry about that now," Corrigan assured him. "Those savages will never know what hit them."

Snell grinned to himself. Neither would this baby-faced officer or the troops he commanded, once the fight with the Indians was over. Snell had already passed the word quietly to the others in his party. When he gave the signal, they would open fire on the unsuspecting soldiers and wipe them out.

Of course, that hinged on finding Willard Carling alive and well in the village. . . .

As they came in sight of the village, Lieutenant Corrigan drew his saber from its scabbard and lifted it in the air. "Charge!" he called as he swept the saber down and kicked his horse into a gallop. The others thundered toward the village with him.

The Indians heard and saw them coming, of course, and there was no mistaking the intention of the riders. Arrows began to fly through the air as the inhabitants of the village attempted to mount a defense. They were too startled to put up an effective resistance, though, as ruthless attackers swept into the village for the second time in about twenty-four hours.

Those soldier boys didn't *know* this was the second attack, though. Snell grinned as he thought about how skillfully he had manipulated things into going his way. Guiding his horse with his knees, he lifted a pistol in each hand and blasted two of the warriors right into the spirit world.

"Watch out for the prisoners!" Corrigan bellowed to his men. "See that they come to no harm!"

The attackers had to make every shot count. Snell jammed the empty pistols into his saddlebags and lifted the rifle that was slung on his saddle. He yanked his horse to a halt and lifted the rifle to draw a bead on a warrior who was charging at him brandishing a tomahawk. He pulled the trigger and sent a ball crashing into the Indian's chest. The red bastard never had a chance—and that was just the way Snell wanted it.

All around him, the other trappers were fighting with the same deadly efficiency, each of them accounting for two or three of the Teton Sioux defenders. The soldiers weren't quite as effective. Some of their shots missed. But they did a good job of skewering the Indians with the bayonets attached to the muzzles of their rifles.

In a matter of two or three minutes, most of the warriors left in the village had been either killed or wounded badly enough so that they were out of the fight. All that was left now was mopping up, and Snell and his men handled that with brutal dispatch, cutting throats and blasting pistol balls through heads. One of the last defenders to fall was a big, ugly warrior with a scarred face and a little bit of an ear missing. Snell recognized him as Bites Like a Badger, one of old Hairface's sub-chiefs. Snell hadn't seen any sign of Hairface, and wondered if Badger had become the chief of this band now.

Badger wasn't anything anymore except meat. He'd been shot twice in the chest and had a bayonet buried in his guts. He lay on his back in a spreading pool of blood, sightless eyes staring up at the sky.

Most importantly, Snell hadn't seen any sign of the prisoners. He couldn't figure out where they had gone, and he was beginning to get worried. If Carling wasn't here, then it was all for nothing.

When all the warriors were either dead or too badly wounded to fight, the soldiers began going from lodge to lodge, rounding up the women and children and old people and herding them to the center of the village. Snell stalked along with them, still looking for the prisoners. His worry grew as none of them were found.

Then he spotted a white face as a tall, skinny man limped out of one of the tepees, using a crutch to get along because of a wounded leg. Snell recognized him as either Tom or Ed Ballinger, although he didn't know which.

"Ballinger!" he said as he hurried over to the lodge, since it didn't really matter which one the man was. "Where the hell are the others? Where's Carling?"

"Gone," Ballinger replied. "He left early this mornin' with

Preacher and a few others. They went after the Crows who captured Miss Carling and that fella Sinclair."

Snell bit back a curse and thought fast. It was bad enough that Carling was gone, but now Ballinger was spilling things Snell would have rather hadn't been known just yet. "What Crows?" he demanded loudly in an attempt to lessen the potential damage.

"The ones who attacked the village yesterday," Ballinger replied.

Wingate walked up in time to hear that. "What?" he exclaimed. He turned toward Snell. "You didn't say anything about any Crows attacking the village."

"I didn't know anything about it! We saw smoke and knew there was a fire, but that's all we knew." There, Snell thought. Nobody could disprove that statement. He went on. "We thought you boys were prisoners of these Sioux. We just been waitin' for a chance to bust you out o' here."

Ballinger shook his head. "We started out as their prisoners." His voice caught a little. "They killed poor Ed when they jumped us. But then Preacher fought their chief, Bites Like a Badger, to a standstill, and they called a truce and let us go."

Corrigan had come up, too, and now the lieutenant said, "I'm confused by all this."

Snell grunted. "So am I. Looks like we was mistaken about what's been goin' on. We thought sure that the folks from that expedition were captives, and we didn't know anything about any Crow raiders."

Wingate scratched at his beard and asked, "Who's left alive?"

"Well, Mr. Carling and that journalist fella, Hodge," said Ballinger. "And Preacher and Rip Giddens. Poor old Switchfoot and Hammerhead Jones are both dead. Crows got 'em yesterday. And of course, Miss Carling and Sinclair. But the Crows carried them off, along with some Sioux prisoners."

Corrigan took off his shako and ran his fingers through his hair as he frowned. "So you weren't prisoners here anymore, but two members of your party *were* captured by these Crow Indians you mentioned?" Clearly, he was struggling to understand.

"That's right," Ballinger said. He looked around bleakly. "I'd say that you killed all these folks for nothin'. . . ." His face and voice hardened. "Except for the fact that they killed my brother and planned on torturin' the rest of us to death when they first grabbed us. I can't bring myself to feel sorry for them."

"Well . . ." Corrigan was a little pale and queasy-looking now. "They *were* hostiles," he went on. "And we had only the best intentions in attacking the village."

Wingate spat. "Road to hell," he said curtly. No explanation was needed.

Corrigan put his hat back on and said, "The important thing is that we still have to find the remaining members of the expedition. You say they've all left here except for you?"

Ballinger nodded. "I reckon those Crows are headin' back to their usual huntin' grounds, north and east of here, out on the plains. They were Medicine Bull's band, accordin' to Badger."

"I know where to find 'em," Wingate said. "Preacher will, too."

"Then we'll follow along and try to catch up to them," Corrigan decided. "That's the only acceptable course of action."

"You lost a couple of men in the fightin'," Wingate pointed out. To Ballinger, he said, "How many in the Crow war party?"

"Lord, I don't know. I think Preacher said somethin' about fifty or sixty warriors."

"We'll be rather heavily outnumbered. . . ." Corrigan mused.

Snell said, "We'll go with you, Lieutenant. You can count on us." He looked around, and the men with him nodded, even Vickery. Fate had taken some odd twists and turns, but they could still salvage this situation and come out of it as rich men.

"I appreciate that, Mr. Snell," Corrigan said, "but I can't order you to—"

"Beggin' your pardon, Lieutenant, but you ain't orderin' us to do nothin'. We're volunteerin'."

"That's very decent of you." Corrigan nodded. "Very well. I accept your offer. We'll continue our pursuit of the surviving members of the expedition as soon as possible."

And the rest of them would continue their pursuit of being rich, Snell thought.

Chapter Twenty-six

Preacher found the canyon where the Crows had left their horses before attacking the village. He had suspected that the raiders were mounted, but this confirmed that suspicion and prompted him to say, "This is gonna make things even harder."

"Why is that?" Willard Carling wanted to know.

"If they'd all been on foot, they would have had to move a mite slower," Preacher explained. "From the looks of the sign they left behind, the prisoners are still walkin', even though the members of the war party are ridin'. That'll keep them from movin' too fast, but they'll still get along quicker'n they would have otherwise."

"Yeah," Rip agreed, "they'll make those prisoners trot to beat the band."

"Or kill them if they can't keep up," Carling guessed.

Rip looked like he wished he hadn't said anything. "I'm sure it won't come to that," he declared, trying to reassure Carling.

Preacher wasn't sure of any such thing, but he didn't say so. He just said, "Come on. Let's get movin'."

He had no trouble following the trail left by the Indians and their captives. As they pressed on through the day, their route wound through some heavily wooded hills, but overall, the landscape was beginning to flatten out.

When Jasper Hodge commented on that, Preacher said, "Crows are Plains Indians. They live mostly off hunting buffalo and from raiding other tribes. They don't come into the mountains much. Most of the Sioux bands, like the Hunkpapa and the Ogallala, are the same way. Fact is, those Tetons, like Badger's bunch, are about the only Sioux who spend most of their time in the mountains. It's more often the Shoshone, like Mountain Mist and Sparrow, that you find up here in the Rockies."

"Will we be out on the plains before we catch up to them?" Carling asked.

"Could be," Preacher replied, "and that ain't necessarily a good thing, either. There ain't nearly as much cover out there, and it'll be a lot harder to sneak up on 'em."

"That's why we have to hurry, then, to try to catch them before they get out of the mountains."

"Yep. But the odds are against it."

"I don't care about the odds," Carling said. "I just want to get my sister back safely, whatever it takes."

When they stopped to rest the horses along about the middle of the afternoon, Rip caught a moment alone with Preacher, out of earshot of the other three men, and said, "You reckon Carling knows his sister's prob'ly gonna be abused by those redskins before we catch up to 'em?"

"Maybe she won't be," Preacher said. "Now that ol' Medicine Bull's got what he came after, maybe he'll be in such a hurry to get back home that he won't let them take the time for such shenanigans."

"It don't take all that much time," Rip pointed out grimly.

"I know," Preacher said with a sigh. "I'm just hopin' for the best. Right now, that's about all we can do."

Faith dreamed that she was back in Boston, back in her own bed, in her own room, in her brother's house on Beacon Hill.

She sighed and snuggled deeper into the warm comforter . . . only to sneeze when something tickled her nose.

That sneeze brought her out of her slumber, and as she woke up, terror flooded in on her brain. She gasped and jerked her head up. She saw that it had been the hairs of Chester Sinclair's beard that had tickled her nose, and to her utter mortification, she realized that she was practically lying on top of him, cradled in his strong arms.

He had been asleep, too, and he yelled out as her reaction startled him awake. But he didn't let go of her, even when she put her hands on his broad chest and pushed herself halfway upright.

"What . . . what are you doing?" she asked. She looked around wildly, saw the other prisoners and the Crows who had captured them, and everything came back to her, almost overwhelming her with despair.

"I . . . I'm sorry," Sinclair said as he finally released her. She scooted away from him, only to hurriedly move close to him again when one of the Crow warriors glared at her. "I don't know how that happened," Sinclair went on. "I wasn't aware that I was . . . was holding you like that. We must have . . . rolled together in our sleep . . ."

That made sense, Faith supposed. Since both of them were prisoners of these savages, and the only whites among the captives at that, it was only natural that they would reach out to each other. It didn't mean anything except that they were alone and scared—very, very scared, as any normal person would be in this situation.

The Crows had kept the prisoners trotting along the previous evening until they were so exhausted they were about to drop. At least, Faith had certainly felt that way. When the war party had stopped for the night, she had slumped to the ground, stretched out, and immediately fallen asleep, not even thinking about the fact that she hadn't eaten all day and her stomach was empty. She guessed that Sinclair had lain down beside her, and that during the night . . .

A sudden rumbling in her belly, accompanied by sharp

pangs, reminded her of how hungry she was and took her mind off the position in which she had found herself when she woke up. She shivered a little as she leaned her shoulder against Sinclair's and asked, "Do you think they're going to give us anything to eat this morning?"

"I hope so, but I wouldn't count on it," he said.

His words proved to be prophetic. The captives were prodded to their feet with lances and angry words from their Crow captors. They were allowed to drink from the small stream beside which the war party had paused for the night, but no rations were forthcoming. Soon, they were on the move again, trotting along as the Indians surrounded them.

"I can't do this all day," Faith moaned, "especially with no food."

"Don't talk," Sinclair advised. "Save your strength." He took hold of her arm and squeezed it for a second. "Don't worry, I won't let you fall behind."

His words encouraged her, and she didn't even mind the boldness of his action in touching her. She realized just how glad she was that Chester Sinclair was here with her. If he hadn't been captured, too, then she would have been alone, with no one who spoke her language, no one who understood what she was going through. . . .

She felt a surge of unaccustomed guilt. She shouldn't be glad that Chester was a prisoner, too. That was a terrible thing to wish on anyone.

And yet she couldn't help it. When she glanced over at him, she felt a little better for some reason. She knew that he was only one man and that he couldn't really stop the Indians from doing whatever they wanted to do . . . but she was glad he was here anyway.

Uphill and down, through sheer-walled canyons, across rocky stretches that hurt her feet even through the boots she wore . . . all day long Faith was forced to keep moving with the others. The lack of food made her light-headed, so at times it seemed she was imagining this whole terrible ordeal. But then, sharp pains would stab through her feet from the blisters that had been rubbed there, and she knew it was real, all too real. She began to cry, but when she saw how badly her sobs upset Chester, she stifled them and assured him that she was fine. He had his own problems, and she didn't want to add to them. Such a feeling of consideration for someone else was new for her, but genuine.

They stopped for the night a bit earlier that evening than the previous one, but it was still well after sunset before the captives were allowed to slump to the ground. A couple of the warriors moved among them, tossing something onto the ground. The prisoners scrambled to get their hands on the items. Chester grabbed two of them, one for Faith and one for himself.

"What is it?" she asked when he handed her what appeared to be a small piece of darkly tanned leather.

"Jerky," he told her. "Food."

She had been hoping that this would be something to eat, but it didn't look very appetizing. She tried to take a bite, only to find that the jerky was as tough and unyielding as leather, too. "Ow," she said as clamping down on it with her teeth made them hurt.

"It's a small enough piece you can put the whole thing in your mouth," Sinclair said. "Do that and let it soften up for a while before you try to chew it again."

"This is *disgusting*."

"It's better than starving to death," Chester pointed out.

Faith supposed he was right—although this bit of tough, dried meat was so small, she doubted that it would do much to relieve her hunger.

Exhaustion threatened to overtake her again, but she forced herself to stay awake until she had let the jerky soften in her mouth to the point that she could chew it. Sinclair was doing likewise. As his jaws worked, he said thickly, "It's really not too bad."

Faith just gave an unladylike grunt as she ground away at the stuff. Chester was right in a way; the jerky didn't taste too bad, especially to a starving person. But Faith hated to think that she might have to live on the dreadful stuff from now on.

While they were eating, one of the Crow warriors came toward them. From the way the guards stepped aside respectfully from the man and the Sioux prisoners cringed, Faith got the idea that he was somebody important, perhaps the chief. As he came closer, she recognized him as the warrior who had tapped Chester with the coup stick and stopped the others from killing him.

The Indian stopped in front of Chester and spoke in a loud, harsh voice. The words were just gibberish to Faith, utterly meaningless. She knew that Chester had picked up a little of the Sioux language through his friendship with the warrior called Panther Leaping—in fact he had tried, unsuccessfully, to teach her a few words of it—but from the look on his face he didn't understand what this Crow warrior was trying to tell him. Chester shook his head, and that angered the Crow. He lashed out, striking a hard blow on the side of Chester's head with his open hand. Faith gasped in surprise at the sudden violence.

Without thinking about what she was doing, she leaped to her feet and said, "Here now! There's no call for behavior like that! You have no right to bully us—"

That was as far as she got before Chester grabbed her. As his arms tightened around her waist, he swung around, lifting her off the ground and turning her away from the Indian. Faith gasped again, this time in outrage at being manhandled this way.

"Stop it!" he hissed in her ear. "He's their chief. You can't talk to him like that! He'll kill you!"

"But he struck you! And put me down, blast it!"

Chester lowered her to the ground and went on. "Let me do the talking." He turned back to the Indian and said something in what Faith supposed was the Sioux tongue. He moved his hands, too, in that outlandish sign language she had seen him practicing with Panther. The Crow warrior signed back furiously.

That went on for a minute or so before the Indian grunted

and motioned curtly for Chester to sit down. He did so, taking hold of Faith's arm and pulling her down beside him.

"You're getting awfully cavalier about the way you lay hands on me, Mr. Sinclair," she told him coldly.

"I'm just trying to save your pretty little hide," he growled. What he said, and the way he said it, combined to make Faith's green eyes widen with surprise.

For a moment, she didn't trust herself to speak. Finally, as the Indian turned and stalked away, she asked in a low voice, "What was that about, anyway?"

"Well . . . I'm not certain. I only understood bits and pieces of what he said, although the sign language was pretty clear. I gather that he's Medicine Bull, the war chief of the Crows. He's claimed me as his slave, and he hit me when I indicated that I was no man's slave. I know, that was a foolish thing for me to do, but I couldn't help it."

"It was a brave thing," Faith said, the anger that she had felt toward him easing.

"Brave, foolish, under the circumstances it really doesn't matter." Chester shrugged. "Anyway, that's what it was about."

"Did . . . did he say anything about me?" Faith was almost afraid to ask.

"He said that since I was going to be his slave . . . my woman . . . would be given to his wives to be their slave."

Faith stared at him in the dusk. "*Your* woman?"

"That's what they think."

"And did you disabuse them of that incredible notion?"

"I did not," Chester declared. "I thought you might be safer if that's what they believed."

"These savages don't care about a thing like that!" Again, to her surprise, she found herself unable to stay angry with him. "But I suppose you were just trying to do what you thought was best."

"That's right," Chester said. "I haven't given up on getting away from them, so I don't want anything to happen to you before we get a chance to escape."

They were silent for a moment, and then Faith asked,

"What did he tell you there at the end, when he was gesturing so vehemently?"

This time Chester sounded faintly amused as he replied, "Medicine Bull told me that my woman has a temper as much like fire as her hair. He said that you were loud and rude and that if you were one of his wives, he would beat you until you behaved yourself better. In fact, he advised me to take precisely that approach."

"He said *all that* just by flailing around with his hands?"

"Sign language is very expressive," Chester said dryly.

Faith sniffed. "Well, don't you get any ideas, Chester Sinclair. In the first place, I'm not your woman, and even if I was, I would never allow you to try to paddle me back into line as if I were an unruly child. In fact, if you ever lay a hand on me again—"

He did exactly that, just then, picking up her right hand in both of his and clasping it gently. "If you were my woman, Faith, and if I laid a hand on you, it wouldn't be in anger or to teach you a lesson. It would be out of love."

"Oh." She suddenly felt warm and flustered, so much so that it made her forget for a moment about their perilous situation and how frightened she was. She forced a light, casual tone into her voice as she said, "Oh, well, in that case . . ."

There was nothing light or casual about the way she felt, though. In fact, the feelings that had sprung up within her were decidedly unsettling.

Or maybe it was just that awful jerky, she told herself. Yes, that was it. It had to be the jerky.

Chapter Twenty-seven

Wingate tried to keep an eye on Luther Snell at all times. Because of what he knew about Snell and the other trappers, Wingate didn't trust them, not even for a second. He didn't have any choice but to play along with them, however. He had to think about Miss Carling and that Sinclair fella. Their lives were in danger as long as they were in the hands of the Crows, and Snell and the others could help rescue them.

Lieutenant Corrigan didn't seem to have any trouble trusting Snell. In fact, they had become downright friendly now that the lieutenant had other guides besides Wingate. Snell was deliberately worming his way into Corrigan's confidence, Wingate decided, but again, there was nothing he could do about it until after they had freed the prisoners from the war party.

As they moved out onto the Great Plains a couple of days after joining up with Snell's bunch, Wingate brought his horse alongside the lieutenant's and said, "We'll have to be a mite more careful now. There's not much cover on this prairie, and it's so flat you can see a long way on it. If those Crows spot us comin', they might kill all the prisoners before we can catch up."

Snell was riding on Corrigan's other side. He said, "Maybe

what we ought to do is get ahead of 'em and lay an ambush. We can move faster'n those Injuns can, since we ain't saddled with a bunch o' prisoners."

"Taking advantage of the element of surprise is a sound military tactic," Corrigan said. "That's an interesting idea, Mr. Snell."

"Except it won't work," Wingate put in. "If you try to circle around them like that, the Crows are liable to spot the dust from the horses and figure out that somethin' is up. You won't be takin' 'em by surprise."

Corrigan had turned his head to look at Wingate as he listened to the red-bearded trapper's argument. Now he turned back to Snell and asked, "What do you think, Mr. Snell? Is what Mr. Wingate says correct?"

Snell scowled. "Well, it's been sort of a dry spring," he admitted. "The horses might kick up enough dust that the Crows would notice. But they're kickin' up dust now. Nothin' we can do about that."

"There'll be more dust if you gallop hard enough to get all the way around the war party," Wingate pointed out. "And they'll be more likely to see it if it's in front of them, too."

Corrigan said, "Well, then, Mr. Wingate, what's your suggestion? What tactics should we adopt when we catch up with the savages?"

"We ought to catch up to Preacher and them others before we do with the Crows. I'd let him figure it out. He's a little on the young side, but there's nobody better at fightin' Injuns on the whole frontier."

"Preacher." Snell snorted. "Hell, I been out here just as long as Preacher, maybe longer, and I'm still alive and got all my hair. I can come up with a plan just as good as he can."

"Well, continue to mull it over if you would." Corrigan looked back and forth between the two frontiersmen. "To tell the truth, I need the counsel of both of you, and Preacher, too, if I can get it. I'm not ashamed to admit that I'm a novice at this Indian fighting."

The fact that Corrigan wasn't too proud to admit he needed

help meant that he and his troops had a chance of living through this, Wingate thought. Maybe not a great chance, but any was better than none.

"Besides," Corrigan went on, "it's absolutely vital that we rescue Chester Sinclair from the Indians. He's the reason my men and I were sent out here, after all."

That made Wingate frown in puzzlement and surprise. He recalled what Corrigan had said the day they first met about a fortune riding on the lieutenant's mission. He had assumed that Corrigan was talking about Willard Carling. Carling was the one who was rich . . . wasn't he?

Suddenly, as he glanced at Snell and saw the new gleam in the man's eyes, Wingate wished that Corrigan would just shut up. That wasn't going to be the case, though, because the lieutenant went on. "I suppose it's time you fellows know the truth, since you're risking your lives to help me fulfill this assignment."

"You just go right ahead and tell us anything you want to tell us, Lieutenant," Snell urged.

"You see, my orders are to locate Chester Sinclair and return him safely to St. Louis, where he'll be met by legal representatives of his late uncle."

"His late uncle?" Wingate said.

"Yes. Senator Ambrose Sinclair. Are you familiar with the name?"

Wingate had heard of Ambrose Sinclair, all right. So had Snell, who said, "Politician from back East somewhere, right? And a mighty rich man, to boot."

"That's correct. And his entire estate is going to his nephew Chester."

Snell let out a low whistle. "I figured he was just a servant hired by that artist fella. He sure acted that way. He let Carling boss him around all the time and never said nothin' about havin' a rich uncle."

"From what I understand," Corrigan said in a confidential tone, "there was a split in the family, some sort of argument between Senator Sinclair and his brother—Chester Sinclair's father—when they were both young men. The family was still very poor at that time. The two men never saw each other or had anything to do with each other again. Chester's father remained poor, but Ambrose Sinclair went on to become wealthy and eventually entered the political arena, where he became even richer and more influential. It's possible that Chester Sinclair never even knew that Senator Sinclair was his uncle."

"So he was workin' as Carling's assistant without havin' any idea that someday he'd be even richer than the fella he was workin' for?" Snell asked avidly.

"I assume that was the case. Willard Carling is certainly well-to-do, but with his new inheritance, Chester Sinclair could buy and sell Carling several times over. And *that*, gentlemen, is why I've been sent to fetch him back. Senator Sinclair had a great many friends in the War Department, all the way up to the Secretary, and they want the senator's wishes to be carried out."

Wingate scratched at his beard and tried not to let the concern he felt show on his face. This revelation by the lieutenant made things even worse than they had been before. Snell had figured on kidnapping Willard Carling, but now it appeared that grabbing Chester Sinclair could result in an even bigger windfall. Snell wasn't going to let such an opportunity pass without trying to seize it.

It looked to Wingate like rescuing Sinclair and Miss Carling from the Crows wasn't going to be the end of danger, but just the beginning. . . .

As Preacher and his companions sat in a cold camp after night had fallen, making a meager supper on pemmican and jerky, Rip Giddens said, "There's a good chance we're gonna catch up to that bunch tomorrow, Preacher. Got any idea what we're gonna do then?"

"I've been thinkin' on it," Preacher said. "There's no way we can slip in, free the captives, and sneak back out again without the Crows noticin' us. There's just too blamed many of 'em. That didn't work with the war party that grabbed you folks in the first place, and it was a lot smaller."

Panther Leaping said in Sioux, "It shames me that I was part of that war party. When Hairface was chief, our people were always friends to the whites. But when he died and Bites Like a Badger became chief, everything changed."

"That wasn't your fault, Panther," Preacher told him. "You and the other warriors had to go along with Badger."

"We could have challenged his plans to make war on the whites. We could have spoken against him in the council of elders."

"Maybe . . . but that's over and done with. We're on the same side now, and maybe by the time we get back, Badger will have decided not to go to war after all."

Panther nodded slowly. "I will pray to the Great Spirit that it will be so."

Willard Carling smiled faintly and said, "I don't know what the two of you are talking about, Preacher, but it sounds awfully solemn."

"Panther was apologizing for the way his people treated you folks at first," Preacher explained.

"Well . . . it was awfully frightening being their prisoners. But I understand now that the chief was to blame for most of that, and besides, they treated us quite well after you and Badger had your little fight. Tell Panther that we don't bear any grudges toward him or the others."

"Speak for yourself," Jasper Hodge muttered. "I still bear plenty of grudges."

"Anyway," Rip said, "back to what we're gonna do when we catch up to that war party and try to get them prisoners loose . . . Preacher, it seems to me what we need is somethin' to keep those Crows busy."

"Too busy to come after us once we free the captives." Preacher nodded. "I was thinkin' the same thing. And the best idea I've come up with is to start a fire."

"What good will that do?" Hodge asked.

"A prairie fire is just about the scariest thing that can

happen out here on the plains," Rip explained. He seemed to like Preacher's idea. "Well, other than a buffalo stampede or a cyclone," he went on, "but we can't count on one o' those happenin' when we need it to. A fire is somethin' we'd have a little control over."

"Damned little," Preacher said. "But maybe enough."

Carling leaned forward, interest on his face. "How would this work?" he wanted to know.

"Depends on which way the wind's blowin'. One of us will have to get downwind of the war party and start a fire. When it springs up, the Crows will see the smoke and know they have to get out of its way in a hurry. When they run, the rest of our bunch will gallop in, grab the prisoners, and head whichever way the Crows don't. They won't have time to turn around and come after us, because if they do they'll be riskin' gettin' caught in the fire."

"We'll be racin' that fire ourselves," Rip pointed out. "Plus whoever starts the blaze is gonna find himself in what they call a mighty precarious position. But I sure can't think of anything else that'd be more likely to work."

Hodge said, "I've heard about these prairie fires. You're willing to burn up a vast area just to serve as a distraction?"

"It'll be more than a distraction," Preacher said. "If we can get the fire between the prisoners and the war party, it'll serve as a shield, too. By the time the flames burn themselves out, we'll be far enough away the Crows probably won't come after us."

"I suppose it might work," Carling said. "We don't have enough horses for all the prisoners to ride, though."

Preacher glanced at Panther. "I had in mind just grabbin' Miss Carling and Sinclair. But in all the confusion, the Sioux prisoners ought to have a chance to slip away, too." He shook his head. "I know it ain't a perfect plan. But it may be the best we can do."

"All right. I'll go along with the idea and do whatever I can to help, Preacher. But what about Panther? Have you explained it to him?"

"Not yet." Preacher turned to Panther Leaping, and over

the next few minutes he laid out the plan in the Sioux language. The warrior looked concerned over the fate of the prisoners from his band, as Preacher expected that he would. But in the end, Panther nodded and spoke briefly.

"He says he agrees," Preacher translated. "He says once the dung-eaters are distracted by the fire, the Sioux prisoners will be able to escape. That's what I'm hoping, too."

"It's agreed, then," Rip said. "The question now is, who's gonna start the fire? That's the fella who's gonna be runnin' the biggest risk."

"I'll do it," Preacher said quietly. "It was my idea, so I ought to be the one to handle that part of it."

Rip shook his head. "I don't think so. You need to be with the bunch that frees the prisoners. That's the most important part of the job. *I'll* start the fire."

Preacher might have argued the point, but at that moment Panther Leaping tapped himself on the chest with a loosely balled fist and said in English, "I will start fire."

Preacher frowned. It had to be one of the three of them; Carling and Hodge couldn't be trusted with something so vital to the success of the plan. Preacher nodded slowly and said, "All right, Panther, the job's yours."

"Wait a minute," Rip said. "You'll let him volunteer, but not me?"

"He's got the fastest horse," Preacher said. "That means he'll have the best chance o' gettin' out of the way of the fire."

Rip scratched at his beard and frowned, then finally said, "Well, yeah, I reckon that's true." He looked at Panther and added, "Good luck. You're gonna need it."

"We all will," Preacher said. "But if luck is on our side, by this time tomorrow night we'll be on our way back to the village with Miss Carling and Sinclair and I hope some of the other prisoners. In the meantime . . . let's get a good night's sleep."

Chapter Twenty-eight

The haze of dust that hung in the air a couple of miles ahead of them around noon the next day indicated to Preacher that they had finally caught up with the Crow war party. While it was possible that something else was raising that dust, like a herd of buffalo on the move, Preacher's gut told him otherwise.

"Let's get close enough we can see them," he said as he heeled his mount into a faster pace. He wished he had Horse under him. He trusted his old friend's speed and stamina more than he did that of the animal he was riding. But he hadn't seen Horse and Dog since he had been captured by the Sioux more than a week earlier, and he was starting to worry a little about them.

Right now, though, he had bigger worries, like surviving the afternoon.

The group pushed on faster, and a short time later they came within sight of a dark mass on the flat, grassy horizon in front of them. "That's them," Preacher said, relieved that his hunch had been confirmed.

The wind was out of the south, blowing steadily at a fairly high rate of speed. Panther Leaping pointed in that direction and said to Preacher, "That is where I must go to start the fire."

Preacher nodded. "I'd get a little bit ahead of them, if I was you," he advised. "Once you get it started good, head for the war party as fast as you can. We'll meet you there."

"Stay ahead o' them flames," Rip added in his badly accented Sioux.

Panther didn't smile or make any speeches. He just raised a hand in farewell, gave them a solemn nod, and galloped off toward the south, veering a little east as well.

"Do you think he'll be able to start the fire and then get away from it?" Carling asked.

"He'll give it his best," Preacher said. "That's all anybody can do."

The rescue party, now four men instead of five, continued closing in on their quarry. Their approach had to be timed carefully. They couldn't get too close before Panther started the prairie fire, or the Crows might spot them and be warned that something was going on. But they had to be near enough to be able to dash in and free the prisoners once the Indians began their hurried flight from the flames.

Preacher was counting on a little panic setting in among the Crows. They knew as well as anybody how dangerous a fire on these plains could be. The flames moved fast and spread out into a juggernaut of destruction. Preacher hoped the Crows would forget all about guarding their prisoners and flee wildly in an attempt to get out of the path of the fire.

They would know soon what was going to happen, he thought as the time since Panther had ridden off approached a half hour. The Teton warrior ought to just about be in position by now.

A couple of minutes later, that prophecy came true as a thin column of dark gray smoke began to rise into the arching vault of blue sky. The smoke spread quickly until it was a swiftly rolling black cloud. The war party was less than half a mile ahead. Preacher dug his heels into the flanks of his mount and leaned forward in the saddle. "Come on!" he called to the other men. The time for stealth was over. Now the situation called for swift action.

Approximately a mile behind Preacher and his companions rode Wingate, the troop of soldiers commanded by Lieutenant Corrigan, and the group of trappers led by Luther Snell. Wingate and Snell had already seen the dust being raised by the Crow war party and pointed it out to Corrigan. Now Wingate leveled an arm and said worriedly, "Look yonder to the south at that smoke!"

"What is it?" Corrigan asked, adding rather naively, "A fire of some sort?"

"It's a prairie fire!" Snell said. "And look how fast it's spreadin'!"

It was true. The smoke cloud had grown to an impressive size in less than a minute.

"What do we do now?" Corrigan asked, seemingly forgetting that he was technically in charge of this party.

"Wind's out of the south," Wingate said. "It'll sweep that fire right up over the war party and the prisoners if they don't get out of the way. We'd better get up there and see if we can help them—*fast!*"

He and Snell both kicked their horses into a gallop. Corrigan followed suit, yelling over his shoulder, "Come on, men!"

The group of men, nearly thirty strong, charged toward the Crow war party, which by now was probably milling around in utter confusion and fear.

Sinclair heard the shouts of alarm from the Indians and lifted his head, shaking off the dull weariness that gripped him after more than half of another day of being forced to move quickly on foot over the prairie. Faith trudged along beside him, and her head was down as well. She didn't lift hers, though, evidently not realizing that something was wrong.

"Faith!" Sinclair said sharply, causing her to jerk her head up. "Faith, be ready! This may be our chance!"

She blinked rapidly and looked around in confusion. "Our chance?" she repeated. "Our chance for what?"

"To get away!"

That got her attention. She clutched his arm and asked, "What's happening?"

"The Crows are upset about something—" Sinclair turned his head, scanning the plains around them. "And I think I see what it is!" he went on. He pointed. "Look over there!"

"It's just some smoke," Faith said. "So something's on fire. What does that mean?"

"Look around us. See how dry the grass is? And the wind is blowing from that direction."

Faith's mouth rounded as she realized what Sinclair was talking about. "Oh, my God!" she exclaimed. "You mean that fire's going to come this way?"

"It's already doing it, and fast, too." Some of the Crow warriors galloped their horses past, heading east, while others wheeled their mounts and raced back to the west. It looked to Sinclair like their captors were panicking. He went on. "We've got to get out of here!"

"Can we outrun the fire?"

"We can sure try!" He grabbed her hand and pulled her into a run, turning so that they were headed back the way they had come from. He couldn't tell for sure, but he thought they would be more likely to be able to get out of the path of the fire by going in that direction.

All around them was sudden chaos. Some of the Teton Sioux women who had been taken prisoner screamed in terror, and most of the children were crying. Captives raced here and there, ignored for the most part by the Crows. A few of the warriors tried to keep them herded into a bunch, but it was a hopeless task. Panic raced through hearts and minds as swiftly as those onrushing flames leaped across the prairie.

Keeping a tight hold on Faith's hand, Sinclair fought his way through the confusion. They were jostled by other prisoners and nearly trampled by some of the fleeing Crows. Sinclair tried to keep one eye on the steadily advancing smoke, but a sudden angry shout made him wrench his head around the other way. He saw one of the warriors riding straight toward him and Faith, and as the Indian galloped closer, Sinclair recognized the hate-distorted face of Medicine Bull, the Crow war chief.

Clearly, Medicine Bull didn't want his prize slave to escape.

And judging by the tomahawk he held in his upraised hand, ready to strike a deadly blow, he would rather kill Sinclair than allow that to happen.

The smoke from the fire had risen so high and spread so much that it blotted out a large portion of the southern sky. If not for the rolling thunder of hoofbeats, Preacher thought they might have been able to hear the crackling of the flames. He couldn't see the fire itself yet, but he knew that was only a matter of minutes away.

He had expected the Crow war party to remain together, at least to a certain extent, and flee in one direction, hopefully east. But that wasn't happening, he saw, as riders in buckskins and feathers galloped toward him and his companions. Fear had gotten the best of the Crows, and they had scattered, every warrior for himself.

That fear wasn't so overwhelming, though, that none of the warriors noticed the four white men. Several of them did, and they veered their horses toward Preacher, Rip, Carling, and Hodge, screaming out their hate as they attacked.

"Rein in!" Preacher shouted to the others. "Stop and use your rifles! Make your shots count!"

He knew that Faith Carling and Chester Sinclair were still up ahead somewhere, and he hated to slow down before he and the others had found the prisoners. But if they got themselves killed by the Crows, they couldn't help anybody, so he hauled back on the reins and brought his mount to a skidding halt. Instantly, he was out of the saddle, planting his feet firmly on the ground as he lifted his rifle to his shoulder and cocked it. Rip, Carling, and Hodge followed his example.

Preacher settled the rifle's sights on the chest of one of the galloping Indians and pressed the trigger. With a gout of flame and a puff of smoke, the weapon roared and bucked against his shoulder. Blinking through the haze of smoke, he saw his target driven backward off the racing horse by the heavy ball that smashed into his chest.

Rip's rifle blasted, too, followed a second later by those of Carling and Hodge. Two more Indians fell. Preacher didn't know which of the men had missed and didn't care. All that mattered was that the rest of the Crows who had paused in their flight to attack the white men now peeled off and galloped away to the northwest, leaving Preacher and his friends to mount up and race eastward again without taking the time to reload the rifles.

Preacher slung his rifle on his back and drew his pistols as he guided the horse with his knees. The sixty or so warriors and the two dozen prisoners were spread out all over the prairie now. Preacher searched for Faith Carling's red hair, knowing he ought to be able to spot it. He hadn't seen her so far, though, and she and Sinclair were still unaccounted for as more of the Indians raced toward Preacher, savagely whooping at the top of their lungs.

He let them close to within pistol range and then blasted two of them off their ponies. He heard more shots and glanced over his shoulder to see that Rip, Carling, and Hodge had spread out and were emptying their pistols into the Crows.

An arrow cut through the air beside Preacher's ear. He jammed the pistols behind his belt again and unslung the bow from his back. With deft motions born of long practice, he plucked an arrow from the quiver and nocked it, then pulled the bow taut and let fly. He was rewarded by the sight of the arrow lodging deep in the chest of another Crow. The wounded Indian toppled off his horse and landed on the ground so that the arrow was pushed all the way through his body. Preacher caught a glimpse of the bloody arrowhead emerging from the Crow's back.

Then he raced on past, that particular killing already forgotten. There were more Crows to deal with, and the two prisoners he was looking for still hadn't been found.

Not to mention the huge prairie fire that was still bearing down on them, the flames racing closer with every passing second . . .

Sinclair gave Faith a hard shove that sent her spinning off her feet and leaped the other way, putting a little distance between the two of them. Medicine Bull galloped through that opening, slashing viciously at Sinclair's head with the tomahawk. The blow barely missed as Sinclair went rolling on the ground.

He scrambled up as Medicine Bull reined his pony to a halt and wheeled the mount around for another charge. Sinclair wasn't going to just stand still and let the chief come to him, though. Instead, he raced across the grassy space and leaped in the air, tackling Medicine Bull before the chief knew what was happening. The impact drove the Crow off his horse and sent both men crashing to the ground.

They rolled over and came up on hands and knees at the same time. Sinclair saw that the fall had knocked the tomahawk out of Medicine Bull's hand, but that was the only lucky break he had gotten. The chief seemed to be unharmed, and he hated Sinclair as much as ever. As both of them leaped to their feet, Medicine Bull lunged at Sinclair, his arms outstretched as his hands reached for the white man's throat.

Sinclair was taller and perhaps a little heavier, but the chief had lived a long, hard life on the frontier and knew how to fight. He was also a little too fast for Sinclair. He shrugged off the punch that Sinclair landed on his chest and got his hands on his enemy's throat. As they locked in place, Medicine Bull hooked a foot behind Sinclair's ankle and jerked his legs out from under him. Sinclair went down with Medicine Bull on top of him. The chief's iron-hard fingers were clamped around his throat, and Sinclair couldn't get any air past them into his lungs. He stared up wide-eyed into Medicine Bull's face and saw the ugly killing grin that stretched across the chief's mouth.

Sinclair knew at that moment that he was only seconds away from death.

Chapter Twenty-nine

With the thick cloud of gray smoke boiling up to their right, Wingate, Corrigan, Snell, and the rest of the soldiers and trappers saw the Crow warriors galloping across the prairie in front of them. "Fire!" Corrigan shouted, and he wasn't talking about the hellish blaze to the south. He was ordering his men to start shooting at the Indians. Corrigan probably couldn't distinguish between Crow and Sioux, but this time he was unwittingly doing the right thing. The Crows who had raided the Sioux village were all mounted on horseback, and those were the ones the soldiers opened fire on.

It was a skirmish that quickly turned into a full-fledged battle as more and more of the Crows arrived on the scene. Wingate knew they had to be running away from the path of the fire. He would have done the same thing. He had once seen an entire herd of buffalo, thousands upon thousands of the massive, shaggy creatures, stampede right off the edge of a bluff to their deaths rather than face the swift-moving terror of a prairie fire.

Wingate blew one of the Indians off his pony with a rifle shot, then downed another with a pistol. He rode among them, hacking right and left with his tomahawk. Even while he was fighting, he kept an eye out for any of the prisoners.

When he saw a Sioux woman stumbling along and holding tightly to the hand of a little boy, he called to them in their own tongue. "Over here!" he said. "I'll help you!"

He brought his horse to a stop and swung down from the saddle. The woman seemed frightened of him at first, cringing as he grabbed the little boy and lifted him onto the horse's back. Then he gestured for the woman to mount. She did so, realizing at last that he was trying to help them.

He would have climbed up behind the woman, turned the horse around, and gotten all three of them out of there if something hadn't struck him in the back at that moment, knocking him forward against the horse. Knowing that he was hurt, he grabbed the reins, hauled the horse's head around, and snatched off his hat. He slapped it against the animal's rump and sent it leaping away from him in a gallop that carried the woman and the little boy back to the west, away from the fire.

Then Wingate's strength deserted him and he slumped to his knees. He reached behind him, trying to feel for an arrow. When he didn't find a shaft, he figured that he had been shot. He pitched forward onto his face, trying to fight off the blackness that threatened to overwhelm him.

Somebody thrust a foot under his shoulder and rolled him roughly onto his wounded back. Wingate cried out in pain, and then cursed as he stared up blearily into the bearded face of Luther Snell.

"Sorry about shootin' you, Wingate," Snell said, but the grin on his face told Wingate that he wasn't sorry at all. "I seen in your eyes that you know too much about me and my plans. Can't have you talkin' to the lieutenant and ruinin' everything, so I reckon you have to die instead. Shame about you gettin' hit by a stray bullet while we was fightin' them Crows."

Wingate knew Corrigan would believe that lie. The lieutenant would have no reason not to, since he didn't know the truth about Snell. Wingate tried futilely to push himself up, but he lacked the strength.

"So long," Snell said. "No more Rendezvous for you."

Then he stalked off, leaving Wingate lying there with his life's blood running out on the ground.

A red haze swam before Sinclair's eyes as he struck futilely at Medicine Bull but was unable to loose the chief's grip on his neck. He was about to send up a prayer for his own soul and for Faith's safety when he heard a solid *thunk!* and Medicine Bull suddenly spasmed. Sinclair heard the noise again as the pressure from the Crow's fingers finally eased. Medicine Bull let go completely and then toppled over to lie motionless on his side. Sinclair pushed himself up and looked over at the chief.

The head of a tomahawk was lodged firmly in the back of Medicine Bull's skull. Someone had hit him twice with his own weapon, and on the second blow the tomahawk had gotten stuck.

"Is . . . is he dead?" Faith asked, and when Sinclair looked at her he saw the blood splattered on her hands from the first blow.

He got up, breathing heavily and rubbing at his neck for a second. Nodding, he rasped, "He's dead, all right. You saved my life, Faith."

She closed her eyes for a second and shuddered. "I couldn't let him kill you. Let's get out of here, Chester."

That sounded like a fine idea to Sinclair. He grabbed Faith's hand and they started hurrying toward the west again.

Just in the few minutes Sinclair had struggled with Medicine Bull, the smoke cloud had grown and the fire had raced even closer. Sinclair could smell the smoke now, an acrid scent that stung the nose. It made his eyes water, too, and with every deep breath he drew, he could feel it irritating his lungs. He coughed as he stumbled onward.

A shrill yipping made him glance around in alarm. A couple of Crow warriors had spotted him and Faith and were coming after them, obviously bent on riding them down.

"Run!" he gasped, but even as he clung to Faith's hand and pulled her along with him, he knew it was hopeless. They couldn't outrun the Indian ponies.

More hoofbeats sounded. Sinclair looked over his shoulder again and saw that a third mounted figure had edged up between the first two.

This was no Crow warrior, though, despite the buckskins and the long black braids and the eagle feather worn in a headband that the newcomer sported. He lashed out with the tomahawk in his hand at the Crow to his right and sent that man falling to the ground with the well-aimed blow. As he tried to twist around and strike at the other man, though, that warrior thrust a knife into the newcomer's body, driving the blade deeply between his ribs.

"Panther!" Sinclair shouted in horror as he saw his friend suffer that wound.

Panther Leaping lived up to his name in that moment, throwing himself off his pony and crashing into the second warrior who threatened Sinclair and Faith. Both men fell heavily and rolled over and over when they hit the ground. Panther had dropped his tomahawk, but as he reared up he grasped the handle of the knife buried in his side and pulled the weapon free. Blood welled from the wound. Panther lunged forward and drove the knife into the chest of the Crow warrior, pinning him to the ground and then collapsing across his body.

Sinclair and Faith had stopped running when they saw Panther attack the two Crows. Now Sinclair had the presence of mind to grab the reins of Panther's pony as it started past them. All of his strength was needed to haul the animal to a halt.

"Get on!" he told Faith.

"But I . . . I can't!"

"Yes, you can, damn it! I don't know where Panther came from, but he showed up just in time to save us, and I'm not going to let his sacrifice go to waste. We're both getting out of here!"

Faith let out a little cry as Sinclair took hold of her and practically lifted her onto the back of the Indian pony. She had to ride astride, with her skirt pulled up on her thighs. Sinclair pressed the reins into Faith's hands and told her, "Wait for me!"

He ran over to where Panther had fallen. "Panther!" he cried as he dropped to his knees beside the Teton Sioux. He grasped Panther's shoulders and rolled the man onto his back.

Panther grimaced in pain, but then he managed to grin up at the white man. "Sin . . . clair," he said. "Get your woman . . . go . . ." He lifted a bloody hand. "Preacher . . . that way!"

"Preacher's here?" Sinclair leaned over Panther. "Come on, I'll help you. We'll get you out of here, too."

Panther shook his head. "No . . . nothing to . . . go back to . . . tell Preacher I felt . . . the death of my people . . . knew then . . . I would never return." His hand caught hold of Sinclair's and squeezed. "You . . . good friend . . . never forget . . . Panther . . ."

His head fell back, and the fingers that clasped Sinclair's hand relaxed and slipped limply away.

"Damn it!" Sinclair shouted. "Damn it, it's not fair—"

"Chester!"

Faith's voice penetrated Sinclair's grief. He raised his head and looked around.

"Chester," she called, "we need to get out of here. That fire . . ."

He turned his head and saw the flames dancing hellishly to the south, only a few hundred yards away now. Faith was right. There was no time to waste, and no way they could take Panther's body with them.

He stood up and ran over to the pony, catching hold of the hand that Faith extended toward him. He swung up behind her and reached around her to take hold of the reins. Banging his heels against the pony's flanks, he shouted as he sent the animal lunging forward in a run.

It was a race now, a race for life against the onrushing fire.

* * *

Preacher still hadn't seen Sinclair or Faith, but he had spotted some of the other prisoners. He called out to them in Sioux and told them to run hard to the west. Then he pulled his horse to a stop and looked around some more, his gaze sweeping the plains.

He saw Rip Giddens, Willard Carling, and Jasper Hodge about fifty yards away, all of them calling out to terrified captives and urging them on. Riderless ponies milled around, spooked by the smell of smoke, which was growing stronger all the time. Preacher heeled his horse into motion and started rounding up the ponies. He drove half a dozen of them toward Rip and the two Easterners.

"Get those people mounted up!" he shouted to them. "Get 'em out of the way of the fire!"

He whirled his horse around and headed east again as he saw Rip and Carling and Hodge following his orders. He still had to find Sinclair and Faith, and he wanted to see if Panther Leaping had made it, too.

The smoke had blown northward well ahead of the actual flames, and the dense gray coils were beginning to make it difficult to see. Preacher coughed and waved a hand in front of his face. A figure on foot loomed up out of the smoke and clutched at his stirrup. He recognized her as a Sioux woman, one of the captives from the village. As he extended a hand down to her, Preacher said, "Come with me! I'll help you get away!"

She grabbed his hand and eagerly scrambled up behind the saddle. Preacher kept a tight rein on the horse, which was dancing around skittishly because of the smoke and the approaching flames. He stood up in the stirrups and looked around, swiveling his head as he searched for Faith Carling and Chester Sinclair. He knew they had to be here somewhere.

A flash of dark red hair caught his eye, about two hundred yards away. He saw two people riding double and thought one of them might be Faith. Before he could be sure, smoke drifted in front of him, hiding them from his sight. He said,

"Hang on!" to the woman behind him, then kicked the horse into motion and plunged into the smoke.

The thick, choking stuff seemed to hold him back with phantom fingers, but after a few seconds that seemed longer, he broke free of it and rode out into the open again. He saw the two people on horseback he had spotted a moment earlier, and now he was sure that they were Faith and Sinclair. He was about to open his mouth and shout to them when another rider galloped up behind them. Preacher stiffened as he recognized the newcomer.

What the hell was Luther Snell doing out here?

Preacher didn't have time to ponder that question. Snell was bearing down on the horse carrying Faith and Sinclair, and he had a pistol in his hand. Preacher charged forward, hoping he could reach them in time to stop Snell from shooting them.

Faith and Sinclair saw him coming and recognized him. Sinclair shouted something, probably Preacher's name. They rode toward him, seemingly unaware of the threat coming up behind them.

Preacher recalled that Snell had planned to kidnap Willard Carling. Had he been following them all along? Did he already have Carling in his hands and now was trying to get rid of any witnesses? Preacher didn't know. He waved his free hand at Faith and Sinclair, trying to get them to turn aside, out of Snell's line of fire.

The riders had almost all come together before Preacher realized that Snell was aiming at *him*, not at Faith and Sinclair.

And then it was too late to do anything, because the pistol in Snell's hand suddenly gouted smoke and flame. An instant later, the horse underneath Preacher jerked and staggered. The animal's front legs folded up. It collapsed abruptly, sending Preacher and the Indian woman sailing through the air over its head.

Preacher's head slammed into something hard as he landed. That was the last thing he knew. A black nothingness swallowed him whole.

Chapter Thirty

Luther Snell couldn't believe his luck. Not only had he found Chester Sinclair, who was going to make him a rich man, but he had gotten rid of his archenemy Preacher, too. And grabbing that pretty redheaded gal so he and the boys could have some fun with her was just a bonus.

He knew that several of his men were right behind him. He waved them forward, and Euchre, Baldy, Vickery, and the Dimock cousins swept around him and surrounded the startled Sinclair and Faith as they sat on an Indian pony.

"Get 'em outta here!" Snell bellowed. "Don't let anything happen to Sinclair!"

The others leveled pistols at Sinclair and Faith. Euchre said, "You heard what he said! Come on! We gotta get out of the way o' that fire!"

There was no time to waste. The flames were closing in with breathtaking speed. Snell cast a glance at the motionless forms of Preacher and the Indian woman. They hadn't moved since the dying horse had thrown them. Obviously, the fall had knocked them unconscious.

Snell would have liked to kill Preacher slowly and painfully, but he supposed he would have to settle for knowing that Preacher had burned to death. He wheeled his horse around and followed the others as the fire roared closer. The flames were leaping a good fifty feet into the air as they greedily gobbled up the prairie.

Snell and the others were out of sight before Preacher stirred. He lifted his head and shook it groggily. The fire was close enough now that he could feel its heat on his face. He pushed himself onto his hands and knees, then reeled to his feet. His head spun dizzily for a second or two before settling down. He looked around, grimly taking stock of the situation.

His horse was dead. Faith and Sinclair were gone, as was Snell. The smoke was so thick that he couldn't see very far, but nothing was moving in his line of sight except the racing flames. The Sioux woman he had tried to help lay close by, unconscious. It looked like he wasn't going to be able to save her after all. He wasn't even going to save himself. There was no way he could outrun the flames on foot.

That was when a tall, lean figure came stumbling out of the smoke, leading a horse.

"Preacher!" the man croaked.

"Wingate!" Preacher hadn't expected to see the red-bearded trapper. For all he'd known, Wingate hadn't been within a hundred miles of here. Preacher sprang forward as Wingate started to fall and caught him. He caught the horse's reins, too.

When his hand touched the back of Wingate's buckskin shirt, he realized that it was soaked with blood. Wingate was badly hurt, maybe dying.

"What are you doin' here?" Preacher asked.

"Followin' . . . Snell," Wingate gasped. "Bastard . . . shot me . . . in the back . . . so I couldn't tell . . . about him kidnappin' . . . Sinclair."

"You mean Willard Carling?"

Weakly, Wingate shook his head. "Sinclair," he insisted. "Turns out . . . he's a hell of a lot . . . richer'n Carling . . . if Snell's got him . . . prob'ly kill him . . . and the girl, too . . . sooner or later."

Preacher wasn't sure what was going on, but Wingate

seemed to know what he was talking about. They could hash it out later, if they got clear of the fire.

"Let's get you in the saddle—" Preacher began.

"No need," Wingate said. "I ain't gonna . . . make it . . . you get on this horse . . . take that squaw . . . get outta here . . ."

Preacher became aware that the woman had regained consciousness, sat up, and was now chanting her death song. He eased Wingate to the ground as blood trickled from the corners of the trapper's mouth.

"Me dyin' is just one more reason . . . for you to settle the score . . . with Snell!" Wingate gasped. "Find . . . Lieutenant Corrigan . . . go after Snell . . ."

Lieutenant Corrigan? Who the hell was Lieutenant Corrigan? Preacher realized there must have been a lot going on that he hadn't known about.

But again, it simply didn't matter right now. Not with that fire closing in so rapidly.

Wingate grinned up at Preacher. "Shinin' times," he rasped. "Shinin' . . . times . . ."

His head fell back as death claimed him.

Preacher lowered him the rest of the way to the ground and then turned swiftly to the Indian woman. He didn't say anything, just grabbed her and practically threw her onto the horse Wingate had brought him. He leaped up behind her, said, "Hold on tight!" and kicked the horse into a gallop. Riding parallel with the onrushing flames, he headed west.

Faith wasn't sure what was going on. Nothing made sense anymore. First had come that awful moment when she had been forced to pick up the tomahawk Medicine Bull had dropped and hit him in the head with it to keep him from choking Chester to death. She had killed Medicine Bull . . . she, who had always prided herself on her gentle nature, who had devoted her life to the beauty of poetry . . . she had picked up a tomahawk and buried it in some savage's brain.

And it had felt so good for a second, striking out to protect someone who had grown to be important to her. She had felt almost like a savage herself. She knew she ought to be ashamed of that fierceness, but somehow, she wasn't.

Then, just as Preacher had shown up at last and it looked like he would lead them to safety, that awful Luther Snell had come out of nowhere, and he and his men had taken her and Chester prisoner again.

How many times, Lord? she asked herself. How many times were they going to be pressed into captivity?

Seven or eight men in addition to Snell rode around them, forcing them to continue galloping out of the path of the prairie fire. All of them glanced nervously over their shoulders from time to time, checking on the progress of the conflagration. They were afraid that the flames might still catch them, and Faith couldn't blame them for that. She felt the same way herself.

The smoke was thinner where they were, though, and it looked to her inexperienced eye that they might be getting clear of the flames. As long as the wind didn't shift to a more easterly direction, they ought to be all right, she decided.

So she and Chester wouldn't burn to death—but they were still prisoners of a band of obviously brutal men. Snell had shot Preacher's horse right out from under him and left him and some Indian woman lying there to be consumed by the flames.

Faith turned her head and asked despairingly, "Chester, where are they taking us?"

"I don't know," he said.

"What do they want with us?"

"I have no idea, Faith." Chester's voice was grim and angry. "They murdered Preacher and that poor woman by leaving them there, though."

Faith knew that was true, and whatever Snell and the others had in mind for her and Chester, she was sure it wouldn't be anything good.

Ever since she had come out here to the frontier, she had found herself in one dangerous situation after another, she thought. What *had* her brother been thinking when he dragged her along on his ill-fated expedition? Why had Willard insisted on coming out here in the first place? True, the scenery was spectacular, and the Indians, despite their savage ways, did have a certain nobility about them. And many of the trappers, although rough-hewn, possessed a zest for life that made most of the men she had known back in Boston seem pallid and hollow by comparison. Even Chester, who had never impressed her before—whom she had barely noticed most of the time, in fact—had blossomed out here, becoming more of a man than she had ever realized he could be.

But were those benefits worth the constant peril?

Faith was surprised to realize that she didn't know the answer to that question.

And depending on what their captors had in mind for them, she might never get the chance to find out.

She looked back over her left shoulder and saw that they were definitely getting clear of the fire now. Chester's sudden exclamation made her look forward again, and she was shocked to see several soldiers clad in blue-and-red uniforms riding toward them. Relief washed through her. Whatever nefarious plans Snell and his cohorts had, they wouldn't be able to carry them out now. She and Chester could look to the soldiers for protection.

One of the men, an officer to judge by the gold braid on his uniform, held up a hand in greeting. "Mr. Snell!" he called out. "There you are! And you've rescued the prisoners!"

"That's right," Snell said as the two groups came together and reined their mounts to a halt. "Seen any more Crows?"

The young officer smiled. "I believe most of them are dead, and the ones who aren't are no longer a threat to us. They've all fled from that terrible fire."

"You lose any men?"

The officer's smile disappeared. "Unfortunately, yes. These are all the troops that remain in my command."

"This is all of you, eh?" That news seemed to please Snell

for some reason. He leaned forward in the saddle and said sharply, "All right, boys—*now!*"

Snell and the men with him lifted rifles and pistols, and with a roar that was stunning in its loudness and unexpectedness, they fired a volley of shots that smashed brutally into the soldiers. Most of the men, including the young officer, were driven off their horses by the impact of the shots. A few managed to stay in their saddles, but they were too badly wounded to fight back. Their spooked horses ran away, and one by one the men swayed and toppled off to land in limp sprawls on the dusty ground.

Faith screamed when the shots blasted out, and she became aware that she still had her mouth open and the back of her hand pressed to it a few seconds later, as the echoes of the reports rolled across the prairie. Chester's arms tightened around her. There was nothing they could have done to prevent this slaughter, but both of them were horrified by it.

And having witnessed it, Faith was now more convinced than ever that some sort of horrible fate awaited her and Chester at the hands of these ruthless men.

Snell turned toward them and grinned. "Don't worry, folks," he said as if reading Faith's mind. "No harm's gonna come to you. You're worth a whole hell of a lot to me. Well, you are, anyway, Sinclair."

"Me?" Chester said.

"Yeah. You don't know it yet, but you're a rich man . . . and you're gonna make me and all my friends rich, too."

"You're insane!"

"Nope," Snell said with a shake of his head. He had been reloading his pistol as he spoke, and now he tucked the weapon behind his belt. "Come on. We'll circle around to the south o' where that fire burned and head for Saint Looey. When we get there, you'll see what I'm talkin' about."

Chester said stiffly, "Whatever mad plan you have, I won't cooperate with you, Snell."

The man edged his horse closer and chuckled. "Oh, I reckon you will," he said. He reached out and touched Faith's hair, curling some of it around one of his fingers. "That is, if you don't want to see this pretty little gal suffer more than she ever would have in the hands o' them Injuns."

"Chester . . ." Faith said, her voice trembling with fright.

A couple of tense seconds ticked by. Then Chester said thickly, "All right, damn you. Whatever you want. Just don't hurt her."

"I figured you'd come around to my way o' thinkin'," Snell gloated. "Let's get movin'. We got a long way to go. But when we get there, we'll all be rich."

Somehow, Faith knew that she and Chester weren't included in that. When Snell had gotten what he wanted out of them, the only thing they would be—was dead.

Preacher felt like the whole left side of his body was cooked good and proper by the time he and the Indian woman got clear of the fire. The flames were so close, they pounded against the two pitiful humans and the horse in waves of searing heat. If the horse had stumbled and fallen, they would have all been goners.

But as it was, they galloped past the western edge of the blaze when the flames were less than twenty yards away. The fire roared on by behind them as Preacher gradually slowed the horse to a walk. He looked around, hoping to see some more survivors.

"Preacher! Preacher!"

At the sound of a voice shouting his name, Preacher turned to see Rip Giddens, Willard Carling, and Jasper Hodge riding toward him. The faces of all three men were grimy from the smoke, and their clothes were stained with blood in various places. But they were alive and none of them seemed to be badly wounded.

As they came up to Preacher, Rip said, "Lord, it's good to see that you made it out. Have you run into Panther?"

Preacher shook his head. "I was hopin' he was with you boys."

"No," Rip said, "ain't seen any sign of him. Damn it, I reckon he didn't make it."

Preacher looked at Carling and Hodge. "How about you two?"

"We're fine," Carling answered without hesitation, although Hodge looked like he might have disagreed on that point. The journalist didn't say anything, though. Carling went on anxiously, "Did you find Faith and Chester?"

"I saw 'em," Preacher replied grimly, "but they ain't with me."

"Oh, no," Carling said in a hollow voice. "Oh, dear Lord, no."

"I don't know that they're dead," Preacher went on quickly. "Fact is, there's a good chance they're not. But if they're not, then Luther Snell's got 'em."

"Snell!" Rip burst out. "What's he doin' up here?"

"At one time, he was after Willard here, you'll recollect," Preacher said with a nod toward Carling. "Now it looks like he kidnapped Sinclair, because ol' Chester's really rich."

"What?" Carling exclaimed with a frown. "Chester doesn't have any money except what I pay him, and Lord knows that's not much!"

Preacher shrugged. "I'm just goin' by what I heard. Maybe it was wrong and Snell figured if he couldn't grab Willard, he'd get his sister instead."

"I'll pay any amount to get her back safely," Carling said.

"Could be that's what Snell's countin' on."

"Well . . . we have to find them! What are we doing here? Let's start looking!"

"Just a minute," Preacher said. "Where are the Sioux prisoners who got away?"

Rip pointed toward the west. "Over that way. I don't know if they all got out of the fire or not, but there's more'n a dozen of 'em."

Preacher spoke to the woman in her own tongue, telling her to go after the rest of the prisoners. He would have taken her to them, but they couldn't spare the time. Carling was right: They needed to start searching for Snell's bunch. The women and children wouldn't be moving so fast that the woman Preacher had rescued couldn't catch up to them.

She slid down from the horse, caught hold of Preacher's hand for a moment, and pressed it in gratitude. Then she started walking in a swift, steady pace after the others from her tribe who had been carried off by the Crows.

"You look like you been roasted on a spit and somebody forgot to turn you," Rip commented as the four men rode north along the path of the fire.

"I'd be roasted clean through if it wasn't for Wingate," Preacher said.

"Wingate! I didn't know he was anywhere in these parts."

"Neither did I."

Rip frowned. "He didn't make it out neither, did he?"

"Nope. Snell shot him. Before he died, though, Wingate told me about Sinclair really bein' a rich man. He said somethin' about a Lieutenant Corrigan, too."

"Who?" Rip shook his head. "By the Lord Harry, I'm confused."

"I have no earthly idea what's going on," Hodge put in.

"I'm a mite puzzled by it all, too," Preacher admitted, "but I reckon we can boil it down to where it's simple. More than likely, Snell's got Miss Faith and Sinclair and for whatever reason is holdin' 'em prisoner. But either way, it's long past time I found that son of a bitch and killed him."

Chapter Thirty-one

Now that the fire had moved well north of where they were, leaving behind a scorched and blackened plain, Preacher and the other three men waited a short time for the ground to cool, then rode across the devastation, backtracking to the spot where he had encountered Faith Carling, Chester Sinclair, and Luther Snell.

The burned body of the red-bearded trapper named Wingate still lay there, starkly grotesque. It bothered Preacher that they had to leave Wingate there without a proper burial, but there wasn't time for that. Nor did they have time to search for Panther Leaping, whose body no doubt lay somewhere in the path of the fire. That disturbed Preacher, too, but he knew both Wingate and Panther would have wanted them to get on with the chore of rescuing Faith and Sinclair.

The fact that all the grass had been burned off made it even easier to follow the tracks left by the mounts of Snell and his men. The trail led northwestward, out of the charred path of the flames. Less than half an hour after they started following it, Preacher spotted something up ahead.

"Those are saddled horses roamin' around," he said. "Let's see if we can figure out where they came from."

He rode ahead quickly, with Rip, Carling, and Hodge

doing their best to keep up. When Preacher came closer, he could tell that the loose horses he had seen were wearing military saddles. That tied in with Wingate's comment about a lieutenant named Corrigan.

"Up ahead!" Rip said suddenly, pointing. "There's some folks!"

The four men galloped on. Preacher saw a few men sitting on the ground, while others were stretched out motionless on the prairie. They wore red-and-blue uniforms—but some of the red came from the bloodstains on those uniforms.

One of the men stood up unsteadily with his right hand clutching his left arm, which hung limp and useless at his side. As Preacher came closer he saw the gold braid on the man's uniform that signified he was an officer. "Lieutenant Corrigan?" he asked as he reined in.

The man stared at Preacher in astonishment. "You know me?" he said.

"Wingate told me about you. I'm Preacher."

"Preacher! I've heard of you. And these men are . . .?"

"Rip Giddens, Willard Carling, Jasper Hodge," Preacher introduced his companions.

"Mr. Carling," Corrigan said. "Thank God you're alive, sir, if not exactly unharmed."

"Don't worry about me," Carling said. "Have you seen my sister?"

"Yes, sir." Corrigan swayed a little, but remained on his feet. "She was with Mr. Sinclair. They were . . . prisoners of a man called Snell."

"We know about Snell," Preacher said grimly. "What happened to you fellas?"

"Snell and his men attacked us," Corrigan replied, his voice drawn taut with strain from the pain he was in but also edged with bitterness. "We thought we were all on the same side, but they took us by surprise and cut us down. Everyone was killed except for myself and two of my men."

"You trusted Snell," Preacher said. "That was your mistake."

"I know that now." Hope brightened Corrigan's pale face a little as he went on. "Are you going after him?"

Preacher jerked his head in a nod. "Damn right we are. We want to get Miss Carling and Sinclair away from him, and I got a score to settle with Snell. More than one, in fact."

"Take me with you," Corrigan said.

"Looks like you're wounded," Preacher said, gesturing at Corrigan's limp, bloody arm.

Grimacing, Corrigan reached across his body with his right hand, grasped his left hand, and tucked it behind his belt. "Yes, but I can ride," he declared. "And I can fire a pistol, too."

"We ain't got time to hold back," Preacher warned.

"I won't slow you down. Just catch one of the horses for me. I'm ready to go."

The other two soldiers helped each other to their feet. "So are we," one of them said.

Corrigan turned and frowned worriedly at them. "You men are injured—"

"Beggin' your pardon, Lieutenant, but so are you. And maybe worse than us."

Preacher thought that might be true. One of the men had a gash on his side where a pistol or rifle ball had grazed him, but other than being bloody and messy, the wound didn't appear to be too serious. The other man had been hit a little harder in the leg, losing a chunk of meat from his thigh. But if the wound was bound up and he was helped into the saddle, he could ride, and both hands were all right. Chasing after Snell's bunch would be painful for all three of the surviving soldiers, but they could do it.

"Rip, make sure the rest o' those fellas are dead," Preacher said, making up his mind. "I'll round up some horses for the lieutenant and the other two."

"Thank you," Corrigan said. "I don't care how hard it is or how long it takes, I'm going to see to it that Snell and his men are brought to justice."

Within minutes, the rescue party was ready to ride out. Rip

had confirmed that all the other soldiers were dead, and nothing could be done for them. The responsibility of Preacher and his companions lay with the living.

Again, the trail wasn't too hard to follow. Snell probably believed that he had wiped out everyone behind him who might give chase.

He was going to find out—and soon, Preacher hoped—just how wrong he was about that.

After riding for a short distance to the north, the men turned their horses to follow the trail as it curved back to the east, across the burned-out path of the fire. Smoke still rose in the distance to the north, but it wasn't as thick as it had been earlier. The fire was finally dying out. It had probably reached a river or a creek that had halted its progress.

The trail continued to turn until the tracks led southeastward. "They're plannin' on leavin' this part of the country behind," Preacher speculated. "Probably headin' for Saint Looey as fast as they can get there."

"Indeed," Lieutenant Corrigan agreed. "That's where representatives of Mr. Sinclair's late uncle are waiting."

"Yeah, you ain't explained about that yet. Who's Sinclair's uncle?"

"The late Senator Ambrose Sinclair. I'm sure you've heard of him."

Preacher shook his head. "Nope."

Both Carling and Hodge had heard of Senator Sinclair. They brought their horses alongside Preacher and Corrigan, and Willard Carling asked in amazement, "Did you just say that Senator Sinclair is Chester's uncle?"

"Was," Corrigan corrected. "He passed away a few weeks ago."

"That must have been after we left Boston," Hodge said, "and word of his death hadn't gotten to St. Louis before we left there."

"Senator Sinclair was one of the richest men in Massachusetts," Carling said.

"Yes, and he left his entire estate to his nephew Chester,"

Corrigan explained. He went on to tell the others about how the senator and Chester Sinclair's father had been estranged as young men.

"This is incredible," Carling said. "And Chester had no idea of these circumstances?"

Corrigan nodded. "That's my understanding."

Preacher said to Carling, "Snell's had his sights set on kidnappin' you ever since the Rendezvous, but I reckon he's changed his mind now that he knows Sinclair is worth even more. I expect he'll keep Miss Carling a prisoner until he's forced Sinclair to pay up."

"Yes, Chester is enough of a gentleman so that he wouldn't allow a woman to come to harm if he could help it."

Preacher grunted. "There's a hell of a lot more to it than that. Sinclair's in love with your sister."

Carling stared at him for a second before saying, "What? Chester is in love . . . with Faith?"

"Reckon you just never did see it because you were too busy lookin' at whatever you were paintin'," Preacher said dryly.

Carling shook his head and murmured, "I never knew. I just never knew."

Rip put in, "Sinclair'll do anything for Miss Faith, even give up his whole fortune that he didn't know he had."

"But that likely won't save her, or him," Preached added grimly. "Snell won't want to leave anybody behind to testify against him. As soon as he's gotten what he wants, he'll kill both of 'em."

"We have to stop them!" Carling said.

Preacher nodded. "That's what I figure on doin'."

Snell kept them moving at a fast pace all day, but at least Faith and Sinclair were mounted this time, instead of being forced to trot on foot as they had been while they were prisoners of the Indians. They were exhausted anyway, though, by the time Snell finally called a halt for the night.

The area that the prairie fire had burned was miles and miles behind them now. After sunset, but while the western sky was still red with its glow, they came to a small stream bordered by cottonwoods, and that was where Snell decided to make camp.

"Reckon we can have a fire?" one of the men asked Snell as everyone dismounted. He was bald and seemed rather slow in his thinking.

Snell shook his head. "No, there's too damned many Sioux and Arikara and Pawnee in these parts. Might even be some more Crows come down this way from the north. We ain't takin' any chances. It'll be cold camps for us for a while."

There was some complaining from the men about that, but not too much. None of them wanted to cross Snell openly and risk making him mad. They all seemed to know how ruthless he could be.

Sinclair slid down from the horse first and then reached up to help Faith dismount. Even under these dire circumstances, he liked the feel of her trim waist under his hands. As they stood there beside the horse, Snell approached, his hand on the butt of his pistol.

"Hardcastle, you and Singletree tie these two up," he ordered. "Sinclair first."

"You don't have to do that," Sinclair said. "We won't try to escape."

Snell's lip curled in a sneer. "You don't expect me to believe that, do you?"

"Where would we go?" Sinclair waved a hand at the vast prairie around them. "I don't know where we are. I wouldn't have any idea how to get back to the nearest outpost of civilization. It would be utterly foolish for us to try to escape."

"Maybe so." Snell shrugged. "You're gonna be tied up anyway, just because I don't trust you."

Sinclair seethed inwardly as his hands were jerked roughly behind his back and lashed together with rawhide thongs. "At the very least, you don't have to treat Miss Carling this way," he said.

Snell chuckled. "Don't you worry about the lady. She'll be took care of just fine."

Faith's eyes widened with fear at the sound of that, and Sinclair went cold all the way through. The other men laughed softly and exchanged glances. Sinclair knew they planned to abuse Faith. So did she.

He had to try to prevent that. Quickly, he said, "Whatever it is you want from me, I promise you that I'll never cooperate if you lay one finger on Miss Carling. I'll die first."

Snell gestured to one of his men, who kicked Sinclair's knees out from under him and forced him to sit down on the ground next to one of the cottonwoods. Once he was there, a rope was wrapped around his chest and the trunk of the tree, tying him securely to it.

"You really don't know why we grabbed you, do you?" Snell asked. "You ain't got any idea just how rich you really are."

Sinclair stared at him, completely confused now. "I'm not rich. I'm just Mr. Carling's servant, and trust me, the wages he pays me have never been extravagant."

"You damn fool! Your uncle was Senator Ambrose Sinclair."

Faith gasped in surprise. She was still untied, but a couple of the men stood near her, ready to grab her if she tried anything. However, she was too stunned to do anything except look at Sinclair and ask, "Chester, did you know anything about that?"

He shook his head, every bit as shocked by the news as she was. "I . . . I knew that the senator and I had the same last name, of course, but Sinclair isn't *that* uncommon a name. My parents never said anything about it."

"Those soldier boys came out here lookin' for you," Snell went on, "because the senator died and left all his money to you. His friends in the War Department got the Army involved. The lieutenant was supposed to take you back to Saint Looey and turn you over to the lawyers who represent your uncle's estate." A grin spread across his face. "Instead, *we're* gonna take you back, and you're gonna be so grateful to us for our help that you're gonna have a bunch o' money sent to one of the banks there so's you can give it all to us."

Too much had happened. Sinclair was having trouble wrapping his mind around all of it. But he managed to say, "What's going to happen if I don't cooperate with you?"

He was afraid he already knew the answer to that. Snell confirmed the hunch by saying, "Then it'll be too bad for this pretty redheaded gal. Now, I won't lie to you. We're gonna be takin' turns with her all the way back, so she's gonna be pretty hard-used by the time we get there. But she'll be *alive*. You just think on that, Sinclair. She'll be alive. And if you want to keep her that way, you'll do as you're told."

A whole gamut of emotions had ranged over Faith's face as Snell spoke, ranging from terror to loathing to outright revulsion. Now her features were set in angry lines as she said, "Don't listen to him, Chester. My God, let them go ahead and kill me now! I'd prefer that to the humiliating fate this little toad is describing."

Snell's cocky grin disappeared, and his hand moved to the handle of the knife sheathed on his hip. He didn't like being called a toad. "You better watch your mouth, bitch," he snarled. "I want to keep you alive. That don't mean I can't do some carvin' on you if I'm minded to."

Faith's chin rose defiantly. "I'm not afraid of you," she said, even though Sinclair could tell that she certainly was.

"Stop it," he said sharply. "Snell, listen to me."

Snell stopped glaring at Faith and switched his hostile gaze to Sinclair. "You ain't in any position to be givin' orders, mister."

"You have to have my cooperation in order to get your hands on any of that money," Sinclair pointed out. "I'd say that gives me some say in what happens."

"The only thing you got any say in is whether or not this gal lives or dies."

Sinclair shook his head. "No, that's not true. Unless *you* cooperate with *me,* then somewhere on the way back to St. Louis, I will do something that forces you to kill me. Either that, or

I'll leap off a cliff, or throw myself in a river, or something else that results in my death. Listen to me, Snell, and understand: If anything happens to Miss Carling—*anything!*—I'll make sure that you never see a cent of any inheritance I have coming to me." He looked around at the others. "All of you understand that? I'll cooperate freely . . . as long as Miss Carling is completely unharmed."

"Gettin' ridden ain't gonna harm her," one of the men growled.

"Shut up!" Snell snapped. With his eyes narrowed menacingly, he glared at Sinclair and went on. "I don't like bein' threatened."

"Neither do I," Sinclair returned calmly. "And I won't have Miss Carling threatened, either."

"You're a damn stubborn bastard, ain't you?"

"You don't know how stubborn," Sinclair said.

Snell spat disgustedly. "The hell with it! Have it your way, Sinclair." He looked at the other men. "Nobody bothers the lady."

Again, they looked like they wanted to complain, but no one did.

Snell turned back to Sinclair. "But make no mistake about this, mister . . . you better cooperate when we get to Saint Looey, or else what those Injuns had planned for this gal will look like a damned picnic in the park compared to what I'll do to her!"

Chapter Thirty-two

Snell was moving fast, pushing himself, his men, and his prisoners at a hard pace. Preacher had hoped to catch up to them before nightfall, but when it got too dark to continue tracking, he estimated that Snell and the others were still several hours ahead.

Willard Carling didn't want to stop. "We know where they're going," he said. "Why can't we just keep heading in the same direction?"

"Because we might lose the trail and go right past 'em in the dark," Preacher explained. "Or else we could stumble into the middle of 'em and get ourselves killed, not to mention your sister and Sinclair."

Carling sighed and said, "That makes sense, I suppose. Still, I hate to think of Faith being in the hands of those . . . those barbarians any longer than she has to be!"

Preacher nodded. "I understand. Reckon we all do. But it'll be a different story tomorrow."

They made a cold camp, ate sparingly of the rations they had brought with them from the Sioux village, and then stretched out on the ground to get a little sleep. Preacher and Rip took turns standing guard during the night. No one seemed to feel very rested when they set out again early the next morning before the sun came up, as soon as there was enough gray light in the sky for Preacher to be able to see the tracks left by the horses they were following.

The three wounded soldiers began lagging behind, despite Lieutenant Corrigan's promise the day before that they wouldn't hold back the rescue party. Preacher finally had to fall back and tell Corrigan, "You fellas push on as best you can, but we're goin' on ahead."

Corrigan nodded wearily. "Yes, of course. I understand, Preacher. We'll keep coming along and try to catch up later."

Preacher returned the nod and wheeled his horse. He galloped ahead to rejoin Rip, Carling, and Hodge.

"So it's just the four of us again," the journalist said.

"We'll see," Preacher said. "Maybe that'll be enough."

It was around midday when Carling suddenly exclaimed, "Oh, my God! I see something. Is that them?"

"Yep," Preacher replied. "I spotted 'em a ways back but didn't want to say anything until I was sure." He pulled back on the reins and brought his horse to a halt.

The other three men followed his lead, but Carling said anxiously, "What are we stopping for? Shouldn't we be riding even faster, so that we can catch up to them?"

"Out here on these plains, they'd see us comin' for a long way," Preacher said. "They'd be ready for us before we ever caught up to 'em. We've got to hang back now, out of sight, until night falls again and they've made camp."

"Then what?"

"Then Rip and me slip in there and kill all those bastards," Preacher said.

Carling stared at him. "Just like that?"

Preacher nodded. "Just like that."

Faith had been tied to one of the trees the night before, just like Sinclair was, and although he had grown angry when she winced in pain as she was lashed to the cottonwood's trunk, at least she hadn't been molested otherwise. Sinclair didn't know if his threat would keep her safe all the way to St. Louis, but right now he was just grateful that they had survived another night with her honor intact and both of them reasonably healthy.

During the day, the group continued traveling southeastward. Snell said, "We'll hit the Missouri River in a few days, and we can follow it all the way down to Saint Looey. Shouldn't take us more'n a couple o' weeks."

The thought of spending two more weeks as the prisoners of these men was almost more than Sinclair could bear, but they might not have any choice.

"We're gonna run short of supplies before then, Luther," the bald man said. Sinclair had learned that he was called, not surprisingly, Baldy, and he wasn't as dimwitted as he seemed on first impression.

"We'll be all right," Snell said confidently. "We can do some huntin'. In fact, next game we come across, we'll see if we can get us some fresh meat."

That afternoon, they spied a herd of antelope about a quarter of a mile away. Snell picked out several of the men and told them to try to bring down a couple of the animals. "Don't waste a lot of powder and shot, though," he warned them.

The men rode off toward the herd. A few minutes later, Sinclair heard shots as they fired at the fleet-footed beasts. Spooked by the shooting, the antelopes bolted, raising a cloud of dust as they raced off. But two of them were left behind on the ground, never again to run gracefully across the plains. Snell's men set to work dressing out the carcasses. "Fresh meat tonight," Baldy said gleefully, clapping his hands together like a child.

Once the men had harvested all the meat they wanted from the slain antelopes, the group pushed on. They made camp beside another stream as evening began to settle down once more over the prairie.

"We'll risk a fire," Snell decided, "but get that meat cooked in a hurry, because I want the fire out before it gets good an' dark."

While Baldy tended to that, several of the men tied Sinclair and Faith to trees, as they had been bound the night before. The smell of the roasting meat made Sinclair's stomach clench tightly, reminding him of just how little he had eaten for days now. It had been barely enough to keep him going.

Tonight, though, there was plenty of food. Tied up as they were, Faith and Sinclair couldn't feed themselves, but Snell and Baldy cut off pieces of antelope steak, speared the chunks of meat on their knives, and fed the two prisoners that way. Faith wrinkled her nose a little at the somewhat gamy smell and taste of the meat, but she was hungry enough that it didn't stop her from eating.

As Snell had ordered, the fire was extinguished before full darkness had fallen. Comfortable, and with full bellies for the first time in a while, most of the men stretched out on the ground and fell sound asleep in a matter of minutes. Snores filled the air.

Snell was still awake, though, as was the man called Vickery. They had the first guard shift. Even though Snell had mentioned several times that he wasn't worried about anybody coming after them, out here it was always possible that a wandering band of Indians would stumble on them. If that happened, the men would need as much warning as possible so that they could fight back. That was the reason for the guards.

The moon hadn't risen yet, but there was enough light from the stars for Sinclair to be able to see Faith as she sat on the ground several feet away from him, her back pressed against the tree trunk. Even though she couldn't move very much because of the tightness of her bonds, she shifted around as much as she could, trying to find a comfortable position. Sinclair wished that he could take her in his arms and let her rest her head against his shoulder. He was sure both of them would sleep better in each other's embrace. The odds were against them ever getting an opportunity to make that happen, however.

Sinclair wanted to stay awake as much as he could, just to make sure that none of the men got any ideas about trying anything with Faith during the night, but weariness stole over him, making his eyelids heavy and forcing his head to droop forward until his chin rested on his chest.

But he came instantly awake when he suddenly felt the kiss of cold steel against the skin of his wrists.

Somebody was cutting the rawhide bonds that held him to the tree.

The sound of shooting during the afternoon had driven Willard Carling almost into a frenzy.

"They could have run into more Indians!" Carling exclaimed as he bounced up and down a little in the saddle. "We ought to go and see! They may need our help! Faith could be getting scalped right now!"

Preacher reached over and gripped Carling's arm, squeezing hard enough to penetrate the artist's near-hysteria. Carling yelped in pain, but settled down.

"Take it easy," Preacher advised. "I've heard the shots from plenty o' battles in my time, and that doesn't sound like one to me. It's more likely they're doin' some huntin'."

"Hunting?" Carling repeated with a frown.

Rip said, "Yeah, they're prob'ly runnin' short on supplies, just like us. Could be they came across a herd o' buffalo or antelope and went after some fresh meat."

"You really think so?"

Preacher nodded. "Yeah. Listen, the shootin's already stopped."

"What should we do now?"

"The rest of you stay here," Preacher decided. "I'll get close enough to take a look and make sure there wasn't any trouble."

While Rip and the two Easterners waited, Preacher dismounted and scouted ahead on foot, dropping to hands and knees and crawling when he got close enough so that Snell's bunch might have spotted him otherwise. He worked his way close enough to see several of Snell's men skinning and dressing out the carcasses of a couple of antelope. He and Rip had guessed correctly.

Carling heaved a sigh of relief when Preacher returned and reported what he had seen. "Did you see Faith?" Carling asked. "Could you tell if she was all right?"

"Her and Sinclair were ridin' double," Preacher said. "Looked like their hands were tied. But as far as I could tell, they both seemed to be fine other than that."

"Thank God."

Rip said, "It's good that they shot them antelope."

Preacher nodded in agreement.

"Why?" Jasper Hodge asked with a frown. "What does it matter?"

"Because tonight when they stop to make camp, they'll likely cook some steaks and have themselves a little feast," Preacher said. "Man with a full belly sleeps sounder than one who's on short rations."

"Oh," Hodge said, seeing the light. "You mean it'll be easier to sneak up on them."

"That's what I just said, ain't it?"

They continued following the larger group of riders. At dusk, the smell of roasting meat drifted to their nostrils. Preacher and Rip exchanged grins.

"Goodness, that smells delicious," Carling said. "I hadn't realized how hungry I am until I caught a whiff of those . . . what did you call them, antelope steaks?"

"That's it," Preacher said.

Rip added, "And if we're lucky, it'll be the last meal for those ol' boys."

That comment cast a grim air over the four men as they rode slowly across the plains. A few minutes later, Preacher had them dismount.

"Now we wait," he said.

Time dragged by as the sunset glow faded from the sky and stars began to appear in the deep blue-black vault of the heavens. Darkness cloaked the landscape, and still Preacher waited.

Finally, when several hours had passed, he said quietly, "Here's what we'll do. Rip and I will go in first, bein' mighty quiet about it, and try to get to Sinclair and Miss Faith before anybody knows we're there. We'll cut them loose and send them out of the camp before we open up on Snell and his pards. When you fellas hear the shots, you come chargin' in on horseback. You'll be leadin' the other two horses. Come a-shootin' . . . but make sure you know *who* you're shootin' at before you pull the triggers."

Hodge asked, "Can't we just try to free Sinclair and Miss Carling without killing all those men?"

"If we leave 'em alive, they'll be right behind us on our trail, just itchin' to kill us," Preacher said. "I don't know about you, but I'm tired o' messin' with 'em. They opened this ball. They can damn well dance to the tune they called."

"Damn right," Rip added with a solemn nod.

"I agree," Carling said. "These are evil men, Jasper, and I, for one, intend to deal with them in the manner in which they should be dealt."

Preacher grinned and clapped a hand on Carling's shoulder. "You've got more sand than I gave you credit for at first, Willard. I reckon you'll do."

Carling rested a hand on the butt of his pistols and said, "Jasper and I will be ready when the time comes for us to make our move, Preacher. You can count on us."

"Yep. I believe I can."

With that, Preacher and Rip stole off into the darkness, heading for the camp on the bank of the stream. They worked their way around so that they could approach the place from downwind.

The fire had been out for hours, but a faint, mingled scent of burning wood and roasting meat lingered on the night breeze. Preacher and Rip moved in utter silence, not needing to talk to know what they were doing. Both men had crept through the night intent on dealing death on other occasions. They split up, moving through the tall grass about ten yards apart with such stealth that it appeared the blades were simply rustling in that breeze.

Several of the men in the camp were snoring loudly. That would help to cover up any slight sounds Preacher and Rip might make. It was an indication, too, of how soundly the kidnappers were sleeping.

Preacher raised his head enough to get a look at the camp in the starlight. He located the trees where Sinclair and Faith were tied and pointed them out silently to Rip. Then they resumed their slow, careful approach. Preacher drew his knife from its sheath with the barest whisper of steel against soft leather.

He was behind the tree where Sinclair was tied. As he reached it and began to saw through the rawhide bonds, he heard the sharp intake of breath from Sinclair and saw the way the man jerked a little as he came awake. Preacher's mind went back to how Sinclair had reacted when the Sioux were holding the Easterners prisoner and Preacher had tried to free them. That night, Sinclair had provoked a bloody battle by yelling out.

This time, though, after the first startled inhalation, Sinclair was silent. Preacher finished cutting the bonds, and then came up on his knees so that he could put his mouth next to Sinclair's ear and whisper, "It's Preacher. When I tell you, get up, grab Miss Faith, and run. Get across the stream if you can. And stay low. Lead's gonna be flyin'."

Sinclair turned his head. "I can stay and fight," he breathed. Even though his hands were now loose, he hadn't brought his arms around in front of him yet. He just flexed the muscles in them, getting the feeling back but not revealing to anyone who might be looking that he was free.

"No," Preacher said. "Get the girl. Get outta here."

After a second, Sinclair jerked his head in a little nod of agreement. Preacher glanced over at the tree where Faith was tied. He couldn't see Rip because his fellow frontiersman was on the other side of the tree. But Faith was sitting up straighter now and seemed to be wide awake, although it was difficult to be sure in the dim light.

Preacher sheathed his knife and stood up, staying as close to the tree trunk as he could so that he would blend in with its shadow. When he was on his feet, he wrapped his fingers around the butts of his pistols and pulled them from behind his belt. With his thumbs looped over the hammers, he said softly to Sinclair, "Go!"

Sinclair lunged upright, leaped across to the other tree, and grabbed Faith as she shook off the bonds that Rip had just cut. One of Snell's men yelled, "Hey!" He surged up off the ground as Faith and Sinclair splashed into the shallow stream. "They're gettin' away!"

Preacher stepped away from the tree, leveled his right-hand pistol, and fired at short range, the double load blowing a hole right through the man.

Time for the killin' to commence.

Chapter Thirty-three

One of Rip's pistols boomed a second later, and another man yelled in pain as he was ventilated by hot lead. Preacher swung to his left and lifted the pistol in that hand. Two more of Snell's men had jumped up in alarm, and were dumb enough to be standing close together. Preacher pulled the trigger. The double-shotted pistol roared and both men were thrown backward by the impact of the heavy balls that struck them. One was hit high in the chest, while the other doubled over against the horrible pain where his gut was ripped open.

Preacher dropped the empty pistols and yanked out knife and tomahawk as Rip's second gun blasted. Whirling, Preacher slashed a man's throat and caved in another's skull with the tomahawk. At that moment, hoofbeats thundered and four horses raced into the camp, two being ridden by Willard Carling and Jasper Hodge, the other two being led by the Easterners. Several of Snell's men had to leap aside to avoid being trampled. Carling shot one of them and kicked another in the chest. That kick sent the man staggering backward so that Rip Giddens could loop an arm around his neck from behind, jerk his chin up, and swipe a keen knife blade across his throat, cutting so deep the steel grated on the luckless man's upper spine. Rip flung the blood-gushing corpse aside.

Preacher heard Snell bellowing curses. He didn't know how many of the enemy were left, but a couple of the men broke and run, undoubtedly terrified by this unexpected, bloody raid out of the darkness. Preacher didn't think either of them were Luther Snell, so he was willing to let them go.

They didn't go far, though, because more shots rang out and more hoofbeats sounded. Preacher lifted his tomahawk, ready to throw it, as three men rode into the camp. He relaxed a little when he recognized them as Lieutenant Corrigan and the two wounded soldiers, who had finally caught up with Preacher and the others just in time to cut down the fleeing men.

"Where's Sinclair?" Corrigan asked as he reined his horse to a halt.

"Where's Faith?" Carling added.

Preacher started to reply that they had fled across the creek when a frightened scream came from that direction. The voice belonged to Faith Carling.

"Faith!" her brother yelped in alarm.

Preacher was the closest to the stream. He splashed across it and saw a couple of figures lunging around as they struggled desperately with each other. He heard Snell cursing in a low voice and figured that was Chester Sinclair he was wrestling with. "I'll kill you!" Snell babbled. "Kill you both!"

Willard Carling ran past Preacher, yelling, "Faith! Faith!"

"Willard!" she cried. She was sprawled on the ground not far from Sinclair and Snell. Carling dashed over to her and caught her up in his arms.

Preacher warily circled the battling men. He couldn't risk a throw with his knife or tomahawk for fear of hitting Sinclair. The Easterner was bigger than Snell, but he wasn't as experienced and didn't fight with the same sort of maniacal fury as the smaller man. Starlight suddenly flashed on steel as Snell managed to sink his knife into Sinclair's body. Sinclair gasped in pain and staggered back a step as Snell ripped the blade free. Sinclair lost his balance and fell. Snell loomed over him, ready to strike again.

That was when Preacher stepped in front of him and said, "Luther."

Snell looked up, raising his head slightly. He opened his mouth to say something, perhaps Preacher's name. His eyes widened—

Then the head of Preacher's tomahawk struck squarely between them, cleaving flesh and bone and burying itself in the putrid mass of Luther Snell's brain.

Preacher let go of the tomahawk and stepped back. Snell stood where he was for a second, twitching as the rest of his body caught up to the fact that he was dead. Then he folded up like a rag doll, crumpling onto the ground never to rise again.

Preacher turned away, no longer caring about the lifeless hulk that had been Luther Snell. He had felt an instant of fierce satisfaction as he avenged the death of Mountain Mist, but that was over now. He had other things to worry about.

Kneeling next to Chester Sinclair, he helped the big Easterner sit up. "How bad did he get you?" Preacher asked.

"Not . . . too bad . . . I don't think," Sinclair rasped. He had a hand pressed to his left side, with blood welling darkly between the fingers. "Faith . . . is Faith . . .?"

"I'm here, darling," she said as she threw herself down on Sinclair's other side. She put her arms around him and hugged him close, sobbing in mingled relief and fear. "Oh, God, Chester," she sniffled, "don't you die on me! Don't you dare die on me!"

Sinclair chuckled through his pain and said, "I don't reckon . . . you'll get rid of me that easy."

Preacher put a hand on his shoulder and squeezed. "You'll be all right, Chester," he said. He got up and turned back toward the others, who had all come across the creek from the corpse-littered camp. "Rip?"

"They're all dead," Rip answered, knowing what Preacher was asking. He scratched at his beard. "You reckon it's really over this time, or will we have to fight some Injuns a time or two 'fore we get to wherever we're goin'?"

Preacher threw back his head and laughed. "Hell," he said, "I don't even *know* where we're goin'!"

In the end, they went to St. Louis, because Lieutenant Corrigan insisted on it. But that wasn't until they had buried Snell and the other dead men and spent several days camped a short distance downstream from the site of the battle, allowing the wounded members of the party to heal a little before resuming their journey.

Chester Sinclair had a deep gash in his side, but with Faith nursing him night and day, Preacher had little doubt that Sinclair would be just fine. The same held true for Corrigan and the two soldiers, although they didn't get the same sort of loving care that Sinclair did.

When Corrigan started making noises about doing his duty and delivering Sinclair to St. Louis, Sinclair said bluntly, "I don't want to go." He held up a hand to forestall Corrigan's inevitable protest. "But I will. I'll meet with my uncle's lawyers and sign anything they need me to sign, but I'm not staying in St. Louis and I'm not going back to Boston."

Corrigan frowned at him. "Then what are you going to do?"

"I'm coming back out here."

"That's a splendid idea!" Willard Carling said. "While I'm in St. Louis, I'm going to outfit a whole new expedition, since I didn't get to finish the first one. Chester, I'll still need an assistant. . . . No, wait a moment. You're a rich man now, I hear. I don't suppose you'll want to be my assistant anymore."

"I could be your partner," Sinclair suggested. "I'll furnish all the supplies, and you can furnish the talent . . . Willard."

Carling grinned and stuck out his hand. "It's a deal!"

Faith pointed out, "Neither of you have asked my opinion about this."

Both men instantly looked crestfallen. Sinclair said, "I really want to go back to the mountains, Faith . . . but I suppose if you have your heart set on returning to Boston . . ."

She smiled and shook her head. "I'd prefer not to live in the wilderness permanently . . . but after everything that's happened, I think I can manage for a while longer."

Rip turned to Jasper Hodge and asked, "How about you, Mr. Hodge? You goin' back to the mountains with the rest of us?"

"Good Lord, no," Hodge said without hesitation. "I already have more than enough material for the book I plan to write." A little shudder went through him. "The sooner I put this savage country behind me, the better." He suddenly looked thoughtful. "The savage country . . . you know, that might just work as the title of my book."

Carling turned to Preacher and said, "You'll come with us, won't you, Preacher?"

"Yeah, I believe I will," he replied. With a grin, he added, "Somebody's got to come along and keep you folks out of trouble."

Rip nudged him in the side with an elbow and grinned. "Seems to me like you're the one trouble's followin' around, Preacher. It pops up pert-near ever'where you go."

"Yeah," Preacher said slowly as he rubbed at his bearded jaw and frowned. "It does, don't it?"

Two months later . . .

Preacher already knew that the Teton Sioux village was gone. Lieutenant Corrigan had told him about how the soldiers, along with Snell's men, had attacked the place and killed Badger and the rest of the warriors. Preacher wanted to hate Corrigan for that, but the lieutenant had been taken in by Luther Snell. Corrigan had been duped, but he wasn't evil.

Preacher was glad, though, when the young officer stayed in St. Louis. Corrigan had some more growing up to do before he would be ready for another assignment on the frontier. Preacher hoped his superior officers had the sense to see that.

Willard Carling painted a picture of the remains of the destroyed village. Preacher thought it was mighty fine and said so. Carling nodded and said, "I want people to see this for themselves. It's the beginning of the end for the Sioux and all the other red men, isn't it, Preacher?"

"More than likely," Preacher agreed. "This is a mighty big country and ought to be big enough for everybody . . . but you can already see signs that ain't the way it's gonna be."

"A vanished way of life," Carling murmured. "But I'm going to capture as much of it as I can, so that people won't completely forget it."

That struck Preacher as a good thing to do.

The best thing that came out of his return to this scene of so much tragedy and death was his reunion with Horse and Dog. Both animals had been waiting for him. They had been living off the land for a couple of months, but they were both fat and happy since it was summer and the grass and the rabbits were plentiful.

One evening as the sun was going down, Preacher climbed to the top of a small hill overlooking the camp that had been set up down below. He heard Faith and Sinclair laughing together, and saw Willard Carling standing in front of a canvas propped on an easel, hard at work on a landscape depicting a setting sun over the rugged, beautiful mountains. Preacher sat down on a rock, and Dog sat on the ground beside him. He scratched behind the big cur's ears. He would stay with the expedition for the rest of the summer, he supposed, but come fall, the others would be returning to St. Louis and ultimately Boston. Faith had already started talking about a wedding sometime during the winter, and Sinclair sure wasn't disagreeing with her.

They would go back without Preacher, though. He had missed most of the spring trapping season, and didn't intend to miss the one this fall.

He had been thinking, too, about what Rip had said about trouble following him around. His mind went back over the years, and he knew it was true. Ever since the night he had slipped out of his folks' house back on the farm and started walking away from that settled life, he had seen more trouble, more blood and death, than most men would see in several lifetimes. And as he gazed off into the evening shadows, he seemed to see even more ahead of him. Phantom images danced in those shadows . . . beautiful women and evil men, stalwart friends and those who would betray him, good and bad, hope and despair, love and death . . .

And always, always, in those fading shadows, the blaze of guns . . .

Beside him, Dog whined softly, and Preacher shook those phantoms out of his head. "You're right," he told Dog. "It's about time for supper."

He stood up, and together they went down the hill.

Frank Morgan, The Last Gunfighter,
is back in this action-packed new novel!
Turn the page for an exciting preview of:

THE LAST GUNFIGHTER: AVENGER

From *USA Today* bestselling author
William W. Johnstone with J. A. Johnstone

Coming in March 2007!

The Last Gunfighter: Avenger
ISBN 0-7860-1737-6
Available wherever Pinnacle Books are sold

Chapter One

Once, for a brief moment in time, this place had been a boomtown, a trail-drive town, the railhead where thousands upon thousands of cattle had been loaded on trains to begin their long journey to the slaughterhouses of Chicago.

But then the railhead had moved on farther west, taking the hell-on-wheels with it, and in the twenty-some-odd years since then, the town had settled down into a sleepy little farming community where nothing much ever happened.

On this Tuesday morning, that was all about to change.

Six men rode in about eight o'clock. The eastbound train was due at nine. The men tied their horses at the hitch rack in front of the depot and walked across the street to the hash house run by the Chinaman, Ling Wo. They had flapjacks, scrambled eggs and bacon, and coffee as they sat at a table and talked quietly among themselves. Nobody paid much attention to them. At first glance, they were ordinary-looking men.

That was because their coats covered the butts of their six-guns. Those guns gleamed with care, and the walnut grips were well worn from long use.

The men took their time eating. Around five minutes to nine, one of them took out a big fancy pocket watch, flipped it open, and checked the time. He looked around the table at the other men, nodded, and snapped the watch closed. As he stood up, he slipped the timepiece back in his pocket. The other men got to their feet as well.

The purposeful way in which they moved toward the door of the hash house was the first hint that something might be wrong. The strangers were brisk and businesslike now. As they stepped out of the building, the sound of a train whistle came clearly through the morning air. The easthound was on schedule.

Hell, it was even a couple of minutes early.

The men crossed the dusty street to their horses and shucked Winchester repeaters from saddle boots. Then they walked around the red-brick depot building to the platform, instead of going through the lobby. A few townspeople stood on the platform, waiting to either board the train or meet somebody who was getting off. Some of them glanced curiously at the strangers.

A couple of older men, who had been to see the elephant a time or two in their lives, looked with narrowed eyes at the strangers and then turned to walk quickly into the depot, as if they were getting out of the way of something.

The train was in sight now, chugging steadily toward the station from the west, black smoke rising from the diamond-shaped stack on the big Baldwin locomotive. The man who had checked his watch stepped to the edge of the platform, leaned out slightly to peer along the tracks, and then nodded in satisfaction. He turned to the other five and repeated the nod.

Inside the station, one of the old-timers was talking quickly and earnestly to the stationmaster. The stationmaster frowned dubiously at first, but after a minute, he nodded and gestured to one of the boys who worked at the depot. He gave some quick instructions to the boy, who then hurried across the lobby, banged through the doors, and took off at a run down the street, in the direction of the marshal's office.

He wasn't going to get there in time. The train was already pulling into the station.

Frank Morgan's long legs were stretched out in front of him and his hat was tipped down over his eyes. He never slept very well on a train, so, earlier that morning, after he'd gotten some coffee and a bite to eat in the dining car, he'd returned to his seat for a nap. He didn't fall completely asleep, but he rested a little while remaining alert. That habitual caution was ingrained so deeply within him that it would always be a part of him, he supposed.

When the train began to slow, Frank felt it and raised his head. He opened his eyes and saw the conductor coming along the aisle. The conductor called out the name of the town where the train was about to stop. It didn't mean much to Frank. The train was somewhere in Kansas; that was all he knew.

Frank thumbed his hat back on thick dark hair streaked liberally with gray. He wore a faded blue work shirt with the sleeves rolled up a little on his muscular forearms. The legs of his denim trousers hung outside the tops of well-worn horseman's boots.

His clothes might be nondescript, but his ruggedly handsome face possessed a power that sometimes made folks look twice at him. He didn't appear to be a wealthy man—but he was. One of the richest hombres west of the Mississippi, in fact, with business interests scattered from the Rio Grande to the Canadian border. Frank Morgan didn't pay much attention to those business interests, though. He had a whole passel of lawyers and accountants in Denver and San Francisco to do that. He watched them just closely enough to know that nobody was trying to cheat him.

No, judging by appearances, Frank Morgan was little more than a saddle tramp. A drifter.

But the Colt Peacemaker on his hip told a different story. He wasn't just a drifter. He was *The* Drifter. A fast gun whose fame had spread across the frontier for years. A gunfighter in an era when civilization was on the ascendant and men such as Frank Morgan mostly had been bypassed by time.

Not completely, though. Frank wasn't obsolete just yet.

The conductor knew who he was and approached him with obviously mixed emotions. Frank could have sat on the board of directors of this railroad if he had chosen to do so, which meant the conductor had to treat him with some deference. On the other hand, Frank was a known killer who had gunned down countless men, and that made him an abomination to the conductor's civilized nature. In the end, the man's respect for money won out over his distaste for violence, and he forced a polite smile onto his face as he asked, "Everything all right this morning, Mr. Morgan?"

"Just fine," Frank said quietly in a deep, controlled voice. The train lurched a little as its brakes began to take hold. "We going to be stopped here long?"

"No, sir, just long enough to take on any passengers and freight we've got waiting for us."

Frank nodded. "Long enough for me to get out and stretch my legs a little, though? I'm a mite stiff after last night."

"We would have been happy to find a sleeping berth for you, Mr. Morgan—"

"You mean you would have kicked somebody out of a berth they had reserved," Frank cut in. He shook his head. "I'll sit up all the way to Chicago before I'll do that."

"Well, ah, in answer to your question, we'll be stopped here for at least five minutes if you want to walk around a little."

"Thanks."

The conductor moved on as the train rocked to a stop. Frank glanced over through the windows by the seats on the other side of the aisle. That was the side the station platform was on. He saw six men standing there with rifles in their hands. As Frank watched, the group split up, three going toward the front of the car, three toward the rear.

"Oh, hell," he said softly.

He came swiftly and smoothly to his feet, his brain already

racing as he decided on his course of action. The vestibule at the rear of the car was closer, so he turned in that direction. He wanted to get out of the railroad car as quickly as possible, out where he would have more room to move and where not as many innocents would be endangered by the lead that was about to fly.

Several people turned their heads to look as Frank strode down the aisle. He heard a few startled mutters behind him as some of the passengers realized that something might be wrong. Then he reached the vestibule, stepped through it, and out onto the car's rear platform. His hand was already reaching for the Peacemaker on his hip as he turned toward the station platform.

The three rifle-toters got there at the same time. Their eyes widened as they looked up at him and saw that he was ready for them. One of the men yelled, "Rance! He's back here!"

Then they jerked their rifles up.

Frank's Colt whispered from leather. He fired from the hip, putting a bullet in the chest of the man who had shouted. The lead punched the man backward a couple of steps before he lost his balance and fell.

Frank turned slightly and fired again, so fast that so that none of the riflemen had had a chance to get a shot off yet. His second bullet shattered the shoulder of a would-be killer and sent the man spinning off his feet.

The third man managed to fire the rifle in his hands, but he rushed the shot and the bullet spanked off the brass fitting at the corner of the railroad car. Frank's Colt blasted a third time. The last of the gunmen who had come in this direction doubled over as the slug tore agonizingly into his belly. He dropped his rifle, clutched his stomach, folded up, and collapsed on the station platform as blood welled over his fingers.

Frank spun around and leaped off the other side of the train. He landed agilely and dropped into a crouch. There was open ground on this side of the train, and no place to hunt some cover. He ran toward the front of the car, bending low.

As he ran he glanced underneath the car, hoping to spot the

legs of the other three men who wanted to kill him so that he could tell what they were doing. All he could see, though, was the raised station platform.

He had nearly reached the front of the car when two of the assassins bounded across the platform at the back of it and began firing at him. He whirled toward them and went to one knee, squeezing off a couple of shots as he crouched.

One of the riflemen lurched, blood spurting from the side of his neck where Frank's bullet had ripped it open. He stumbled around wildly for a second before falling in a limp sprawl.

The other man was hit in the body, but somehow he managed to stay on his feet and keep firing. His aim was none too accurate. Bullets from the Winchester whistled over Frank's head.

Frank's problem now was that the gun in his hand was empty. Under normal circumstances, like riding on a train, he carried it with the hammer resting on an empty chamber, and he had expended all five rounds that the cylinder held. There were fresh cartridges in the loops on his belt, but he would need a few seconds to reload, preferably when slugs weren't coming so close to him that he could hear the wind-rip of their passage beside his ear.

He threw himself to the side, rolling over the rail and under the train. The rough gravel of the roadbed poked at him through his shirt. Coming to rest on his belly, he opened the revolver's cylinder, dumped the empties, and reached behind him to pluck live rounds from the loops of the shell belt. As he began to thumb them into the cylinders, he heard a man shout over the low rumble of the engine, "The bastard's under the train, Rance!"

"Well, find him, damn it!" came the reply in a harsh, gravelly voice.

Frank snapped the Colt's cylinder closed and crawled toward the rear of the car. The sound of the engine would cover up the crunching of the gravel underneath him as he moved. He looked over and saw the booted feet of the man who was searching for him. The gunman was moving slowly and carefully toward the front of the car. Frank could have broken his ankle with a shot, but instead he planned to wait until the assassin had gone on by, then roll out behind him.

That plan fell apart before it had a chance to develop. The rumble of the engine suddenly got louder, and the drivers clattered as they engaged. The train began to move, rolling slowly eastward. Frank's cover was leaving.

The leader of the killers, the man called Rance, must have run up to the engine and climbed into the locomotive's cab. A gun at the engineer's head would force him to move the train.

Frank jammed his gun back in its holster and rolled onto his back. He probably had time to slip out from under the car before the train started moving too fast, but instead he reached up and grabbed hold of the undercarriage. He lifted his feet and twisted his ankles around a pipe. As he pulled himself up he came clear of the roadbed. The train carried him along as he hung on tightly.

He clung there like a burr until he judged that the caboose was clear of the station. Then he dropped off, timing his move so that he would fall between cross-ties and ignoring the pain that shot through him as his back jolted heavily against the roadbed. The rest of the train passed over him, and when its shade was gone, the morning sunlight jabbed abruptly against Frank's eyes. He squinted and rolled onto his belly again, drawing his gun as he did so.

The man he had wounded a few moments earlier was standing beside the tracks, across from the station platform, looking around in confusion. Clearly, he had expected to find Frank lying in the roadbed once the train was gone.

"Hey!" Frank called.

The man whirled toward him, bringing up the rifle, but before he even started to line up a shot, the Peacemaker in Frank's hand cracked. The range was a little long for a handgun, but Frank had plenty of experience at making such shots.

The slug thudded into the killer's chest and drove him backward as if he had been punched by a giant fist. His arms went up in the air and the Winchester flew from suddenly nerveless fingers. He crashed down beside the steel rails.

With that threat disposed of, Frank leaped to his feet and turned toward the train.

He saw immediately that he'd been a little too slow. Rance had already climbed down from the cab of the locomotive, bringing the engineer with him. He had his left arm looped tightly around the man's neck, and his right hand held a pistol with the muzzle pressed hard against the engineer's head.

"Drop your gun, Morgan!" Rance yelled as he forced the engineer closer to Frank. "Drop it or I swear I'll blow this poor bastard's brains out!"

Chapter Two

Frank tried not to look into the engineer's eyes, which were wide with terror. Instead, he kept his gaze fixed on the gunman and said, "You know I can't do that, Rance."

"You know me?" Rance looked a little surprised at that.

As a matter of fact, Frank had never seen the man before. He had seen the type, though, too many times to count. A hired gun, a cold-blooded killer. Maybe a little smarter than the run-of-the-mill shootist, judging by the way he'd had his men approach the train. But in the end he was just another gunman.

Frank didn't say that. He said, "Sure. I know if I drop my gun, you'll ventilate me a second later. So I can't do it."

Rance pressed harder on the engineer's temple with the gun barrel. "I'll kill him!"

Frank's shoulders rose and fell in a minuscule shrug. "That's too damned bad, isn't it? Maybe what you should do is drop *your* gun. Your boys are lying back there at the station, either dead or shot up so bad they're out of this fight, and I'll wager that the local law is on its way. But you haven't done anything today that's a hanging offense. You haven't killed anybody. So unless you're wanted for something else, you can surrender and live through this, Rance."

There was no emotion on Rance's weathered, rugged face. "The hell with that," he said. "I took money to do a job. I aim to do it."

"Took money from who?" Frank asked. He had a pretty good idea of what the answer was, but some confirmation of his hunch would be nice.

"Go to hell, gunfighter."

"I hope you enjoyed spending Dutton's money," Frank said.

The slight widening of Rance's eyes told Frank that he'd been right about who hired the killers. Then Rance jerked his gun toward Frank and fired.

The shot went wild because the gun in The Drifter's hand had roared a shaved instant of time earlier. Frank's bullet had already sizzled past the engineer's ear, aimed at the narrow slice of Rance's face that Frank could see. It struck Rance in the right eye and bored on into his brain just as the gunman pulled the trigger. The .45 slug went all the way through and burst out the back of Rance's skull in a spray of blood, bone splinters, and gray matter. He stood there for a second with his arm still around the engineer's neck, before the rest of his body caught up with the fact that he was dead. Then he let go, slid down to his knees, and toppled onto his side.

The engineer fell the other direction, passing out from fear and strain and the sudden relief of realizing that he was still alive.

Before Frank could holster his gun, a man's voice called from behind him, "Drop it! Drop that gun, mister! I got a scattergun pointed right at you!"

Frank didn't move. He asked, "Are you the law?"

"That's right. I'm the town marshal here, and I got a shot-gun and two deputies that're armed, too. You gonna put that gun down, or do we have to shoot?"

"Take it easy, Marshal," Frank said. He bent forward and carefully placed the Colt on the roadbed. Then he straightened and lifted both hands to shoulder level. "I'm turning around now."

"Do it slow and careful-like, and don't try nothin' funny."

Frank did as he was told, and saw that the marshal was a stocky, middle-aged man with graying red hair. He was flanked by a couple of much younger and more nervous deputies. They worried Frank more than the marshal did. The local badge had the look of an experienced man who wouldn't panic and start shooting unless he had good reason to.

"It's all over, Marshal," Frank said, keeping his voice calm and steady. "Why don't you tell your deputies to lower those Greeners? I'd hate for one of them to go off accidentally."

"Won't be nothin' accidental about it if you try anything," the lawman warned.

"I'm not going to. All I did was defend myself. Those men met the train with the sole intention of killing me. They were hired guns."

The marshal frowned. "Who the hell are you, that somebody would send six bushwhackers after you?"

"My name is Frank Morgan."

That meant something to all three of the star-packers. The eyes of the younger men got even wider. "Hell, he's The Drifter!" one of the deputies exclaimed. "He's in some o' those yellowbacks I read!"

Frank tried not to sigh. Not for the first time, he thought there ought to be a law against pasty-faced scribblers making up a bunch of rubbish about real people and publishing it in dime novels.

"The Drifter, eh?" the marshal said. Without taking his eyes off Frank, he ordered his deputies, "Lower those scatter-guns. Unless he's got another gun hid somewhere on him, he's unarmed, and I ain't never heard nothin' about Frank Morgan carryin' a hide-out." The lawman tucked his own Greener under his arm. "Now, what's all this about, Morgan?"

"I'd be glad to come down to your office and tell you all about it, Marshal, but only if you can convince the conductor to hold the train for me. I don't want to have to wait until the next eastbound comes through to be on my way."

"I'll see what I can do . . . but don't forget, you ain't the one givin' the orders here." The marshal turned his head and snapped at one of the deputies, "Go check on them fellas who got shot. Some of 'em might still be alive. Josh, you go fetch the doc." As the deputies hurried to carry out the commands, the marshal asked Frank, "Did Endicott get hit?"

"Who?"

"Cleve Endicott. The engineer."

"Oh." Frank shook his head. "No, I don't think he's hurt. Looked to me like he just fainted."

For the first time, a hint of amusement appeared on the lawman's rugged face. "Swooned like a gal, eh? He'll get some ribbin' about that. I might've done the same thing, though. I saw that shot you made just as I was gettin' here. That bullet couldn't have missed him by much more'n an inch."

"That was enough," Frank said.

The marshal grunted. "Yeah. Come on, Morgan. Let's go talk to the conductor."

The conductor didn't like holding the train, but he agreed to for half an hour. The engineer had to be brought around, anyway, and given a little while to recover from his fainting spell.

The marshal, whose name was Harry Larch, walked down to his office with Frank. Larch had Frank's Colt tucked behind his belt, and Frank had retrieved his hat from the roadbed where it had fallen off.

As he brushed dirt from the Stetson and settled it on his head, he asked, "Am I under arrest?"

"Not yet. I just want some answers, is all. There hasn't been any real trouble here in my town for a long time, and I want to know why folks started dyin' this morning all of a sudden."

The dying hadn't started this morning, Frank thought. This was just the latest installment.

The marshal's office was in a small, blocky building that also served as the town jail. A coffeepot sat on a cast-iron stove in the corner. After putting the shotgun back on the rack, Larch offered Frank a cup, and Frank accepted gratefully.

"I used to do some cowboying, and that's where I learned to boil coffee," the marshal said. "So this is pretty potent."

Frank smiled. "Just the way I like it."

Larch poured coffee for both of them and waved Frank into a chair in front of the battered, scarred desk. He took Frank's gun from behind his belt and placed it on the desk. As he settled down in a swivel chair, he said, "Now tell me why somebody wants you dead, Morgan . . . other than the fact that a man like you must have a lot of enemies to start with."

Frank took a sip of the strong black brew and nodded in appreciation. Then he said, "Those gunmen were sent to intercept me by a man in Boston named Charles Dutton."

"Why would this fella Dutton do that?"

"Because he knows that I'm on my way to Boston to kill *him*."

Larch's bushy eyebrows rose in surprise. "Simple as that, eh?"

Frank nodded. "Simple as that."

But it wasn't simple, not really. Not at all. And the beginnings of it went back years. Maybe even decades, depending on how you looked at it.

It went all the way back to when he had met and fallen in love with and ultimately married a beautiful young woman named Vivian. Her father had been opposed to the marriage, and eventually had succeeded in having it set aside legally. But he couldn't do anything about the child Vivian had been carrying when she and Frank parted, and even though Vivian had wound up marrying somebody else who had raised her son Conrad as his own, the boy was Frank's and that connection would always exist between them.

Years later, they had met again. Vivian Browning was a widow by this time, and a very rich widow, to boot. It was then that Frank had learned for the first time he had a son. Conrad Browning's dislike for Frank had made Frank's reunion with Vivian a bittersweet one, but given enough time, things might have improved all around.

They didn't get the chance to, because Vivian had been betrayed and set up by one of her attorneys, a man named Charles Dutton. Because of Dutton's treachery, Vivian had been cut down by an outlaw's bullet, ending her life and driving a wedge between Frank and Conrad that threatened to become permanent.

Fate had cast the two men together again on several occasions, and Conrad had overcome his resentment of his true father to form a grudging respect for Frank. They had even worked together to ward off threats to a railroad Conrad was building down in New Mexico Territory. They were partners whether they wanted to be or not, since Vivian's will had left a large share of her business holdings to Frank and the rest to Conrad.

Frank had met Charles Dutton briefly, before Vivian's death. He knew the man was responsible for what had happened, even though Dutton hadn't actually pulled the trigger himself, and he was aware that Dutton had fled back to Boston. Frank had intended to go after him and settle the score, but other things had gotten in the way, keeping him from getting around to it.

And then, while Frank was embroiled in a bloody range war down Arizona way, a hired killer had come after him and forced a showdown. Frank had emerged triumphant from that shoot-out. As the gunman lay dying, he had revealed that Charles Dutton had hired him to kill Frank. Clearly, Dutton felt that Frank's very existence posed too much of a continuing threat and had decided to have him eliminated.

Instead, the attempt on his life had served as a reminder for Frank, a reminder that he had unfinished business to take care of. Now he was on his way east, and nothing was going to sidetrack him until he had looked into Charles Dutton's eyes and avenged Vivian's death.

He quickly sketched in this background for Marshal Harry Larch, then said, "I suspect Dutton has spies keeping an eye on me. I rode from Arizona up to Denver and talked to my lawyers there, made arrangements for my horse and my dog to be taken care of while I was gone, and bought a train ticket to Boston. I see now that was a mistake, though."

"How come?" Larch asked, clearly fascinated by Frank's story.

"How come it was a mistake? Because if Dutton knows that I m coming for him—and I'm sure he does—he'll his damnedest to try to stop me. Hell try to have me killed before I can get anywhere close to him. He's got the money to hire plenty of gunmen, too . . . money he stole from my late wife."

"What's that got to do with you riding the train?"

"I'm an easy target on a train," Frank explained. "There's no room to move, and there are too many innocent people around. Not only that, but the men who are after me will always know where to find me." He shook his head. "What I've got to do is throw them off the trail. That's my best chance of getting to Dutton."

Larch rubbed his jaw and frowned in thought. "Even if you make it to Boston, it won' t be easy gettin' to Dutton. He'll probably have himself a bunch o' bodyguards."

"I expect so," Frank said with a calm nod.

"So you're willin' to fight your way through a whole army o' hired guns and guards just to take your shot at this hombre."

"That's about the size of it."

The marshal laced his hands together and leaned back in his chair as his frown darkened. "There's one thing you're forgettin', Morgan . . . No matter how justified you may feel in seekin' revenge, what you're really talkin' about is murder. This is a civilized country now. You can't just walk up to a man and gun him down, no matter what he's done. If you can prove that Dutton is responsible for your wife's death, you need to go to the law and let them handle it."

Frank nodded. "I wouldn't expect you to tell me any different, Marshal. And what you say would be mighty good advice for most people. But I'm in the habit of stompin' my own snakes, and I reckon I'm too old to change now."

Larch sighed and reached out to rest his hand on Frank's gun. He shoved the Peacemaker across the desk toward The Drifter. "All I can say is that I'm damn sure glad this fella Dutton is in Boston and not here in my town. This is gonna be some other lawman's worry."